SPECIAL EDITION

**from *New York Times* and *USA TODAY*
bestselling authors**

"When I started writing for Special Edition,
I was delighted by the length of the books,
which allowed the freedom to create,
and develop more within each character and
their romance. I have always been a fan of
Special Edition! I hope to write for it for many years
to come. Long live Special Edition!
—Diana Palmer

"My career began in Special Edition.
I remember my excitement when the SEs
were introduced, because the stories were so rich and
different, and every month when the books came out
I beat a path to the bookstore to get every one of them.
Here's to you, SE; live long, and prosper!"
—Linda Howard

"Congratulations, Special Edition,
on thirty years of publishing first-class romance!"
—Linda Lael Miller

THE DOCTOR'S NOT-SO-LITTLE SECRET

CINDY KIRK

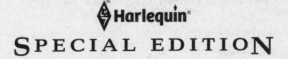

Harlequin®

SPECIAL EDITION

ISBN-13: 978-0-373-65666-0

THE DOCTOR'S NOT-SO-LITTLE SECRET

Copyright © 2012 by Cynthia Rutledge

THE ANNIVERSARY PARTY
Copyright © 2012 by Harlequin Books S.A.

The publisher acknowledges the following writers who contributed to THE ANNIVERSARY PARTY: RaeAnne Thayne, Christine Rimmer, Susan Crosby, Christyne Butler, Gina Wilkins and Cindy Kirk.

Recycling programs for this product may not exist in your area.

CONTENTS

CINDY KIRK

has loved to read for as long as she can remember. In first grade she received an award for reading one hundred books. As she grew up, summers were her favorite time of year. Nothing beat going to the library, then coming home and curling up in front of the window air conditioner with a good book. Often the novels she read would spur ideas, and she'd make up her own story (always with a happy ending). When she'd go to bed at night, instead of counting sheep, she'd make up more stories in her head. Since selling her first story to Harlequin Books in 1999, Cindy has been forced to juggle her love of reading with her passion for creating stories of her own…but she doesn't mind. Writing for the Harlequin Special Edition series is a dream come true. She only hopes you have as much fun reading her books as she has writing them!

Cindy invites you to visit her website, www.cindykirk.com.

Dear Reader,

In every book an author has opportunities to incorporate bits and pieces from their life. In *The Doctor's Not-So-Little Secret,* Kate had a sister who was the family's "golden child." I don't have a sister, but I had a friend who was in the same situation as Kate. She still struggles with feeling second best.

Then there's Chloe's Cabbage Patch Kid. I vividly remember standing outside the local JCPenney store waiting for the doors to open, hoping for a chance to snag one of those coveted dolls.

I wish I could say I'm fabulous on the ice. The truth is I'm closer to Joel's talent level than Kate's. I consider it a good ice skating session if I spend more time standing up than falling down.

And as far as what goes on when a couple is alone in the dark on an observation tower…no comment.

Lastly, I want to congratulate Harlequin Special Edition on reaching their thirty-year milestone. I've always loved reading the heartwarming stories they publish and now I enjoy writing them, too!

Cindy Kirk

Patience Bloom—You're the best editor around, and I'm thankful you're mine!

THE DOCTOR'S
NOT-SO-LITTLE SECRET

Chapter One

Dr. Kate McNeal sat back in her seat by the front window of Jackson Hole's newest coffee shop, enjoying her cappuccino. It was Saturday and, thanks to a very generous on-call rotation schedule at the pediatrics clinic, she had the whole weekend off.

All Dressed Up and Nowhere to Go could be her motto. Kate sighed and took another sip. Although she'd been in Jackson Hole for almost two years, she had no close friends. Oh, she had tons of social buddies, men and women who invited her to their parties and other events. But no one she felt comfortable calling up on a Saturday morning and asking, "Hey, do you want to grab a scone and then do some shopping?"

Part of the problem was that most of the women she knew had husbands and children. Once she'd reached her early thirties, Kate had discovered there weren't many women left in the single, never-married category. But she couldn't blame her current loneliness *all* on her marital status.

As a child, Kate had been painfully shy. While in her professional life she did fine, shyness was still a struggle in social settings. Worse yet, her reticence often led to her being labeled "aloof" or "standoffish" by those who didn't know her well.

She smoothed the skirt of the buttercup-yellow dress she'd purchased last week. Even though most of the coffee shop patrons were wearing jeans or shorts with a casual shirt, Kate liked to dress up. Wearing pretty things made her *feel* pretty, a feeling that had been in short supply during her growing-up years. Unlike her sister, Andrea, who everyone still raved over, it had taken years for Kate's lanky body to develop a few curves and for her teeth to not look too large for her face.

Back in her early twenties, when she was finally reaching out and becoming the woman she was meant to be, her world had fallen apart. Her grandmother had died. Her boyfriend had deserted her. And she'd had to make a decision no woman should ever have to make…alone. A decision she now lived with every day of her life.

Kate choked down the last bite of lemon-curd scone and gazed out the window, wondering if some shopping therapy would help get her out of this funk.

She was ready to give it a try when she saw Joel Dennes heading toward Hill of Beans, his nine-year-old daughter, Chloe, in tow. Even though she told herself to look away, Kate couldn't take her eyes off them.

Thankfully Joel didn't see her staring. Dressed in jeans and a striped cotton shirt that brought out the green in his hazel eyes, the handsome contractor's entire focus was on his young daughter. Joel was tall—at least six foot two—with a rugged outdoorsy build. His child was petite and slender as a reed with delicate features. From the bag Chloe held, it appeared they'd just come from the dance studio down the street.

So far, on this sunny June morning, Kate had seen at least six little girls walk by with their mothers. All carried the same type of "dancer" bag she'd once owned.

The normally reserved Chloe let out a peal of laughter at something her father said, and his eyes crinkled with good humor as he settled his hand on her shoulder.

From everything she'd heard and seen, Joel had been doing his best to be both mother and father to Chloe since the death of her mom two years ago.

As far as Kate was concerned, such actions spoke volumes about a man's character. She admired him for stepping up to the plate, admired him a lot.

She shifted in her seat so that her back was to the window, ensuring if they looked her way, she'd simply be a dark-haired woman in a yellow dress.

"Is Joel why you told Ryan you didn't want to see him anymore?"

Kate shifted her gaze to find Lexi Delacourt standing beside her table, latte in hand, wearing a stylish green-and-brown dress with a short green sweater. Lexi's dark hair hung loose to her shoulders in a sleek bob. The social worker's amber-colored eyes held a knowing look as her gaze shifted from Kate to the front door. If the bells jingling were any indication, Joel and his daughter had just entered the coffee shop.

"C'mon, Kate, spill." Without waiting for an invitation, Lexi took a seat at Kate's tiny table. "Did you break it off with Ryan because you've got a thing for Joel?"

Lexi and her husband were part of the large ensemble of young professionals that Kate considered "social" friends. They held frequent parties and embraced any opportunity to get together.

Kate's ex-boyfriend, Ryan Harcourt, was part of this group. A former championship bull rider, he had gone on to law school, then returned to his hometown of Jackson to practice. He and Kate had dated until recently when she'd told him she thought it best if they didn't see each other anymore.

In truth, she'd have been content to continue dating him. He was smart, fun and helped fill those lonely hours when she wasn't working. But Ryan had begun to push for a physical and emotional closeness that was more than Kate could give.

Because of her past, she found it difficult to be open even with guys she dated. No, *especially* with guys she dated.

Ryan had given their relationship his all. She'd given it as much as she could, but refused to pretend to have feelings that weren't there.

"Be honest with me," Lexi pressed. "Do you like Joel better than Ryan?"

"It's not that." Kate took a sip of her cappuccino, stalling for time, considering how much to divulge. She hated discussing her personal life. "Ryan and I were—*are*—simply friends."

That much was true.

"His feelings go deeper than friendship." Lexi's eyes never left Kate's face. "I know he really likes you."

Kate fought a surge of irritation. Coming from Pittsburgh and then doing her residency in Los Angeles, she still hadn't completely acclimated to living in a small community. Even though Jackson Hole was a thriving tourist destination, it sometimes felt as if everyone knew everyone's business.

"I realize you and Nick consider Ryan a good friend." Kate chose her words carefully, not wanting to offend. While she might travel in their social circle, she hung on to the fringe by a fingernail while Ryan was firmly woven into the fabric of the group.

"We consider you a friend, too, Kate." As if she'd read her mind, the attractive brunette reached over and briefly covered Kate's hand with hers. "As well as Joel."

The sincerity in Lexi's voice touched Kate's heart. Perhaps she should come clean with the beautiful brunette. After all, it wasn't as if there was any big secret underlying her relationship and breakup with Ryan.

Not like there would be if I dated Joel.

Kate inhaled sharply. *Date Joel?* Where had that thought even come from? Joel Dennes was the last person she'd ever consider dating. The.very.last.person.

"I'm sorry," Lexi said unexpectedly when the silence lengthened, her cheeks now a bright pink. "It's none of my concern."

"Ryan is a great guy," Kate said honestly. "But you're right. He *was* looking for something more than I wanted out of our relationship."

Ryan had made it clear he was ready to settle down. He'd been convinced he was in love with her. But how could he be? There was so much about her he didn't know.

Lexi gave a little laugh. "That simply tells me he wasn't 'The One' for you."

"The problem wasn't with Ryan." Kate rose to his defense. "It was me. I'm not ready to settle down."

Kate conveniently pushed aside the promise she'd made to herself that when she turned thirty, she'd put her past to rest and move on. That had proven impossible, especially in Jackson Hole.

"If Ryan had been 'The One' it wouldn't have mattered if you were ready or if this was the right time or not."

Kate opened her mouth to argue the point, but Lexi waved her silent.

"Let me tell you a little story." The social worker's hands encircled her cup, the large diamond on her ring finger glittering in the sunlight. "If you'd asked me three years ago why I wasn't in a relationship, I'd have given the same excuse. I was raising Addie on my own and I was content with that arrangement. Then I met Nick."

Kate envied the happiness she saw in Lexi's eyes and heard in her voice, but she wasn't about to get drawn into a discussion about Mr. Right. She focused instead on Lexi's other comment. Even though someone had once mentioned in passing that Nick wasn't their oldest child's biological father, it was easy to forget. "Your ex-husband doesn't live around here, right?"

While she waited for Lexi's answer, Kate took a sip of her cappuccino and noted that Joel and Chloe had gotten their drinks "to go." Obviously they weren't staying. The tightness in her chest eased.

"Actually there is no ex-husband." Lexi's confession pulled Kate back from her thoughts. "Addie's dad and I never married. When Drew found out I was pregnant, he made it clear he didn't want a baby. His career was revving up and he believed having a child would only drag him down. He offered to pay for an abortion."

"Did you ever consider—"

"Not having the baby?" Lexi shook her head. "Never."

"How about adoption?" Although Kate felt her lips move, the words seemed to come from far away.

"It's a great option, but not for me." Lexi's gaze grew thoughtful. "Still, I have to tell you, being a single mom was no walk in the park. Addie and I endured some pretty lean years. In fact, when I met Nick, I was working two jobs."

"Not every woman could do that," Kate murmured. The scone she'd just finished eating sat like a dead weight in the pit of her stomach.

"Keeping my daughter was easy," Lexi said, "compared to how hard it would have been to give her up."

Kate could only nod.

"What brings you two fine ladies downtown this morning?"

At the sound of the familiar baritone, Kate's heart plummeted to the tips of her toes. Somehow she managed to lift her gaze and smile.

"I rounded at the hospital early and thought I'd check out Cole and Meg's new business." Even though Kate's heart was above the safe number of beats per minute, thanks to years of practice her tone gave nothing away.

"Chloe and I were just talking about how glad we are that they opened a coffee shop just down the street from The Dance Studio." Joel smiled at his daughter. "We've become Saturday morning regulars."

Kate made a quick mental note *not* to come here again on the weekend, then settled her gaze on the nine-year-old. Chloe's straight dark hair, which normally hung past her shoulders had been pulled back into a makeshift ponytail. Like many preteens, her eyes and teeth seemed too large for her thin face. Although it wasn't obvious to the casual eye, Kate saw the promise of great beauty.

"What do you usually get when you come here?" Lexi bestowed a friendly smile on the two.

"Coffee with cream for me." Joel lifted his cardboard cup. "Nothing fancy."

Even though it would have been easy for him to answer

for his daughter, to Joel's credit he merely offered the child an encouraging smile.

Chloe's eyes dropped to the clear plastic cup in her hand. "I got an Italian soda."

"I almost ordered one of those this morning," Kate said, surprising herself by jumping into the conversation. Perhaps because she'd been a shy child and knew how hard it was to have all eyes on you. "My favorite flavor is watermelon."

Chloe lifted her gaze, her eyes wide. "Mine, too."

"Watermelon." Although Joel shook his head in apparent disgust, a smile tugged at her lips. "Must be a girl thing."

Chloe giggled.

For a second, Kate basked in the warmth of the child's pleasure. As Chloe's doctor she'd seen only the little girl's serious side. She'd even spoken with Joel after that first visit about his daughter's reticence, thinking it might be related to her mother's death. But Joel said Chloe had always been shy around strangers.

"Would you like to join us?" Lexi asked. "We could pull up a couple chairs."

Kate remained silent.

Chloe looked up at her father.

Kate held her breath, hoping he would say no, but at the same time wanting them to stay.

"Thanks for the offer," Joel said, sounding sincere. "Unfortunately I have a potential client to meet, so we need to hit the road."

Joel built high-end custom homes in Jackson Hole and from everything Kate had heard, his business was booming despite the economy.

"If that person wants references," Lexi said, "feel free

to give them our number. I know Travis and Mary Karen would also be happy to sing your praises."

"Thank you for that. Much appreciated." Joel shifted from one foot to the other, as if embarrassed by the compliment.

Since Joel's Montana-based company had established a presence in Jackson Hole almost five years ago, he'd built homes in the mountains surrounding Jackson not only for Lexi and her husband, but for Mary Karen and Travis Fisher, as well. Kate knew he was in the process of building one for Cole and Meg Lassiter, the couple who owned the shop where they were seated.

"Daddy." Chloe tugged on his arm. "You promised we'd stop and pick up my new ice skates before your meeting."

"You ice skate?" The question popped out of Kate's mouth before she could stop it. If she truly wanted them to leave—which she did—she was doing a poor job of hurrying them on their way.

"Since I was a little girl," Chloe said with a nine-year-old's maturity. "Do you like to skate?"

"I used to," Kate said. "When I was your age."

For her, skating had been a way to forget her troubles at home. She hoped it wasn't that way for Chloe.

"That's cool," Chloe said, then ducked her head, staring down at her hot-pink sneakers.

Joel pulled his phone from his pocket and glanced at it. "We better get going."

From the distant look in his eyes, his thoughts were already on his next appointment.

Kate kept the disappointment she had no right to feel from showing as she watched them walk out the door.

Or at least she *thought* she'd hidden her disappointment.

"His wife hasn't been gone all that long. From what I

understand they were childhood sweethearts." Lexi took a sip of her latte, a look of sympathy in her eyes. "Give him time. He'll come around."

Kate blinked. "I'm not interested in dating Joel."

"Really?" A tiny smile played at the corners of Lexi's lips. "Could have fooled me."

Even though Kate was absolutely, positively certain she didn't want to date the handsome contractor, she could see where he could catch a woman's eye. "I'll admit he's a good-looking man."

"Oh, you noticed." Lexi looked as if she was trying to keep from laughing. "Even though you're not interested."

After a second Kate chuckled and took a sip of her drink. It was probably best to let Lexi think what she wanted. If she protested too much, her friend's curiosity radar might be activated and she'd ask even more questions.

Questions Kate had no intention of answering.

For now her secret was safe, held close and tight against her heart. And that was just where she intended to keep it.

Chapter Two

Sunday morning, Kate rose early and flung open her closet doors, searching for just the right dress to wear to church. She'd promised herself at the first of the year that she'd start attending services on a regular basis. January had gone well, but by February she'd already fallen off the churchgoing wagon.

She was ready to try again. After all, she couldn't build relationships or meet new friends sitting home alone.

After donning a simple slip dress in a wild swirl of colors, she pulled out a pair of dangling earrings that had been an impulse buy. Even though at the time they seemed a little bold, today they fit her take-charge-of-life mood.

The decision on what shoes to wear took way too long. By the time Kate waltzed through the front doors of the church she usually attended in Jackson, the congregation was already on their feet for the opening hymn.

There was space for her in the back pews, which were normally reserved for parents with babies and small, noisy children. While Kate loved kids, this morning she didn't feel like being surrounded by them.

Instead she strolled down the center aisle looking for a place to sit. As she reached the midway point, a sick feeling had taken up residence in the pit of her stomach. Perhaps this was a sign for her to casually pivot on her designer heels and head for the door.

The escape was already in progress when the sound of her name aborted the flight plan and had her turning back toward a pew she'd just passed.

Chloe gave her a shy smile. Joel motioned to her.

His brown hair, which normally looked like he'd just run his fingers through it, had been carefully combed and the stubble on his cheeks had been shaved away. He looked very business casual this morning in a navy blazer with a blue-sapphire plaid shirt and tan chinos. He also looked very handsome.

While Kate took a hesitant step toward him, he and Chloe moved over. Joel gestured to the tiny space he'd opened up next to him. A space so small that if she accepted his offer, she might as well be sitting on his lap.

Her heart skipped a beat. Her breathing quickened.

Kate rapidly considered her two options. Sit down. Or make some lame excuse and walk away.

Before she could second-guess the rightness of her decision, she squeezed in beside him. It was tight. Very tight. His muscular thigh pressing against her bare leg ignited feelings that had no place in a house of worship.

Joel's gaze lingered on her earrings—or was it a bit lower, say on her breasts?—before turning his attention back to the hymnal.

While slip dresses were popular and no more reveal-

ing than a skirt and tiny tee, Kate suddenly felt exposed.
As though she was caught in one of those horrible dreams
where you leave the house in your underwear and only
later realize you'd forgotten to put on the rest of your
clothes.

It didn't help that someone had set the air condition-
ing on low and she was freezing. Or she would be if Joel
wasn't beside her. The guy was like a blast furnace and
the warmth radiating from him made her yearn to throw
caution to the wind and cuddle close.

It took every bit of control to ignore the spicy scent of
his cologne and his heat, that wonderful heat that wrapped
itself around her like a favorite blanket, tethering her to
him.

Still, she remained in firm control of her emotions until
it came time to share the hymnal with him and Chloe.
Standing beside the tall, broad-shouldered man and the
girl with a ribbon tied awkwardly around her ponytail felt
a little too much like heaven. Or was it hell?

Regardless, it was a vivid reminder of what she'd given
up all those years ago. Breathing became difficult and
tears stung the back of her eyes.

The only way she held it together was by focusing on
the letters and notes swimming on the pages before her.
And by ignoring the man next to her and the child in the
pink jersey dress with the crooked smile on his other side.

By the time they rose for the closing benediction,
Kate's emotions were raw and bleeding and too close to
the surface for comfort.

She needed to put some space between her and Joel.

Between her and Chloe.

The second the minister quit talking she'd say a quick
but polite goodbye, then sprint for the exit. Unfortunately

her escape plan didn't include Lexi Delacourt appearing out of nowhere to block her way out of the pew.

"You look absolutely gorgeous, Kate." The social worker gave her a quick hug, then shifted her gaze to the man now trapped beside her. "Doesn't she look nice, Joel?"

"Beautiful," came the deep rumble behind her.

Something in the way he said the word sent a shiver of awareness up her spine. Or maybe it wasn't the word so much as his warm breath against the back of her neck. Yes, it was definitely time to put some distance between her and the sexy contractor. If only Lexi would move....

"We're all going to The Coffeepot for breakfast while the kids are in Sunday school," Lexi announced, her feet firmly planted in front of Kate. "I hope you two will join us."

"I don't thi—"

"Sure," Joel said at the same time. "I'd like that."

A moment of silence followed. Kate wished sinking through the floor were an option.

"Dr. Kate doesn't want to go with you, Daddy." Chloe's voice came from behind her father. "I don't think she likes you."

"Apologies, Kate," she heard him say and the hitch in his voice made her heart twist. "It wasn't my intent to answer for you."

Lexi's amber eyes remained riveted on Kate, her expression watchful.

Kate swallowed hard. While she'd vowed to keep her distance, she could not, and would not, embarrass this fine man. Besides, it wasn't as if this was a *date*. Lexi had said a whole group was going. It wasn't as if she had to even sit by him.

She turned and met Joel's gaze over her shoulder. "Breakfast sounds wonderful."

Her heart tripped over itself as a smile spread across his face. Kate then focused on Chloe. "Everyone likes your father. He's a great guy."

"Including you?" the girl asked, surprising Kate with her boldness.

Kate didn't even hesitate. "Including me."

"Well, then." Lexi's smile broadened. Relief filled her eyes. "Sounds like we have a plan. July and David are already on their way to nab our usual table at the back. We'll see you two at the café."

As Kate walked down the aisle smiling and saying hello to patients and their families, she felt Joel's hand on the small of her back. Of course, that was only because it was crowded and he was behind her. The gesture was oddly intimate and yet, she found she didn't mind it at all.

When they reached the foyer, Chloe headed downstairs to her Sunday school classroom, leaving Kate alone with Joel. They walked in silence to the parking lot.

"May I give you a ride downtown?" he asked, obviously not wanting to take anything for granted. "Because of the limited parking, it makes sense to take one car. Unless you have somewhere you need to go right after breakfast."

He'd graciously left her an out. All Kate had to do was say the word and she could drive separately. If things were different, she'd be thrilled at the thought of spending some one-on-one time with the handsome contractor. But before making the decision to move to Jackson Hole, Kate had promised herself that she'd keep her distance. From Joel. And from Chloe.

Yet in her deliberations, she'd never considered the

possibility they might end up running in the same social circle or have mutual friends.

This is only breakfast, she reminded herself, *nothing more.*

"We might as well go together," Kate said, stumbling a bit over the last word. "I hope your truck isn't far because I'm starving."

Joel noticed café patrons casting glances their way as he and Kate wove through the crowded dining room of The Coffeepot.

They weren't looking at him. It was Kate. She turned heads wherever she went. She was so pretty. Today, her multicolored silky dress showed off her long slender legs to full advantage. She was wearing her trademark heels. Instead of the black ones she'd worn the other day, these were red with a little strap around her ankle.

Even though it wasn't fair, Joel couldn't help comparing her to his deceased wife. Fashionwise, Kate and Amy were as different as night and day. His wife had always preferred simple attire, dresses that showed very little skin and serviceable shoes with only a slight heel. Her taste in jewelry had been equally conservative. All she'd ever worn was her wedding band and tiny gold hoop earrings.

Amy would never have worn bright dangly ones that couldn't help but draw a man's attention to a woman's slender neck and creamy skin.

Joel shoved the image of Kate aside and replaced it with a vision of Amy with her short curly blond hair and broad smile. His wife hadn't needed jewelry; she'd had a natural glow that made everyone sit up and take notice.

His lips curved upward. Amy had loved people. Loved finding out what made them tick. It didn't matter who:

sales clerks, meter readers, the person standing in front of her in the grocery line. She'd start talking and by the end of the conversation, she had a new friend. Her innate gregariousness had sometimes made it hard for her to understand their daughter's shyness and need for solitude. But she'd been a wonderful mother and had done a lot to make Chloe more at ease in social situations.

Unfortunately when Amy had passed away, Chloe had taken a giant leap backward....

Joel realized with a start that Kate had come to a dead stop. Puzzled, he cast a sideways glance in her direction. Didn't she realize their destination was just a few feet ahead?

If he hadn't been so in-tuned to his daughter's reaction to similar situations, he might have missed the signs.

The hesitation on her face.

The slight furrow to her brow.

The uneven breaths.

Even though Kate projected a bold confidence, he realized that she wasn't cool or aloof. She was...*shy*.

A protective urge rose inside him.

"Walking into a group that's already gathered can be stressful." Joel kept his tone conversational and low, for her ears only.

"I know everyone," she said, but her sexy red heels remained firmly planted on the shiny hardwood.

"Yes, you do. And it's not as if you'll be talking to all of them at once," he said in a matter-of-fact tone. "It'll be just the ones sitting by us."

Us. The word flowed easily from his lips. After all those years of being married, he still thought of himself as part of a couple. Joel hoped Kate didn't take offense.

She hadn't seemed to notice. Her focus was on the battle-scarred table up ahead with its old-fashioned tin coffeepot centerpieces sprouting plastic sunflowers. Even though the table was large—holding twelve or even thirteen if someone took the end—there were only three seats left at the far end and a single open chair next to Lexi. Joel assumed that one was saved for Lexi's husband, Nick.

A middle-aged waitress with a nose ring and orange lipstick had already begun taking orders.

"We better sit down." Joel wrapped his hand around her elbow and gently urged her forward. He took a step away from her before they reached the table.

"Hello, everyone." A smile that didn't quite reach her eyes lifted Kate's lips.

As the greetings flew back and forth, Joel positioned himself at the end with the three open chairs. He waited to see where Kate decided to sit so he could pull out her chair.

For a second her gaze appeared to linger on the chair next to Lexi. But if Kate was hoping to sit next to her friend, that option disappeared when Nick showed up, brushing a kiss against his wife's cheek and slipping into the chair beside her.

Joel and Kate had barely gotten settled and picked up the menus when the waitress asked for their orders. The woman obviously knew they had only an hour before they needed to pick up the children and wanted to keep things moving.

Drinks were already on the table by the time Ryan Harcourt showed up. Unlike the other men at the table who'd come from church, the attorney wore a pair of jeans with holes and a faded navy T-shirt. His thick dark hair was still damp, as if he'd just hopped out of a shower.

Even though Joel tried to steer clear of the whole who-was-dating-who gossip, he'd heard Kate had recently ended a relationship with Ryan. Some speculated it wouldn't be long before the two were back together. Even if they didn't, Joel knew Kate wouldn't be available for long.

The chorus of hellos and ribbing that greeted Ryan's arrival told Joel that Kate's former boyfriend was a regular at these gatherings. Not surprising because, like so many of those congregated around the table, Ryan was a Jackson Hole native.

The attorney glanced around, his gaze initially bypassing the empty seat next to Kate. Although Ryan's cocky grin never wavered, Joel noticed his gaze made a second sweep as if seeking another option before commandeering the last open spot.

"Hello, Joel. Kate." Ryan placed the paper napkin on his lap and gestured for the waitress to bring him some coffee.

"Decided to skip the sermon, eh, Ry?"

Kate's light, almost-teasing greeting surprised Joel. Because the two had recently broken up, he'd expected to see some awkwardness. If Kate felt ill-at-ease, it didn't show.

Ryan took a cup of steaming coffee from the waitress before turning his attention back to his ex-girlfriend, an answering gleam in his eyes.

"I wouldn't be so cocky if I were you." The attorney's gaze settled his gaze on her dress. "At least I didn't get up late and wear a slip to church."

For a second she looked taken aback. Then Kate burst into laughter. "Touché."

Something twisted in Joel's gut at the playful banter. Something that felt an awful lot like jealousy, which didn't make sense. He didn't care if she got back together with Ryan. Didn't care at all.

"I didn't see your car outside, Kate," Ryan said, shortly

after the waitress brought the food. "Is the Subaru back in the shop?"

Kate swept a strand of hair back from her face. "Actually, I rode with Joel."

Ryan's eyes widened in surprise and when he spoke, his gaze was riveted on Joel. "What are you, a miracle worker? She would never come with me. No matter how many times I begged, er, invited her."

"Eat your omelet, Harcourt," Kate said mildly, then promptly changed the subject. "Did I mention to either of you that I agreed to help out at the Jackson Hole rodeo in August? They wanted a doctor available in case any of the kids in the peewee division are injured."

Joel ate his "Hearty Man's Breakfast" of eggs, hash browns, ham and toast and listened with half an ear to the ensuing rodeo talk all the while wondering why Kate *had* come today. More important, why had she agreed to ride with him? He hoped she didn't have any, well, romantic interest in him.

While Kate seemed to be a fine person, she was nothing like Amy. When he did jump back into the dating scene, he would look for a woman more like his wife. A woman of substance.

Although Joel didn't doubt Kate's intelligence or competence as a doctor, he'd noticed that outside of work she rarely spoke of anything beyond the superficial. Personal details were kept to a minimum. Consequently he knew little of her. Even though it didn't really matter, he *was* curious.

After Ryan had finished entertaining them with stories from his bull-riding days, Joel slathered some grape jam on his toast and decided this would be an opportunity to get to know more about his daughter's doctor. "Where did you say you went to medical school?"

Kate took a sip of coffee before answering. "UC Irvine."

"Did you like it there?" Joel asked.

"I did."

He waited for her to elaborate, but she simply stirred some more cream into her coffee. Joel had never pulled teeth, but he had the feeling that would be easier than getting basic information from Kate McNeal.

Ryan doused his omelet with more Tabasco sauce before looking up. "Isn't that in Orange County?"

"That's right." Kate took a sip of coffee, obviously not intending to say more.

Joel couldn't help but smile remembering how excited he and Amy had been when they'd landed at the John Wayne Airport in Orange County on their first and only trip to the West Coast. "My daughter, Chloe, was born at the Women's Hospital in Laguna Hills, which isn't that far from Irvine."

Kate didn't look up, apparently more fascinated by the granola in her yogurt parfait than the conversation.

Ryan took a bite of his omelet, then quickly followed it with a shot of water. "I didn't know you used to live in California."

"Actually, Chloe is adopted. We went there to pick her up and complete the rest of the paperwork." Joel smiled. "When all that was done, we took her home to Montana."

"That's wonderful," Ryan said.

"It is," Kate echoed.

"I remember how beautiful it was there. Are you from that area?" Joel asked Kate.

"I grew up in Pittsburgh."

"Do you go home often?"

"Kate and her family aren't close," Ryan said. "Her parents are still married. She has one older sister, Andrea, who is the family's golden child. Andrea is married with three kids, a boy and two girls."

Kate's brows slammed together and a warning that even Ryan couldn't fail to recognize, flashed in her hazel eyes.

The attorney raised both hands. "Don't glare at me, sweetheart. It took me six months of intense effort to ferret out the basics. I'm simply helping the new guy out. Getting him up to speed."

"I'm not the—" Joel began.

"Thank you, Ryan." The sarcasm in Kate's tone came through loud and clear. "Is there anything else you'd like to share about my life?"

A thoughtful look crossed Ryan's face. "Kate thinks she wants to settle down, but there's something in her background, I never did discover what, that keeps her from—"

"Enough." Her voice cut like a knife. "That's quite enough."

Even though her face was perfectly composed, Joel heard the anger and saw the tremble in the hands she clasped in her lap. Without thinking, he reached over and covered her hands with one of his.

Almost immediately, she pushed it away.

But in the second that his hand had closed over hers, he learned that her skin was soft as silk. Joel had a sudden image of his arms wrapped around her, those hands sliding down his bare chest...

Dear God, what was happening to him? He jerked to his feet, pulled out his wallet and tossed a couple bills on the table. "I need to get back to the church. I don't want Chloe to wait on me."

Only after the words left his mouth did Joel remember he hadn't come alone. Not only had Kate barely made a dent in her yogurt parfait, but there was also plenty of time left to pick up Chloe.

"Go ahead." Kate waved a spoon filled with yogurt in the air. If she seemed disturbed about his impending departure, it didn't show. In fact she appeared almost... pleased.

"I can catch a ride with someone," she continued when he made no move to leave. "Or I may walk. The church isn't far."

Joel knew he should feel relieved, but all he felt was irritated by her cavalier attitude. "I'll wait."

"Go ahead, Dennes." Amusement danced in the attorney's eyes. "I'll take the lady wherever she wants to go."

"I'm not going anywhere with you." Kate shifted her gaze from Ryan to Joel. "I'll be fine."

Ryan heaved a melodramatic sigh and placed a hand on his chest. "Ah, Kate, you're breaking my heart."

Kate rolled her eyes.

Joel experienced a sudden urge to shove a fist in the attorney's smirking face, but that would accomplish nothing. He'd brought this on himself.

"Are you sure?" he asked Kate one last time. "I'll be happy to wait."

"Positive." She held up her cup and took more coffee. "No worries. Go ahead."

"Okay, well, I'll be seeing you around." As he walked away, Joel turned back one last time to look at Kate.

For a second their eyes met and he thought he saw a look of regret. Then she turned back to Ryan, leaving Joel with no choice but to head to his truck.

This time, alone.

Chapter Three

Kate leaned back in her office chair and stretched, grateful the hectic Monday was almost at an end. She hadn't gotten much sleep last night. The incident in church and then at the café had consumed her thoughts.

Her feelings for Joel had taken her by surprise. In the quiet of her bedroom, staring up at the ceiling, she'd admitted to herself that she liked the guy. He was intelligent and hard-working and she respected how much he cared about Chloe. If he wasn't Chloe's father, she'd be hoping he'd ask her out.

But he *was* Chole's dad and she had more important things to think about, like what was up with her last patient.

Emilie Hyland. Kate pulled her brows together. She'd seen the sixteen-year-old last fall for a sports physical. No health issues had been identified on that visit. The vivacious cheerleader had been the picture of good health.

I wonder why she's coming in today?

Normally the receptionist indicated the reason for the visit next to the name, but the field had been left blank.

"Dr. McNeal." Lydia Albrecht, one of the front-office staff, stuck her head inside the door. "I'm sorry to disturb you, but there's a woman at the desk who says she's an old friend of yours. She asked if you might have a few minutes to see her."

An old friend? While Kate didn't have many friends now, she had even fewer that she would categorize as "old." "Did she give you a name?"

Lydia glanced down at the paper in her hand. "Mitzi Sanchez."

Surprise of the most pleasant kind rippled through Kate. She and Mitzi had been roommates all through medical school. This would be the first time Kate had seen her friend since they'd met in L.A. for an afternoon of lunch and shopping right before Kate had moved to Jackson Hole.

Kate rose to her feet. "By all means, send her back."

Less than a minute later, Mitzi stood in the doorway. Even though she'd once told Kate she didn't speak a word of English until she began grade school, with her fair skin and blue eyes, she was far from the stereotypical exotic Latina. Her hair, which had once been down her back and dark brown, now barely brushed her shoulders and was definitely a shade lighter. One thing hadn't changed...the smattering of freckles across the bridge of her nose that Mitzi loved to hate.

The most shocking change was her attire. As Kate crossed the room, her eyes skipped past the blue jeans and simple white cotton shirt to settle on her friend's feet.

The last time she'd seen her friend they'd lunched at Koi, just off Melrose Avenue. That day Mitzi had worn a darling cap-sleeve dress with a pair of Giuseppe Zanotti peep-toe pumps.

"Seriously, Mitzi, *cowboy boots?*"

Her friend chuckled. "Hey, you know me. I bloom where I'm planted."

It was true, Kate realized as she pulled Mitzi close, enveloping her in a hug. Her friend had always been a master at fitting in, no matter where she found herself.

"It's good to see you." Until this second, Kate hadn't realized just how deeply she'd missed her friend and confidante.

"I'm sorry to stop by so unexpectedly," Mitzi began. "You know that isn't my style—"

"Yeah, right." Kate hugged her for another second before releasing her. "You like keeping me on my toes."

Mitzi simply smiled and took a seat in one of the two leather wingbacks facing the desk. Kate slipped into the other.

"I'm surprised you're not in L.A. right now, taking care of the rich and famous." Kate searched her memory. "Didn't you tell me you'd accepted a position with Beverly Hills Orthopedics and Sports Medicine?"

"I did, but they don't need me to start until January."

"This is only June." Kate raised a brow. "You can't go six months without doing surgery."

Mitzi brushed a strand of shiny brown hair back from her face. "That's why I'm here. I'm going to be a locum at Spring Gulch Orthopedic through the end of the year."

Kate squealed. If she'd have been standing, she'd have jumped up and down. "You're staying with me," she said in the no-nonsense tone she often used with recalcitrant patients. "I have plenty of room and I won't take no for an answer."

"Thank you, Kate." Mitzi reached over and squeezed

her hand, appearing touched by the offer. "I was hoping you'd ask."

Thank You, God, Kate thought. *This is just what I needed.*

She exhaled a happy breath. "Who are you filling in for?"

"John Campbell," Mitzi said, naming a prominent surgeon at the largest orthopedic practice in Jackson.

Kate wasn't surprised. According to the medical grapevine, the doctor had recently been diagnosed with advanced cancer.

"I'm surprised they didn't ask you to join them permanently." Even before Campbell was diagnosed, one of the docs in that practice had told Kate they were hoping to add another physician to their busy group.

"They asked." Mitzi lifted one shoulder in a slight shrug. "While it was a fair offer, there's no comparison between that money and what I can earn in Beverly Hills."

"I'm thinking the fact that your best friend lives here should be worth at least half a mil." Kate fought to keep a straight face.

"Oh, if only I wasn't so materialistic," Mitzi said with an exaggerated sigh. "If it's any consolation, your being here was the reason I chose to take this temporary assignment."

Even as her heart swelled with emotion, Kate shot her friend a saucy smile. "Gee, thanks, Mitz. Way to put the pressure on me to show you a good time."

Before Mitzi could fire a comeback, a light knock sounded and Lydia announced that Kate's last appointment had arrived.

"If you want to give me your address and a key," Mitzi said, "I'll head over to your place in my rental car and chill until you get off."

"You'll also need a keycard for the gate." Kate rounded the desk and pulled out the drawer that held her purse. When she straightened, she tossed Mitzi an extra key to her townhome while keeping the fob to her Subaru in her hand. "Walk with me to my car and I'll give you my extra one. The townhome I rent is in a gated community just outside of town, so you'll definitely need it."

Kate had considered purchasing a home, but she wasn't certain how long she planned to stay in Jackson Hole. Being so close to her heart's desire, yet needing to keep her distance had been harder than she'd imagined.

"I've heard it all." Mitzi chuckled as she followed Kate out the back door of her office to the employee parking lot. "A gated community in Wyoming. Why? You need protection from big bad elk and moose?"

The two bantered back and forth all the way to the car. Kate retrieved the keycard from her glove compartment and pressed it into her friend's hand. Unfortunately the good-luck train she'd been riding since Mitzi had walked through her door derailed when Kate saw Joel's red four-wheel drive pull into a slanted parking stall in front of Rallis Orthodontics.

For a second she considered grabbing Mitzi's arm and making a U-turn straight back to the building. Then Chloe hopped out of the truck and Kate saw the child point in her direction.

Her heart dropped when Joel waved and began walking toward them, his daughter skipping behind him.

Mitzi's eyes widened with pure female appreciation. "If the men in Jackson Hole are all like him, it's going to be an enjoyable six months."

Kate had to admit that even dressed simply in jeans, boots and a blue polo, Joel looked good. And Chloe looked adorable in a black-and-white-checkered dress with red piping.

"Who is he?" Mitzi whispered in a low tone as the man and child approached. "More important, is he available?"

"Look, Daddy." Chloe hopped out of the truck and pointed. "It's Dr. Kate."

Joel shut his door before turning, knowing his little girl had to be mistaken. They'd just driven past the area where she was pointing and he hadn't seen anyone who remotely resembled Kate McNeal.

But when he gazed back in that direction he realized Chloe was right. He lifted his hand in greeting, feeling a little awkward about yesterday but surprisingly happy to see the pretty doctor.

As always, Kate looked stunning. Her dark, shoulder-length hair caught the sunlight and she moved with elegance. Under her lab coat she wore a white dress with yellow-and-black bands of color around the waistline. She looked as if she should be walking down a runway rather than tending to sick children.

There weren't many women in Jackson Hole as lovely and intelligent as Dr. Kate. Not that it mattered to him. Like he'd told himself last night, he was a busy contractor with a daughter to raise and a company to run. Even if he had been interested in dating, Amy would always be number one in his heart. Kate McNeal didn't seem like a woman who'd be satisfied with second place.

"Hi, Joel. Chloe." Even though she couldn't have walked more than ten feet across the parking lot, Kate seemed oddly out of breath. It was probably those spiky heels she wore. While they were very sexy-looking, they had to be hell to walk in.

"This is a pleasant surprise." Joel knew her office was

just across the parking lot from Chloe's orthodontist, but he hadn't expected to see her today. He thought she'd be busy inside seeing patients.

"I needed to get something out of my car." Kate brushed a strand of hair back from her face, her cheeks bright pink from the exertion. "When I saw you and Chloe, I thought it would be a good opportunity to introduce you to my friend."

"Mitzi Sanchez." The slender woman offered up a friendly smile. "It's a pleasure to meet you."

"Joel Dennes." He took the hand she'd extended and gave it a perfunctory shake. Although dressed casually in jeans and boots, there was something about this woman that reminded him of Kate. Perhaps it was the directness of her gaze or the firmness of her handshake. Whichever it was, he liked her instantly. He gestured with his head to the little girl at his side. "This is my daughter, Chloe."

"Joel and Chloe Dennes," Mitzi repeated slowly, as if their names were familiar. But because that couldn't be the case, it had to be her way of trying to remember them.

"That's right," Joel said, flashing a smile.

Mitzi shifted her attention to the child and studied her for several seconds, as if looking for a resemblance between him and Chloe. Obviously finding none, she simply smiled. "It's very nice to make your acquaintance, Chloe."

His daughter's gaze dropped to her feet and for a second Joel wasn't sure she would answer. Normally Chloe hated it when a stranger talked directly to her. Just when he'd given up hope, she lifted her head. "It's nice to meet you, too."

A surge of pride swept through Joel. He slipped an arm around his daughter's shoulders and gave a squeeze. *That's my girl.*

He chatted with Kate and Mitzi for a few minutes

about the weather, then the conversation began to lag. Joel resisted the urge to look at his phone to check the time. They were early for Chloe's orthodontic evaluation, so there was no reason to rush. "What brings you to Jackson Hole, Mitzi?"

"I'm an orthopedic surgeon. I'm going to be filling in for Dr. John Campbell." She cast a sideways glance at her friend as if disturbed by her silence. "Kate's going to let me crash on her sofa."

"Actually my guest room has your name on it." The teasing smile Kate shot her friend, brightened her whole face.

Even though the smile hadn't been directed at him, Joel found himself basking in the warmth. He wondered why Kate didn't smile more often. After a second he forced his attention back to her friend. "Will you be staying long?"

"Through the end of the year at Spring Gulch and with Kate as long as she'll put up with me." Mitzi chuckled. "Right now I'm not sure how long that will be. I can be a real pain sometimes. Who knows? I could be gone tomorrow."

"Ah, Mitzi, you know that's not true." Kate reached an arm around her friend's shoulders and gave her a quick hug. "You're my best friend."

"I had a best friend once," a small voice piped up. "When we lived in Billings."

It took Joel a second to realize that it was Chloe who'd spoken. "You have friends here, too."

Chloe shrugged.

"I know how you feel." Mitzi placed a hand on the girl's shoulder. "Good friends—best friends—aren't always that easy to find."

"Savannah and I used to play every day." Chloe's voice

was so low that Joel had to strain to hear her. "I really miss her."

"Mitzi and I haven't lived in the same town for five years." Kate's eyes softened as they settled on Chloe. "And I missed her so much, but we kept in touch. We sent each other funny cards and we talked on the phone."

Joel guessed that her not mentioning the internet was deliberate and he was grateful to Kate. He closely monitored his daughter's time on the web.

"I don't remember Savannah's address or her phone number," Chloe said in the same small voice, pushing the toe of her shoe against the concrete.

"I'm sure I have them." Joel couldn't believe his daughter hadn't mentioned wanting to contact Savannah before now. Or had she? "How about we call her after your orthodontic evaluation?"

"Thank you, Daddy." Chloe flung her arms around him.

Over his daughter's head, his eyes met Kate's. Something in her gaze pulled him right in. Time seemed to stretch and extend. Without his realizing quite how it had happened, their eye contact turned into something more, a tangible connection between the two of them.

Then Kate blinked and looked away.

Joel could feel heat rising up his neck. Dear God, what had gotten into him? You'd have thought he was a lust-struck teenager.

"There's a lot to do in Jackson Hole," Joel stammered, then stopped and took a deep, steadying breath. "I'm sure you'll like it here."

"I have no doubt of that," Mitzi said.

Her smile was open and friendly while Kate's shoulders were as stiff as any soldier's. Of course, right now, his shoulders were feeling pretty tight, too.

"When I was driving around earlier I noticed an indoor ice rink that I'd like to check out," Mitzi added.

"It's very nice." Joel cast a look in his daughter's direction and she nodded her agreement. "We've been there many times."

"So you like to skate?" Mitzi asked.

"Chloe does. She skates very well." Joel hooked a thumb toward his chest. "Me, I spend more time getting up from falling than I do gliding across the ice."

"Oh, Daddy." Chloe exhaled an exasperated breath. "You're not *that* bad. You just need to practice more."

Mitzi cast a sideways glance at Kate as if waiting for her to add her two cents to the conversation. But the doctor only glanced pointedly at her watch making Joel wonder if she had a patient waiting.

"I'm what would be considered an average skater." Mitzi waved a hand. "I can usually make it around the rink without falling, but I don't do any fancy stuff. Kate, on the other hand, can do it all. She's good enough to be a professional."

"Hardly." Kate gave a self-conscious laugh. "But I've been skating since I was old enough to walk, so it stands to reason I'd be somewhat proficient."

Mitzi's gaze shifted to Chloe, then back to Kate. "Something tells me this young lady might be even better than you are when she grows up."

"I might already be as good." Chloe spoke with the blind confidence of youth. "I've never seen her skate."

Kate simply smiled.

"We'd better get going." Joel rested a hand on his daughter's shoulder. "Wouldn't want to keep Dr. Rallis waiting."

Chloe made a face, making it clear she wouldn't mind skipping the appointment.

Kate resisted the urge to tell the little girl that she'd had braces for six months when she'd been her age and that it hadn't been all that bad. In fact, she could give Chloe some pointers to make the experience better. Then Kate remembered that wasn't her place.

She was Chloe's doctor. Nothing more.

As Kate watched the father and daughter walk away, a melancholy sadness, at odds with the sunny June afternoon, settled around her shoulders.

"I've got a patient waiting," she said to Mitzi. "If I don't get back to the office soon, Lydia will track me down and beat me with my own stethoscope."

"I definitely see the resemblance," Mitzi said.

An image of the office assistant flashed before Kate. Gray hair. Round face. Glasses. Without thinking, Kate grimaced. "You really think Lydia and I look alike?"

Mitzi shook her head, sending her hair swinging from side to side. "Chloe."

An icy chill filled Kate's veins. "What about her?"

"Your daughter, Chloe. She looks just like you."

Chapter Four

Even though Kate couldn't stop a rush of pleasure at the words, she had to put a stop to Mitzi's assumption.

"She.is.not.my.little.girl." Kate spoke slowly and deliberately so there could be no misunderstanding. "She is Joel's little girl."

To Mitzi it might seem like a small distinction, but for Kate it was huge. And it was something she needed to continually keep in mind herself. When she'd signed those papers nine years ago, her child had become Joel and Amy Dennes's daughter. She could not, would not, let herself think of Chloe as hers.

Mitzi didn't respond until they were back in the office and the exterior door had fallen closed behind them. "I saw how you looked at her, Kate."

Kate pulled her brows together. "And how was that?"

"With motherly love." A sudden look of tenderness crossed Mitzi's face. "You might tell yourself she's Joel's daughter. You might have even convinced yourself. But in your heart she's yours. And you love her."

Of course Kate loved Chloe. She'd carried her for nine months. She'd given birth to her. When the attorney had walked from the room with the signed relinquishment papers and her baby—her sweet girl—in his arms, she'd cried and cried.

Her love hadn't disappeared simply because the child was now someone else's daughter. Still, Kate thought she'd done a better job of hiding those feelings. A shiver of fear skittered up her spine. "Do you think Joel noticed?"

"Nah." Mitzi shook her head. "He was too busy drooling over you."

"Yeah, right." Kate's laughter was tinged with relief.

Even if Joel was interested in her, nothing would come of it. Kate couldn't imagine anything with more of a potential for disaster than becoming involved with the adoptive father of her biological daughter.

"We can talk more about this later." Kate glanced at the clock on the wall. Emilie had been waiting for almost fifteen minutes. "Right now I have a patient to see."

"Just one?"

Kate nodded.

"How about I wait?" Mitzi leaned over and brushed a piece of lint from her obviously new boots. "We could go for a walk after you're finished, then grab some dinner. I saw an elk refuge on my way into town that I'd like to explore."

"It'll be like old times." Kate had fond memories of all the walking and talking she and Mitzi had done in medical school. She'd shared so much about her life during those walks.

Mitzi cast a pointed glance at Kate's dress and heels. "What about—"

"Gym bag is in the car."

"Excellent."

On her way out the door, Kate waved a careless hand in the direction of a coffee table littered with professional journals, the light reflecting off the red fire opal on her right ring finger. "They're recent issues. Help yourself."

"*Pediatric and Adolescent Medicine? Journal of Medical Genetics?* Uh, no, thank you." Mitzi's voice followed Kate out into the hall. "Do you happen to have *People* or *Entertainment Weekly?*"

The elk refuge on the outskirts of Jackson had been a good choice, Kate decided. The sun shone warm against her face and a light breeze caressed her cheek. She and Mitzi's only company was a herd of bison far in the distance.

Mitzi slanted a sideways glance, studying her for several seconds. "Biker shorts, UCLA T-shirt and a ponytail. I'm proud to be your friend."

"People in cowboy boots shouldn't throw stones," Kate retorted and Mitzi laughed.

On the way to the wildlife refuge, Mitzi had done most of the talking. Kate had been distracted, unable to forget the despair she'd seen in Emilie Hyland's eyes. Even though the teen confided she'd known for months that she was pregnant, her mother had been stunned by the news. They'd both cried and when Kate thought of the difficult decision the sixteen-year-old would soon face, she'd wanted to cry with them.

"I was thinking back to the day you emailed me that you'd hired a detective to locate your daughter," Mitzi said.

"I worried something had happened to her." Kate

hadn't been looking to interfere in the adoptive parents' lives; she'd simply wanted confirmation Chloe was alive and well.

Sympathy filled Mitzi's blue eyes. "I'd have been frantic, too, when her birthday passed with no pictures or updates."

"First time in nine years." Kate had only known Chloe's adoptive parents as Joel and Amy, not where they lived or how to contact them directly. They'd had less information about her. Not even her first name. The correspondence was one way, filtered through the attorney. "Communication simply stopped."

"Joel should have notified you that Amy had passed away," Mitzi said, a hint of censure in her tone. The investigator Kate hired had obtained the death certificate. Complications from diabetes had been listed as the cause of death. "Even if his wife had been the one who'd sent updates in the past, he should have taken over that task. After all, in a semi-open adoption, that's part of the deal."

"Unfortunately there's no recourse if the adoptive parents don't follow through." Kate expelled a sigh, the past a heavy weight on her shoulders. "You know, sometimes I wonder if I'd have made the same decision if my grandmother had been alive. Or if I hadn't been so exhausted from the pressures of—"

"You did the right thing," Mitzi insisted. "You'd just completed your first year of medical school. You'd worked so hard. Keeping her would have cost you everything."

Although Kate had wanted to be a doctor since she'd put a stethoscope over Raggedy Ann's candy heart, the price she'd paid had been steep. "When I look at Chloe and think of all I've missed, it feels as if I *did* lose everything."

"Don't second-guess yourself." Mitzi stopped in the

middle of the dirt path to face Kate. "You agonized over that decision."

"I did." Lots of sleepless nights. Lots of prayers.

"Now a miracle has happened. You've been given another chance to be part of your daughter's life."

It took several erratic heartbeats for Kate to find her voice. "I gave up that right nine years ago, Mitzi. And after being here for so long, it would be too confusing to Chloe to break my silence now."

"I'm not saying to tell them who you are. I simply think both Joel and Chloe could use a friend like you."

"It makes sense, but—"

"No buts." Mitzi placed a hand on her arm, her voice a gruff rasp. "You put Chloe first when you gave her up. You need to put her welfare first again."

By the time they finished their hike, Kate and Mitzi were hot, sweaty and so tired that everything made them laugh…including the rumble of Kate's stomach. Because it was quick and casual, they decided to eat at Perfect Pizza in downtown Jackson. They ordered their pizza at the counter and had been handed glasses for drinks when Mitzi's phone rang.

In a matter of minutes she was gone, insisting Kate stay behind and wait for the pizza. Since they'd driven separately, it worked. Kate filled her glass with iced tea, tucked the order number under her arm and ambled into the dining room hoping to find a place to sit.

She heard her name and Kate's heart performed a series of flutters at the sound of the familiar baritone. A sense of déjà vu washed over her when Joel motioned her over, his lips lifted in an easy smile. He must have said something to his daughter because Chloe turned and waved, leaving Kate no choice but to head that way.

By the time she reached the booth, Joel was standing, his steady gaze shooting tingles down her spine. He surveyed her from the top of her disheveled ponytail to the tips of her dusty cross-trainers. "You look lovely."

Kate gazed into his eyes, noticing for the first time the green in the hazel depths. Discounting the fact that he was Chloe's adoptive father, there was something about this rugged contractor that appealed to her.

"Where's your friend?" Chloe pushed herself up in her seat and looked around.

"Mitzi is on her way to my house," Kate said. "Her niece was in a car accident this afternoon and she had some calls to make. Once the pizza is ready, I'm headed home, too."

Kate felt it important to make it clear she wasn't eating here. Despite her conversation with Mitzi, Kate still wasn't convinced she should be more involved in Chloe—and consequently, Joel's—life.

"You're welcome to join us while you wait," Joel offered. "We've got plenty of hamburger pizza."

"With extra cheese," Chloe said, sweetening the pot.

There was a beat of silence as Kate hesitated. She felt Joel's gaze on her mouth. Her lips began to tingle.

"Daddy and I were talking about my appointment with the dentist," Chloe said. "He never had braces. Did you have braces, Dr. Kate?"

"I did." Kate moistened her suddenly dry lips with the tip of her tongue and concentrated on the facts. Fact one, she had to wait for the pizza. Fact two, with the dining area so small, it would look like an obvious slight if she sat anywhere else. Fact three, she wanted to sit with them.

"I can move over." Chloe scooted across the bench seat, making room.

Kate turned back to Joel, noticing the five o'clock

stubble on his cheeks. A man's man. "If you're sure I'm not interrupting…"

"Sit down, Doctor." Joel's smile took any sting from the order.

He stepped back at the same moment she moved forward and her arm brushed against his. His body tensed at the brief contact, but Kate pretended she hadn't felt it. Or caught a whiff of his spicy cologne.

She placed the stand with the number card on the edge of the table so it was clearly visible, then slid into the booth next to Chloe. When she turned to drop her hobo bag on the seat, this time it was the little girl who stared.

"You have a ponytail," Chloe said loudly. "Just like mine."

A self-conscious-sounding laugh escaped Kate's mouth. She was about to apologize for her appearance when she saw the pleased look in Chloe's eyes.

"I like my ponytail." Or she had, when it had been all neatly pulled back. Not so much now, with half the strands out of the tail. "Do you like yours?"

"I do." Chloe sounded surprisingly serious. "It keeps my hair off my face. And my neck stays cooler in the summer."

Kate made the mistake of looking at Joel. When his lips twitched, she had to bite the inside of her cheek to keep from smiling. "So true."

Chloe's gaze narrowed. "You don't look like a doctor in those clothes."

Intrigued, Kate angled her head. "Okay, I'll bite. What do I look like?"

Across from her, Joel took a sip of soda. Puzzlement, along with an unmistakable flash of amusement, glittered in his eyes. Apparently he wasn't sure what was going to come out of his daughter's mouth. Well, that made two of them.

Chloe shrugged and took a gulp of milk, suddenly tight-lipped.

Something in Kate told her to let it drop. But curiosity propelled her to offer an encouraging smile. "C'mon, Chloe," Kate urged, "tell me."

"You look—" the little girl took a deep breath then began, again, her hazel eyes staring straight at Kate "—like my mom."

Chapter Five

Kate inhaled sharply.

Joel's pizza slice dropped to his plate.

"Mommy used to wear those black shorts when she went to the gym. Before she got sick." Chloe's voice broke. "Then she died."

Kate swallowed a nervous gasp. For a second, she'd thought that like Mitzi, Chloe had looked at her and seen...

But she hadn't and Kate was relieved. Still, her heart twisted at the pain in Chloe's voice. While some might say it'd been two years and it was time for the child to move on, Kate knew better. Time did make such a significant loss easier to bear, but even after ten years Kate still missed her grandmother. She squeezed Chloe's shoulder. "I can tell you loved your mother very much."

"I did." Tears shimmered in Chloe's eyes. "I miss her so much."

Across the booth, Kate saw Joel stiffen and for a second she thought he might put an end to a conversation. Instead he reached across the table and patted his daughter's hand. The look he shot Kate was filled with unmistakable gratitude. Her breath caught, then began again.

"I bet she loved you just as much," Kate said softly. "I—I know I would if you were my little girl."

Kate clamped her lips shut. *Where had that come from?*

"She told me that she thanked God every day for me." Chloe's voice grew thick. "Didn't she say that, Daddy?"

"You were her world, princess." Joel cleared his throat. "I'll never forget the look on your mommy's face when the nurse put you in her arms. You were only three days old."

Chloe leaned her head against Kate's shoulder and Kate stayed very still, afraid to move and ruin the moment.

Finally Chloe straightened and reached for another piece of pizza, moisture clinging like little crystals to her lashes.

"Do you belong to a gym?"

Joel's question seemed to come out of left field. Not until Kate met his gaze did she understand that while he didn't want to shut down Chloe talking about her mom, he didn't want their evening out to turn maudlin either.

"I joined the Y the month I moved here," Kate said. "I like it there."

"I took swimming lessons at the Y," Chloe said. "One of the girls in my class had her birthday party there. Everyone got to swim and then they had cake and ice cream."

Kate took a sip of tea, missing the feel of Chloe's head against her arm and conscious of the warmth in Joel's eyes that seemed directed straight at her. "Was it fun?"

Two bright spots of pink dotted Chloe's cheeks. "I wasn't invited."

Open mouth. Insert foot.

"Well, if they were trying to keep the party small—" Kate scrambled for a logical answer "—she probably couldn't invite everyone."

"She had pretty invitations that looked like a flower," Chloe advised in a matter-of-fact tone, but Kate saw the hurt in her eyes. "She put them in everyone's cubby at school. All the girls got one except me."

Anger rose inside Kate. What kind of teacher would allow something like that to go on in her classroom?

"How could your teach—" she sputtered, then stopped when Joel shook his head ever so slightly.

"I'm sorry that happened to you." Kate took a deep, steadying breath. "Something similar happened to me when I was your age. It hurts."

Chloe's eyes widened with surprise. "You? They didn't like *you?*"

"Really?" The skepticism in Joel's voice came through loud and clear.

"I was shy," Kate admitted. "We moved when I was eight. My sister, Andrea, had a whole group of new friends the first day. I—I didn't have any. Not for a long time."

Chloe sat quietly for a second, a strange look on her face.

"I have to go to the bathroom." She pinned Kate with her gaze. "You have to move."

"Chloe." A warning sounded in Joel's voice. "Ask, not tell. And say *please.*"

"Please, Dr. Kate." A pleading note sounded in Chloe's voice. "Can you move? I have to go real bad."

"I'm moving." Kate slid out of the wooden bench. "I

need to be leaving anyway. My pizza should be almost done."

"Don't go. You talk to Daddy." Chloe grabbed her hand. "I'll be right back. I promise."

Kate glanced at Joel.

"If you have time…" His eyes seemed to glitter, suddenly looking more green than brown.

"I'll stay," Kate promised the little girl. "And, really, there's no need for you to rush."

"Yes, there is." Chloe hurried off, her legs pressed tightly together.

Only when the child was out of sight did Kate chuckle. "I guess when you gotta go, you gotta go."

"Thanks for agreeing to stay." Unmistakable gratitude flickered in his eyes. "Chloe really likes you."

"I like her, too."

His mouth relaxed in a slight smile. "But please, don't feel you have to make up stories to make her feel better."

"Unfortunately they're true." Kate sighed. "For me, growing up was a painful process. I was gawky, all arms and legs. And very shy."

"Well, you certainly turned out nice." Joel's admiring gaze settled on her. Suddenly her stomach and her heart were involved in a competition for the most flip-flops per minute.

She laughed, a short, nervous burst of air.

"Don't feel like you have to make up compliments so I'll feel better," Kate said teasingly, throwing his earlier words back at him. "I'm well aware of how I look in this outfit."

"You look beautiful." He leaned forward, resting his forearms on the table. The gleam in his eyes sent blood flowing through her veins like warm honey. "Casual. Relaxed. Approachable."

Kate didn't know whether to be insulted or amused. "Are you saying I usually look uptight and unapproachable?"

"Not all the time," he said, with a lopsided smile.

Kate firmly ignored the unsettling flutter in her midsection.

"Your daughter seems like a remarkably well-adjusted little girl," she said, with a studied nonchalance.

Joel didn't smile as she expected.

"Her mother's death hit her hard. And the move here, well, I'm not sure it was the best thing for Chloe." His expression grew somber. "She had a lot of good friends back home. Kids she'd known since kindergarten."

"But surely Chloe has made some new friends by now?"

Joel shook his head. "If she has, I've never seen them. I've noticed girls her age here seem to be much more into adult kinds of stuff than the ones in Montana. Perhaps that's part of the problem."

"You think so?" Kate thought of her patients. Coming from Los Angeles, the children here seemed like such innocents.

"I'll give you an example. A couple of days ago, Chloe asked me for money to buy makeup." The look of bewilderment on Joel's face would have been funny at any other time. "She's nine years old. Who wears makeup at that age?"

"That *is* really young," Kate agreed. "How did she take it when you said no?"

"She just looked at me. There was this expression on her face that I can't even describe."

"Anger? Resentment?"

"Neither. *Crushed* would be more accurate. It would have been easier if she'd been angry."

"Did you ask her why she thought she needed makeup?"

It suddenly hit Kate that they were talking about Chloe the way parents would discuss their child. It seemed so right and, at the same time, so very wrong.

"I didn't think to ask," Joel admitted. "I see now where that would have been a good thing to do."

He looked at her and she felt the impact of his regard all the way down to her feet.

Time to change the subject. "By the way, did Chloe ever get a chance to talk to her friend Savannah?"

"Why don't you ask her?"

"Ask me what?" Chloe asked, sliding into the booth when Kate rose to let her in.

"Did you speak with your friend in Montana yet?" Kate asked.

Chloe smiled broadly, showing her prominent canine teeth. "She was so excited to hear my voice she almost peed her pants."

"Chloe," Joel chided.

"That's what she told me, Daddy."

A half smile tugged at his lips.

Kate leaned forward, resting her arms on the table. "What else did she have to say?"

Chloe had just finished going through the entire conversation sentence by sentence when a red-haired girl with a Perfect Pizza T-shirt and an anxious expression stopped at the table.

"Did you order a large ham and pineapple with cream cheese?" the restaurant employee asked.

Kate smiled at the girl. "I did."

"There was a problem." The teen's cheeks turned as red as her hair. "But the new pizza is in the oven now. It will be ready in about ten minutes. I'm sorry for the delay."

"No worries," Kate said, feeling guilty she wasn't more

distressed. "Just bring it out when it's ready. And if you could put it in a to-go box that would be wonderful."

"Guess you're stuck with us a little while longer," Joel said, not looking sorry at all.

Kate wasn't sorry either. Even though she was still convinced keeping her distance would be best for all concerned, she was enjoying her time with Joel and Chloe. The conversation moved to braces and all things orthodontic. When her stomach growled—even more loudly—Kate finally gave in and accepted a piece of their hamburger pizza.

She'd finished her first piece and had been laughing about something Chloe said when she heard her name being called from across the room.

Sarabeth Brown, one of Kate's patients, waved wildly.

Kate swallowed a groan and waved back. That was one thing she'd quickly discovered after moving to Jackson Hole. Her pediatric patients—and their parents—were everywhere. Restaurants. Grocery stores. Gas stations. It was one reason she always liked to look her best when she went out.

Not today, she thought with a rueful smile. Today she looked…approachable.

As Sarabeth and her mother crossed the dining room, Kate hurriedly wiped her lips with a paper napkin.

"We don't want to interrupt your meal." Mrs. Brown offered an apologetic smile. "Sarabeth saw you and insisted on coming over to say hello."

"Well, I'm happy she did." Kate smiled at the blond-haired child who looked adorable in tan shorts and a hot-pink top. "Hi, Sarabeth. How are you this evening?"

If Kate remembered correctly, the child was about Chloe's age. She wondered if they knew each other.

"Mommy ordered the vegetarian pizza." Sarabeth wrinkled her nose. "I like pepperoni."

"Sarabeth," her mother said sharply. "Dr. Kate doesn't want to listen to you complain when she's out with—"

The brunette paused, her curious gaze settling on Joel.

"Oh, forgive my poor manners," Kate said. "I thought you knew Joel and Chloe."

Before Kate could proceed with introductions, Sarabeth piped up. "I know Chloe, but I didn't know you were her mom."

There was a respect in the little girl's eyes that hadn't been there a second before.

"My mommy died." Chloe tensed beside Kate. "Dr. Kate is—"

"A very good friend," Kate said, looping an arm around Chloe's shoulders.

Sarabeth pulled her sandy-colored brows together. "Oh."

"Honey, your dad is sitting all by himself. We need to go." Mrs. Brown placed a hand on her daughter's shoulder.

"I'll see you tomorrow at day camp," Sarabeth said to Chloe. "Maybe you can be on my kickball team."

"Maybe." Chloe's tone was offhand, but the look in her eyes said she was pleased.

After a few moments more of polite conversation, the mother and daughter headed back to their table.

"Sarabeth is the one who didn't invite me to her party." A thoughtful look stole across Chloe's face. "You know what, Dr. Kate?"

"What, honey?"

"You're a pretty good friend to have."

Joel tucked the sheet up close to his daughter's neck and brushed a kiss across her cheek. Instead of rushing off, like he'd done for much of her young life, he took a seat on the edge of her bed.

When they'd lived in Montana, Amy had done most of the "tucking in." He'd been busy with his business, reviewing blueprints and lining up subcontractors for the next day. On the few occasions when he had gotten Chloe ready for bed, he'd made quick work of it.

It wasn't until Amy was gone and he and Chloe had moved to Jackson Hole that Joel realized how much he'd missed. His wife had tried to tell him how special these end-of-the-day times were, but he hadn't listened. Now he understood. With the lights down low, and quiet filling Chloe's bedroom, conversation and confidences came more easily. It was during these moments that he and Chloe had their best talks.

Like so many nights since moving to Jackson, his daughter gazed up at him. Her lids were heavy, and there was a dreamy smile on her lips. She looked so young in her pink-and-purple-striped pajamas, surrounded by her favorite stuffed animals. "We had fun tonight, didn't we, Daddy?"

"We sure did, princess." Joel thought back over the evening. It certainly hadn't gone as he'd expected. He thought they'd eat quickly and head straight home. Then Kate had arrived and rushing through the meal was suddenly the furthest thing from his mind.

Before the past couple of days, he hadn't really known Kate. Nothing beyond the fact that she was a good and caring doctor. Even though they'd attended many of the same parties, she'd always seemed cool and unapproachable outside of her office. In fact, whenever they *had* spoken, Kate had appeared to have little to say. Of course, she'd usually had a man at her side.

After spending some time alone with her, he realized

she wasn't aloof; she was shy. And she was good with Chloe.

Joel couldn't remember the last time his daughter had smiled so much. He knew her joy this evening had been due in large part to Kate McNeal. The doctor had kept the conversation focused on his child. Chloe had blossomed under all the attention.

"I'm glad Dr. Kate ate with us." Chloe relaxed against her pillow, a smile of contentment on her face.

"That was nice," he said, still disturbed by his attraction to the pretty doctor.

Chloe's lips turned upward. "I liked Dr. Kate's ponytail."

"Uh-huh," Joel murmured.

Normally he'd have been thrilled to have his daughter so talkative, but not when all conversational roads seemed to lead to Kate McNeal. "So how's day camp been going?"

It was the wrong thing to say. The happiness spurted from Chloe's face quicker than water flowing from a just-opened dam. "It's...okay."

Joel remembered Kate asking him if his daughter had any friends. He recalled how embarrassed he'd felt when he had to admit he couldn't say for sure one way or the other. What kind of father didn't know something like that?

"You and Sarabeth seemed to hit it off tonight." He hesitated, feeling as uncertain as a soldier navigating a minefield. "Perhaps you could invite her over to the house to play sometime?"

Chloe turned her face toward the wall. Even without speaking, the defeated slump to her shoulders gave him an answer he didn't want to hear.

"She—they—all think I'm ugly."

Her answer was so soft that Joel didn't understand what she'd said. He thought at first she'd said they all thought she was ugly. But that couldn't be. His precious little girl was beautiful.

"I'm sorry, princess," he said. "I didn't hear what you said."

With great reluctance, Chloe shifted to face him and propped herself up on her elbows. "Can I have money to buy some lip gloss?"

The "no" had already started to form on Joel's lips but he stopped himself.

Did you ask her why she thought she needed makeup? Kate's voice, whisper soft in his memory, helped him refrain.

"Why is it so important to you to have this lipstick?"

"Lip *gloss,* Daddy, not lipstick." Her irritated huff made him want to simply say no immediately, but he silently counted to ten and waited.

"Because *all* the girls wear lip gloss," she said finally. "It makes them look pretty."

While Joel certainly didn't consider himself wise to the ways of nine-year-old girls, he felt very certain that not *all* of the other girls her age were wearing makeup. He had to believe there were still a few sensible parents out there. And it disturbed him that his bright daughter seemed to be such a follower.

"If everyone was jumping off a bridge, would you do it?" The second the words left his mouth, Joel realized it was the same phrase his father had used on him. And he'd always hated it.

"You don't understand." Chloe's eyes flashed. "You don't care about me. All you care about is that stupid job. If Mommy was here, *she'd* understand."

Joel felt as if he'd been shoved to the ground and

kicked in the side with a steel-toed boot. Anger rumbled through him. Didn't she realize how hard this had been for him? Didn't she realize she wasn't the only one hurting?

He opened his mouth to tell her that but came to his senses just in time.

She was the child.

He was the adult.

Chloe's hands clenched into tiny fists. Every part of her body spewed defiance, from her stiffened shoulders to her eyes flashing amber fire.

In that moment, he couldn't see a trace—not even a glimpse—of the sweet little girl who'd insisted he come to her tea parties. The one who'd told him over and over how much she loved him.

But Joel knew, behind all that bravado, that little girl had to be in there someplace. He had to find a way to reach her.

"How 'bout we talk more about this tomorrow, when we're not so tired?" he said with a conciliatory smile.

Chloe thought for a long moment, then nodded, her body relaxing again. In a few minutes her eyes fluttered shut. "I like Dr. Kate," she murmured before falling asleep.

"I do, too," Joel muttered under his breath, the admission only adding to his frustration.

While he'd enjoyed the evening immensely, the unfairness still rankled. It should have been Amy sitting next to Chloe and making her laugh. It should have been Amy casting teasing glances his way.

And it should have been Amy he was trying to impress, not Kate.

Joel let his gaze linger on his sleeping daughter for a couple more heartbeats before jerking to his feet, his odd mood tinged with an even more disturbing realization. Tonight, for the first time since Amy had passed away, his wife hadn't been front and center in his thoughts.

Instead of thinking about her, instead of remembering all the good times they'd had, he'd been fully in the moment with Kate. Her intellect and wry sense of humor had intrigued, her body had tantalized.

Although slender as a willow branch, she had curves in all the right places. The biker shorts had shown off her slender legs to full advantage and her curves had sent his mind careening down a road he had no intention of traveling. He couldn't be interested in Kate. Not in that way. She was Chloe's doctor, for Christ's sake.

Casting one last look at his daughter, Joel stepped into the hall and quietly closed her door. The yearnings he'd experienced hadn't been about Kate, he told himself; he'd simply been without a woman for too long. If he wasn't careful, Widow Dombrowski at the Food Mart was going to start looking good.

He smiled, wishing his attraction to the pretty, young doctor could be so easily dismissed. The truth of the matter was, he liked Kate. He enjoyed her company. And God help him, he found her extremely sexy.

But it had been only two years since Amy's passing, and he and Chloe were still mourning her loss. It was much too soon to get involved with another woman. No matter how attracted he was to her.

Chapter Six

Kate let her hair fall loose from the clip it had been in all day and fluffed it with her fingers before pulling the keys from her purse. Since Mitzi was having dinner tonight with the doctors at her new practice, Kate planned to stop at the store on her way home and do her weekly grocery shopping.

Grocery shopping on a Friday night? Even though it sounded pathetic, it would free up the weekend, which promised to be a busy one. Tomorrow she and Mitzi were shopping during the day and attending Travis and Mary Karen Fisher's summer solstice party that evening. Then Sunday would be church and ice skating in the afternoon. At least if Mitzi got her way.

Kate wondered if Joel would be at the party tomorrow. She hadn't seen or heard from him since she sat with him and Chloe at Perfect Pizza on Monday.

Not that she expected to, of course. He had no reason to

contact her. Which is what she wanted, right? The thought was oddly depressing.

"Dr. McNeal." Lydia stood in the doorway. "I realize you've finished for the day, but one of your patients just showed up. The father thinks she'll need stitches."

Kate hesitated. It had been a long week and she was ready to have it over. Still, if she didn't see the child, the parent would be forced to take her to the E.R., which, depending on the girl's age, could be traumatic.

"Take her to room three, Lydia." Kate dropped her keys back into her purse and locked the drawer. Reaching for her lab coat she rose to her feet. "Who's the patient?"

"Chloe Dennes," Lydia said over her shoulder.

For a second Kate froze. Then she jumped to her feet and hurried down the hall, pulling on her lab coat as she ran. She arrived just as Lydia was ushering Joel and Chloe into the room decorated with dancing hippos in tutus. Chloe's green Earth Day T-shirt was stained with blood, as was the hand towel she held tightly pressed to the left side of her forehead. Joel's face was as white as his shirt.

"Kate." He turned toward her and his eyes lit up. "Thank God you were still here."

Lydia glanced curiously at the handsome widower before returning her attention to Kate. "I'll lock the door on my way out. Unless there's something else I can do for you?"

If the older woman had been a nurse or a medical assistant, Kate might have asked her to stay. But she was a front-office person who'd displayed a tendency to go woozy at the sight of blood. Thankfully the woman kept her gaze averted from Chloe.

"We'll be fine, Lydia. Thanks for offering," Kate told her. "Have a good weekend."

Instead of immediately taking out any supplies, Kate

wheeled a stool in front of where the child now sat. Joel had taken the chair next to his daughter, but Chloe had positioned herself in the seat as if to get as far away from him as possible. Kate also noticed the girl refused to look at him. Very odd.

Kate looked into the girl's tear-filled eyes and her heart overflowed with love. Mitzi had been right. This wasn't just another patient. Kate would do whatever necessary to help her daughter.

"I'm going to take good care of you, Chloe." Kate kept her voice calm and soothing. "Understand?"

The little girl sniffled, then nodded.

With great gentleness, Kate removed the towel Chloe held against her head. In addition to a half-centimeter gash that had stopped bleeding, there was a nasty bruise beginning by her eye. A dark discoloration and swelling that Kate knew would look worse before it got better.

It was the type of injury often seen after a punch to the eye or a hard slap to the side of the face. A sense of unease crept up Kate's spine. She didn't want to be suspicious, but between the injury and Chloe's behavior, something wasn't right.

"Is she going to need stitches?" Joel's eyes were filled with worry, his jaw tight with strain. Splatters of blood dotted his white shirtfront.

Kate forced a smile to her lips. "Joel, would you mind leaving Chloe and me alone for a few minutes?"

"Leave?" His brows slammed together. "Why would I leave? If you're worried I'm going to faint I can assure you that—"

"Nothing like that." Kate placed a hand on his arm and looked into his eyes. "I simply need to speak with Chloe for a few minutes."

"'S okay, Daddy." Chloe's gaze remained on the doctor. "Dr. Kate will take care of me."

Joel reluctantly pulled to his feet. "I'll be right outside in the hall," he said to his daughter, completely ignoring Kate.

Kate knew she'd made him angry but it couldn't be helped. With the cut above Chloe's eye and the surrounding skin starting to blacken, their office protocol—and the law—required she interview the child alone. As much as it pained her to do it, she had no choice.

Opening up an ice pack, Kate handed it to Chloe and had her press the coldness against her rapidly swelling eye. "I need you to tell me what happened."

Chloe's gaze dropped to her lap. "I lost my balance and hit the edge of the coffee table."

That might explain the laceration. It didn't explain the black eye and the way the child was acting.

"What about your eye?"

The child chewed on her lip. "I hit it on the floor when I fell?"

Kate noted Chloe had answered with a question, as if searching for an acceptable explanation. Red flags began popping up in her head.

"Is that what happened?"

Chloe nodded vigorously, then winced.

"What were you doing when you fell?"

The little girl's shoulders lifted together in a shrug. "I dunno."

A shiver of unease rippled through Kate. The fact that Chloe's eyes refused to meet hers when she was answering told her the child was hiding something.

She clenched her hands into fists. If Joel had hurt her…

No, he wouldn't hurt Chloe. There had to be another

explanation. Kate drew in a deep, steadying breath. "Chloe, look at me."

After several long heartbeats the child lifted her gaze. Tears shimmered in the hazel depths.

"Tell me how this happened." Kate spoke slowly, her eyes never leaving the child's. Her tone made it clear not answering wasn't an option. "Don't leave anything out."

"Daddy was holding on to my arm. I pulled away. That's when I fell."

Kate kept her face expressionless. "Why did you pull away?"

Chloe's dark eyes flashed. "He was yelling at me. I didn't want to listen anymore."

Kate waited.

"He's mean."

Kate's heart stopped at the vehemence in Chloe's tone. She leaned forward and took the child's hand in hers. "Does your father hurt you?"

Confusion filled the girl's eyes. "Huh?"

"Does he hit you? Push you?" Kate could barely get the questions past her suddenly stiff lips. "Slap you?"

"What? No." Chloe looked shocked Kate would even make such a suggestion. "Daddy wouldn't do that."

"You said he was mean," Kate pointed out.

"Not in *that way*. He doesn't understand how important—" Chloe stopped and clamped her lips shut.

Kate expelled a frustrated breath. "I guess I'm going to have to ask your dad to come back in, so I can determine what went on."

Chloe shifted her gaze out the window.

Kate rose and opened the closed door. As she'd anticipated, rather than taking a seat in the chair, Joel stood, hands jammed into his jeans pockets, rocking back on his heels.

"May I come in now?" The irritation in his voice said clearly what he thought about being relegated to the hall.

"It wasn't personal." Kate kept her tone professional. "Anytime a child comes in with her type of injury, we speak with them alone."

Confusion blanketed Joel's handsome face. "Why?"

Kate paused, knowing he wasn't going to like her answer. "To make sure the injury was indeed an accident and not the result of…abuse."

"Abuse?" His face turned red and he roared the word. "You thought I hurt Chloe?"

Kate lifted her chin. "It's protocol."

"You know me, Kate. Or I thought you did." His tone turned cold, his eyes practically frosty. "May I comfort my daughter now? Or do you have a protocol for that, too?"

Kate flushed at the sarcasm.

Without waiting for an answer he brushed past her. She opened her mouth to say she was sorry, then shut it without saying a word. She had no reason to apologize. Even though her heart said he was incapable of hurting his child, logic said it was possible. As far as she was concerned he still hadn't been cleared. Which meant before she let Chloe walk out the door with him, all questions would be answered to her satisfaction.

"You haven't even touched her cut," Joel said accusingly. "Chloe lost all that blood and you've done *nothing*."

"Cuts on the head and face always bleed more because of all the blood vessels in the skin," Kate informed him. "The blood loss looks like a lot more than it is."

"Oh," was all he said.

"Chloe, I'm going to clean you up a bit. While I'm doing that, your daddy is going to tell me how you hurt yourself."

Kate fixed her gaze on Joel.

"We were talking. She started to walk away. I grabbed her arm. She pulled away and fell. The gash game from the edge of our glass-topped coffee table. I'm not sure about the eye. It had to happen when she hit the hardwood floor." Regret blanketed Joel's face. "I should have just let her walk away."

"What were you arguing about?" Kate asked.

"We weren't *arguing*. We were *discussing*. Or rather, I was trying to discuss."

"Okay, what were you discussing?" Kate asked, trying to keep the frustration from her voice.

"Don't Daddy, don't," Chloe begged. "Please don't tell her. She'll hate me."

Kate finished pulling on her gloves and paused. Why would Chloe think she would hate her? It didn't make sense.

"She won't hate you, honey," Joel began.

"There is *nothing* you could do that would make me hate you," Kate said with a fierceness that surprised them all.

Chloe's eyes widened. "Really?"

"It's true." Kate began to gently clean the area around the wound, trying to regain her composure. While she'd loved this child when she was born, that feeling couldn't compare to the depth of her love now. Or to the protective urge that made it hard to think rationally at a moment like this.

"Chloe has been after me to buy her lip gloss." Joel cast a sideways glance at his daughter who kept her gaze averted. "While we were in the drugstore this afternoon picking up her allergy medicine, she asked again. I told her no. Apparently she didn't like that answer because she put a tube in her pocket. The manager saw her and stopped us on the way out the door."

A pained expression crossed his face and Kate sensed his confusion and his embarrassment.

"Thankfully Mr. Henderson didn't press charges." He glanced pointedly at his daughter and she flinched. "When we got home, I tried to discuss what had happened, but Chloe didn't want to talk." Frustration underscored the words. "I'm just glad her mother wasn't around to see this."

"Mommy would have understood," Chloe cried out.

"Your mother would never have condoned thievery," Joel roared.

Chloe pushed up from the chair.

"Relax, honey." Kate put a hand on the girl's shoulder. "You need to sit and stay very still for me. Can you do that?"

With tears slipping down her cheeks, Chloe nodded.

"Why don't you tell us why having lip gloss was so important to you." Kate kept her tone light and nonjudgmental. "Your dad and I are going to listen because we really want to understand."

Kate glanced at Joel and he reluctantly nodded.

"All the girls my age wear lip gloss," Chloe began.

Joel opened his mouth, but Kate shot him a warning glance and he shut it without speaking.

"They think I'm ugly." Chloe drew a shuddering breath. "I thought maybe if I had some lip gloss I might be pretty and they'd like me."

"How could anyone think you're ugly?" Joel looked shocked. "You're beautiful."

"You have to say that," the child said in a dismissive tone. "You're my dad."

"Well, *I* don't have to say it and I happen to agree with

him." Kate thought for a second. "I'm wondering if perhaps your father doesn't realize what lip gloss looks like."

The girl and her father exchanged confused glances. Kate wasn't sure what she was doing either. She only knew she had to help these two find some common ground.

"Joel, would you reach into my pocket please?" Kate lifted her arm and gestured to the right side of her lab coat.

He hesitated for a second, then moved closer. The spicy scent of his cologne surrounded her. Her traitorous heart picked up speed, the way it always did around him. He leaned near, careful not to touch her. His tense shoulders and the tight set to his jaw told her that while he was willing to go along with this, he still hadn't forgiven her for banishing him to the hall. Or for practically accusing him of child abuse.

After he'd pulled out the small tube of the neutral-colored lip gloss Kate used over her lipstick for extra shine, he held the small cylinder out to her. "What do you want me to do with this?"

"First I want you to look at my mouth."

"This is ridiculous…" he hissed.

"Please, Daddy, do as she asks."

His gaze dropped to Kate's mouth and her body took on a warmth at odds with the room temperature. When her lips began to tingle, she knew she had to keep the illustration moving. For her sake as well as his.

"What do you see?"

Joel looked at her as if she'd lost her mind. "Lips."

She smiled. Typical man.

"Put the lip gloss on me."

Joel dropped his gaze to the tube, two lines forming between his brows.

"You unscrew the top, then pull the applicator thingy out," Chloe instructed. "That's what you smooth on her lips."

"Shouldn't you be stitching my daughter up?" Joel growled.

Kate smiled and waved a hand. "There's no rush."

With an irritated huff, Joel leaned forward, applying the gloss as if he was painting a fence board with a wide-bristle brush. Still, for several seconds, his face, his lips, were right.in.front.of.her.

Kate's breath hitched. The answering flare of heat in his eyes told her his anger had changed to something a lot more dangerous. At least as far as she was concerned.

"Tell me," she asked when he sat back, "what do you see now?"

"A pretty woman," he said flatly.

Chloe giggled, easing some of the tension.

Kate rolled her eyes, but the truth was, she liked the unexpected compliment. "Focus," she told Joel, "on the mouth. What word comes to mind?"

"Shiny."

"Exactly," Kate said triumphantly. "Shinier lips."

She saw the moment he made the connection.

"This is your way of telling me—of showing me—that Chloe wearing lip gloss should be no big deal." He smiled, a crooked boyish sort of smile that sent her stomach into flips and melted her heart. "Certainly not something worth arguing over."

"Exactly right." Kate shifted her gaze to Chloe. "But stealing, well, that is something worth discussing."

"I know." Chloe let out a beleaguered sigh, then with her bottom lip trembling, she turned to her father. "I'm sorry, Daddy. I promise I won't take anything ever again."

Joel looked as if he wanted to pull her into his arms, but settled for squeezing her closest hand instead.

"When we leave here, I think we should go back to the store," Chloe said. "I want to apologize to Mr. Henderson."

"He'd appreciate that," Joel said. "And maybe we can buy you a tube of this stuff while we're there."

"Really, Daddy, really?"

Joel nodded. "I'm sorry I didn't listen to you before when you tried to talk to me about the lip gloss."

"It's okay." Chloe shifted her attention back to Kate. "Will the stitches hurt?"

"I have good news and bad news." Kate smiled. "The good news is that now that I've had a chance to inspect and clean the wound, no stitches are needed. Instead, we're going to glue the edges together."

"Glue?" Joel looked surprised.

Chloe looked pleased. "Superglue?"

Kate chuckled. "Actually I'll be using a special skin glue that's quite similar. It will keep the edges together until the laceration heals. And it dissolves by itself in seven to ten days, so you don't have to come back."

"What's the bad news?" Chloe asked.

"You're going to have one heck of a shiner."

"You're quite the party animal." Mitzi stood back while Kate perused the dresses at a boutique in downtown Jackson.

"That's me," Kate said with a wry smile. "Wild and crazy."

Moving to Jackson Hole had been quite an education. Kate hadn't known what to expect from this part of the country. What she'd found were people who liked to work hard and play even harder. Tonight, she and Mitzi would attend a party celebrating the change of seasons.

"I've never been to a party heralding the arrival of the summer solstice," Mitzi said. "Being from Los Angeles, I thought I'd seen everything."

"For Mary Karen and Travis, any excuse will do. They love to entertain. Lexi and Nick are like that, too. Because most of their friends have children, kids are usually included."

"Are you telling me there will be toddlers underfoot and babies screaming?" Mitzi wrinkled her nose. "On second thought I may have to stay home and wash my hair this evening."

"Trust me, it'll be fun." Still, Kate couldn't help but remember one event where she'd looked down and seen Connor—one of Mary Karen's twins—dressed in camouflage and crawling commando-style under a coffee table with a toy hand grenade in his hand. But that had been during a book-club meeting, not a full-blown party like tonight. "For the bigger parties, they hire college girls to watch the children. The kids will have their own 'party' in another part of the house."

Mitzi's face brightened. "Okay, so maybe I don't need to wash my hair tonight after all."

With renewed enthusiasm, her friend shifted her focus back to the task at hand. Plunging her hand into a rack of clothes, Mitzi pulled out a dress. "How about this one?"

Oversize violet and yellow flowers decorated the bodice of the ugliest dress Kate had ever seen.

"Uh, no." Kate tried not to cringe. "Those aren't my colors...and they're definitely not yours."

Mitzi laughed and shoved the garment to the back of the rack. "I can't believe you thought I was serious."

"You *did* show up at my office wearing cowboy boots," Kate pointed out.

"It's Jackson Hole." Mitzi winked, an impish gleam in her eyes. "Not New York during Fashion Week."

Before Kate could think of a comeback, she caught sight of another dress, one she hadn't noticed before. Sleeveless and the color of raspberry sherbet, it had a scooped neck and wide jeweled belt.

Kate held it up. "What do you think of this one?"

"Ooh, I love it," Mitzi squealed.

"I'm going to try it on." Dress in hand, Kate turned in the direction of the fitting rooms.

Before she'd taken two steps, Mitzi blocked her path. "Will the fabulous Mr. Dennes be at the soiree this evening?"

"I'm terribly sorry," Kate said in a fake English accent. "I haven't been privy to the guest list."

She held the dress up and studied it carefully.

"But he'll probably be there, right?"

"I really like this dress," Kate said.

"He'll be there," Mitzi said, answering her own question. "You know it and you're glad. Cuz you like him."

Kate groaned. She refused to revisit a subject that had already been beaten into the ground. Bottom line, becoming involved with Joel as anything more than a casual friend would be a mistake on too many levels to count. "Of course I like him. He's a nice guy. But that doesn't mean I want to date him."

"Would you mind if I did?"

Kate jerked her head up from the belt she'd been inspecting. "Date Joel?" She narrowed her gaze. "Are you serious?"

"What do you think?" Mitzi's blue eyes were all wide-eyed and innocent.

"You're not interested." Kate wasn't sure whether to feel exasperated or relieved.

"I may not want him...but you do." Mitzi grinned. "That's what makes teasing you so much fun."

"Read my lips. I'm only interested in Joel Dennes because he's Chloe's dad."

"And because he's got a phenomenal ass."

"Never noticed."

"A ruggedly handsome face."

"He's not ugly," Kate grudgingly admitted, knowing that was an understatement.

"Best of all he's got big hands and feet."

Kate frowned. "What does the size of his hands and feet have to do with anything?"

Mitzi wiggled her brows. "Supposedly men who have big hands and feet have a big—"

"Old wives' tale."

"You're such a priss." Mitzi's saucy smile took any sting from the words. She pulled out a slinky-looking red dress with a slit up the side that would have done a hooker proud. "Does this mean you're not going to spill when you find out if Joel's, uh, size correlates with those big feet?"

"If I did sleep with him—which is absolutely never going to happen—I certainly wouldn't give you details." Kate headed for the dressing room with long purposeful strides, ready to put an end to this ridiculous discussion.

Mitzi hurried to catch up, obviously determined to have the last word. "One of these days you're going to have to admit it, Kate."

"Admit what?"

"You're not just interested in Chloe." Mitzi's gaze met hers. "You're interested in her dad, as well."

Chapter Seven

The "summer solstice" party at Mary Karen and Travis's new home ended up being as much a house-warming event as a celebration of summer's arrival. Most of the guests brought a bottle of wine, a plant or some other small item.

Kate came with a bottle of champagne in hand, knowing it was Mary Karen's favorite beverage. Any woman who daily dealt with a doctor husband and five small children deserved to get something special just for her.

Mary Karen squealed when she saw the gift, then gave both Kate and Mitzi a big hug. After an impromptu tour of the large home, Mary Karen got called to the kitchen. Kate and Mitzi stood around sampling a few of the delectable appetizers Lexi had made especially for the party.

Even while she asked and answered questions, Kate surreptitiously scanned the room for people she knew. Her surveillance activity was briefly interrupted when a woman who was involved in working with Jackson Hole's immigrant population stopped over to say hello. During the introductions that followed, Mitzi mentioned she was bilingual. The woman's eyes had lit up and a discussion of the part Mitzi could play in the medical community was off and running. After a few minutes of polite listening, Kate wandered off.

She found a spot by the floor-to-ceiling stone fireplace and resumed her people watching. Men in casual pants and cotton shirts. Women in colorful dresses and flouncy skirts. Everyone talking and laughing. People she knew and those she recognized. Normally the parties she attended were smaller and more intimate. At those events, finding who she was looking for was easy.

Standing there in her raspberry-sherbet dress and black eel-skin heels, Kate sipped her glass of white wine and wondered if Mitzi might be right about her attraction to Joel.

Even though the anticipation over seeing Chloe again might partially account for the nervous quiver in her stomach, it didn't explain the extra time she'd spent on her makeup and hair.

On her way home from the "Great Dress Hunt," she'd picked up some eye shadow guaranteed to make her eyes dark and mysterious along with a tube of lipstick that matched her dress. While getting ready for the party, rather than leave her hair hanging loose, she'd pulled the dark strands off to one side in a low stylish bun.

Had she really gone to all this extra effort simply to celebrate the arrival of the summer solstice? Kate tightened her fingers around the stem of the wineglass.

Joel was an attractive single man whom she admired, she told herself. She'd admired him even more when he'd called to apologize for his gruffness in the office and to thank her for looking out for his daughter's welfare. Still, that didn't mean she was foolish enough to consider dating him. Or, heaven forbid, sleep with him.

Darn Mitzi for even putting that idea in her head.

Still, reassured by her logic, Kate relaxed her hold, took a sip and decided that rather than continue to survey the room like some spy in a Grade B movie, she would socialize.

With bold confident steps and her head held high, Kate started across the room. She'd barely gone ten feet when a couple crossed in front of her without warning. She abruptly changed course to avoid a collision and ran straight into a broad muscular chest.

Her white wine flew forward. She stumbled backward, teetering on the edge of her four-inch heels. Just when she thought a fall was inevitable, a pair of large hands reached out and steadied her.

Kate looked up into the concerned eyes of Joel Dennes. The gallop in her chest became an all-out sprint.

"I thought you weren't coming," she blurted out.

Joel glanced down at his shirt. A twinkle filled his eyes. "I'm happy to see you, too."

Even with wet splotches of wine across the front of his brown shirt, Joel looked way too appealing. His normally longish hair had been recently trimmed and he'd exchanged his jeans and work boots for khakis and stylish loafers.

"I'm sorry about the wine." Kate mumbled the apology, her tongue thick and unwieldy.

"I'm sorry I knocked you off your feet." He flashed a warm smile that brought back that off-kilter feeling she'd had when she was falling.

They exchanged a smile before his gaze dropped and traveled down her body. When those piercing hazel eyes reached her bodice, Kate felt her nipples strain against her lace bra. As his gaze dropped lower, an almost forgotten heat filled her abdomen.

She felt like protesting when he shifted his attention back to her face, until she saw the look of pure masculine appreciation in his eyes.

"You look nice," he said, his eyes glittering.

"So do you. I mean you did—" Kate gestured toward his damp wine-splattered shirt "—before…"

"A certain beautiful doctor threw a glass of wine at me?"

He thinks I'm beautiful. A thrumming filled her veins. She gazed at him through lowered lashes. "Only because a certain handsome contractor chose to block my path."

A smile slowly made its way across his face. In response, an answering one lifted her lips.

Unexpectedly Joel put an arm around her waist and pulled her close to let a waiter with a platter of tiny sandwiches pass by them. Her heart gave an excited leap.

If she'd been a teenager, having him so near would have made her swoon. She may have kept her composure, but her insides quivered as he maneuvered her through the crowd. "First you block my way, now you're spiriting me off to God knows where."

"Blocking your path was the only way to get your attention." He grinned and shot her a wink before stopping in an alcove just off the main room.

"A tad dramatic." Kate put a finger to her lips. "But I like your style."

She resisted the urge to tell him that she'd been searching for him since she'd arrived. Instead, she gestured to the crowded room. "Look at this party. All sorts of interesting guests are here this evening."

"If you feel that way, why were you alone?"

"I'm better one-on-one."

"Me, too."

"Your daughter seems to do better one-on-one, too." Kate tried to ignore the spicy scent of his cologne. "By the way, how is Chloe?"

"Very well, other than her eye. You were right." Joel shook his head. "She's got quite a shiner."

"Did you bring her tonight?"

"She's downstairs at the kids' party. Lexi's daughter Addie spirited her away the second we came through the door." Joel's gaze turned thoughtful. "I wish Addie were a couple years younger. She and Chloe would be good friends."

Every time Kate thought about Chloe feeling left out, her heart ached. She'd been there. It wasn't a happy place to be. "How are things in the friend arena?"

"If you're asking about day camp…" He shrugged. "About the same. But she's been talking to Savannah every evening and that makes her happy."

A waiter with an empty tray stopped to take Kate's glass.

"May I get you another drink?" Joel asked.

"Do you think that's wise?" Kate spoke with mock seriousness. "Are you sure you want to procure alcohol for a person already proven to be tipsy?"

By the blank expression on his face, she realized he'd missed the point of her pathetic stab at humor. No wonder she'd never been a social success. She lifted one foot and wiggled it back and forth, then pretended to lose her balance. "Tipsy. Get it?"

His gaze lingered for an extra beat on her leg, then he chuckled, a low pleasant rumbling sound. "Got it."

"Mental note," Kate said with a teasing smile. "Spell it out for Joel."

"Hey," he said with mock outrage.

"It's okay." Kate patted his arm. "In the future I'll keep it simple. Make it easier for you to comprehend."

She'd been bantering with Mitzi so much this past week that Kate responded to Joel in the same manner. For a second she worried she'd carried the teasing too far. Until he broke into laughter.

With a smile tugging at her own lips, she shifted her gaze out the window. "It's much too beautiful a night to be indoors. What would you say if I asked you to go outside and swing with me?"

On the tour Mary Karen had given her and Mitzi, Kate had taken note of a porch swing in a backyard gazebo. She didn't feel that it was necessary to explain which swing. Joel had built this beautiful home.

"If you ask me," he said, his expression turning serious, "I will say yes."

There it was again, a connection, a spark, a fiery heat she hadn't felt in years. An intense attraction that should send any woman with her secrets running for the hills. Instead of taking off as fast as her heels would carry her, Kate rested a hand on his arm.

"Would you come outside and swing with me?" she asked in a tone that bordered on flirtatious.

His eyes danced with sudden humor. "I'd love to play on the swings with you, Dr. McNeal."

Play?

Kate found the possibilities intriguing.

Nonononono. What was she thinking? Playing with Joel was too dangerous. Unfortunately if she backed out now, she'd look like a total flake. Or worse yet, a shameless flirt.

Besides, she simply wanted to swing with Joel.

That's all.

How could that kind of play be dangerous?

Feeling reassured, Kate considered the next hurdle—how to get outside without attracting attention. Many of the people at this party were into "couple activities," which meant if they found out where she and Joel were headed, they'd want to join them.

"If we want to make a clean break, the best exit to use would be the one in the kitchen," his voice whispered in her ear.

Kate whirled to face Joel, wondering how he'd known what she'd been thinking.

Even though she hadn't said a word, he tapped the side of his head with an index finger. "Psychic."

Kate rolled her eyes. The man was incorrigible.

Joel gestured to where Mitzi stood halfway across the room still talking to the economic-development woman. "Do you need to tell your friend where you'll be?"

Lifting a brow, Kate smiled. "You're the one who's psychic. You tell me."

"I'd like to hear it from you."

"You're good." Kate laughed. "Actually I doubt Mitzi will notice I'm gone. Because we came in her rental car, even if she does, she'll know I can't be far."

"Chloe knows to have someone call my cell if she needs me, so it sounds like all bases are covered." Joel pointed to a slight break in the crowd. "Looks like an escape route has opened up."

Anticipation skittered up Kate's spine. "Ready when you are, James Bond."

Joel lifted his eyes to the heavens. "The woman asks me to go outside and she doesn't even know my name."

Kate punched him in the shoulder. "Get movin', Sherlock."

Luckily no one stopped them on their way to the

kitchen. They'd barely stepped past the large refrigerator when Joel brought a finger to his lips, whispering there were footsteps headed their way.

"Quick," he urged, "out the back."

By the time they reached the gazebo and plopped into the swing, they were both laughing.

"Ohmigod." Kate wiped tears from the corner of her eyes with her fingertips. "Who knew making a quick getaway could be so much fun?"

"I haven't laughed this much in years." Joel's eyes crinkled with good humor. He gestured to the broad expanse of lawn flanked by tall evergreen trees. "Coming out here was a brilliant suggestion."

Kate exhaled a contented sigh and lifted her eyes to the clear, star-filled sky. "I didn't realize there was a full moon tonight."

Like a huge yellow orb, the moon cast its glow on the earth below. Over the Tetons with snow still lingering on their peaks. Over the trees filling the air with their pungent scent of pine. Over the gazebo with its gingerbread trim.

A breeze caressed Kate's cheek as she swung back and forth, but she wasn't at all cold. How could she be? Heat rolled off Joel in waves.

An image surfaced of Joel covering her like a blanket on a snowy winter's night. Kate shivered, imagining the feel of his bare skin against hers, the touch of his lips—

"Don't tell me you're cold," Joel whispered in her ear.

Kate hoped the dim light hid the heat flooding her face in a warm tide. She shoved aside the stranded-in-a-blizzard-with-a-sexy-contractor fantasy. "Nope, not at all."

He rested his arm on the back of the swing behind her and leaned in close. "Kate, I—"

She wasn't sure what would have happened if the phone in her tiny black purse hadn't begun to vibrate. Kate cast an apologetic glance in Joel's direction and retrieved her smartphone. "I need to take this. I have a patient in the hospital who—"

"Answer it." Joel straightened in his seat. "Do you want me to give you some privacy?"

She shook her head.

"Dr. McNeal." Although she and Joel were the only people in the gazebo, Kate kept her voice low.

"Kate? Is that you?"

"Mother?" Kate stifled a groan. This is what she got for answering without looking at the readout first.

"I'm surprised I reached you," her mother said, sounding peevish. "I was just telling your father the other day that you screen my calls. And don't bother to deny it."

Kate ignored the jab. "I'm surprised to hear from you." She and her mother had already talked on the first of June and Kate hadn't planned to hear from her again until the obligatory call on July 1st. Once a month had always been enough for both of them. "Is everything okay with you and Dad?"

Beside her, Joel stilled.

"We're both fine, although your father's prostate has been giving him fits and my hemorrhoids are a constant battle."

"I'm sorry to hear that." Kate wanted to ask her mother why she was calling, but she held her tongue. Knowing LuAnn McNeal, she'd soon get to the point.

"I suppose you're wondering why I called."

"It crossed my mind." Kate kept her tone light.

"Your Aunt Edith read me the riot act today. She said I should have let you know Elle is in the hospital. I told her it's nothing serious but she insisted I call."

Elle was Kate's niece, the youngest of her sister Andrea's three children.

"Mother, they don't put a three-year-old in the hospital unless it's serious. What's wrong with Elle?"

"They don't know. Not yet anyway." For the first time, her mother sounded uncertain. "But I'm confident they'll figure it out."

Kate's medical training kicked into high gear. "What are her symptoms?"

"Uh, fever and a bad headache," her mother said slowly as if she was trying hard to remember what she'd been told. "She may have a rash, too. I'm not sure."

A chill traveled up Kate's spine. Meningitis. Septicemia. Both of the conditions were serious and required correct diagnosis and treatment for a favorable outcome.

"Is everything okay?" Joel whispered.

"It's my niece," she mouthed, then switched the phone to speaker so she wouldn't have to give Joel a blow-by-blow when she hung up. "Who's her attending?"

"Her what?"

"Her doctor." Kate made a determined effort to keep her mounting irritation out of her voice. "Who admitted Elle to the hospital?"

"Oh, that would be Dr. Markham."

"George Markham?" A sinking sensation filled the pit of Kate's stomach. "The same Dr. Markham that Andrea and I saw when we were children?"

"That's him. I must say it's reassuring to have him be the one taking care of our little Elle."

The general practitioner was a nice guy, but he had to be close to retirement age now. Of course, being in practice for so many years could be an advantage. Or...not.

"If Andrea and Jim would be agreeable, I'd like to call Dr. Markham and speak to him about Elle's case."

"Now, why would you do that?" Her mother sounded truly puzzled.

"Elle's my niece," Kate said with none of the frustration she felt in her voice. "I'm a doctor who specializes in the care and treatment of children."

"Sounds like you think you know more than Doc Markham who has been in practice for forty years." Censure filled her mother's tone. "Bragging is not an attractive quality, Kate. You'd do best to remember that."

Joel's lips twitched.

Kate rolled her eyes. "It's not bragging, Mother, it's a fact. My training, my entire practice is devoted to children and their needs. His isn't."

"Well, I'll mention to Andrea that you offered."

"Is she there? May I speak with her?" Perhaps she was worrying for nothing. For all Kate knew, Dr. Markham may have already called in a specialist.

"Your sister isn't here. She and Jim are at the hospital with Elle. They haven't left her bedside." Her mother made that tsk-tsk noise with her tongue that Kate had always hated. "If you were a mother, Kate, you'd understand that her place is with her child. Nothing is more important."

Kate's cheeks burned as if she'd been slapped. There had been a handful of times over the years when she'd been tempted to tell her mother about the baby she'd given up for adoption. She was glad now that she'd kept silent. She reached up and rubbed her suddenly tight neck muscles. "I'll call Andrea directly."

"Now, don't you go bothering your sister. She's got enough on her plate right now."

Kate clamped her jaw shut and counted to ten. She'd barely reached eight when the sound of shrieks and yelling filled the phone.

"I've got to go," her mother said, sounding relieved. "Jim Junior just slugged Sophie with his plastic bat."

Kate couldn't help but smile. From what she'd heard, Andrea's two oldest had a real love-hate relationship going on. "Keep me—"

The call ended.

"—informed about Elle," Kate finished.

Kate dropped the phone back into her purse, fighting a surge of frustration. Still, from all reports, Andrea was a good mother, and Kate had to trust that if her sister had any questions or wanted her help, she'd call.

"Elle," she informed Joel, "is the youngest child of my sister, Andrea."

"I see," he said, and she wondered if he really did see. His hazel eyes gave nothing away.

"My parents wanted only one child." Resignation, rather than bitterness, filled her tone. "They'd already hit the jackpot. My sister Andrea was a beautiful, intelligent, dutiful child. She grew up to marry the boy next door and give them three lovely grandchildren."

"But you—"

"I, on the other hand, was an oops. A colicky baby who became a scrawny shy little girl who—"

"Grew up to be a successful physician and a wonderful woman and friend." Joel lifted in imaginary drink cup in a mock toast.

"You are so good for my ego." Kate gave him a smile. "An ego which, according to my mother, is already too big."

"Your mother—" Joel paused, apparently holding to the tenet if you can't say something nice, don't say anything at all.

While Kate intended to call Andrea tomorrow and offer her assistance, for now she was content to relax and enjoy Joel's company. She leaned back and inhaled the fresh scent of pine.

"You know if this was a hundred years ago, we'd probably be gathered around a piano drinking lemonade and singing 'Shine On, Harvest Moon.'"

"Sounds like a pleasant way to pass the time." Joel's lips lifted in a lazy smile.

"It is."

Joel lifted a brow.

"My grandmother loved that song. When my sister and I were at her house, she'd usually offer us a glass of lemonade from her cut-glass pitcher. Then Andrea would play the piano and Gram and I would sing. She said the song reminded her of my grandfather."

Now they were both gone. Two loving, caring people who'd never once compared her to Andrea. Who loved them both equally and without reservation.

Unexpected moisture filled Kate's eyes. She blinked and cleared her throat. "Grandad died when I was Chloe's age. Gram passed away the spring before I started medical school."

"Kate."

She blinked a couple times, pulling her thoughts back to the present.

"That had to be tough." Compassion deepened the hue of his eyes. His voice a tender caress on the night breeze. "I know what it's like to lose someone you love."

"Gram was the only one in my family who I could talk with about important things. You know what I mean?"

"I do." His gaze shifted to a point over Kate's left shoulder. Even though he didn't elaborate, she guessed he was talking about his wife.

"I still remember when I got the news that Gram had died in a car accident." Looking back, Kate wondered if she'd have gotten hot and heavy so quickly with Neil if she hadn't felt adrift and alone. And would things have turned out differently if Gram had been around when she'd discovered she was pregnant? She pushed the thought from her head. "Gram called me Katie, not Kate like the rest of my family."

Kate wasn't sure why she'd even mentioned that fact.

"How 'bout we sing a stanza of her favorite song in her memory?" Joel squeezed her shoulder and began to sing.

Kate joined in, her heart tripping over itself. Not only did he know words to a song written almost a hundred years ago, but this lovely baritone blended extremely well with her soprano. Anyone hearing them would have assumed they'd been singing together for years.

The old-fashioned words and melody wrapped around Kate like a favorite sweater. While they sang, she was transported back in time. She saw her grandmother's smile, felt her love and reveled in her approval once again. It was a heady feeling.

"…for me and my gal."

The last note hung in the air.

"Kate."

She turned to find Joel staring. Somehow, without her quite realizing how it had happened, she'd moved closer to him—or maybe he'd moved closer to her—while they'd been singing.

Her gaze met his. For a moment he didn't speak and time seemed to stretch and extend.

"Thank you," she stammered. "That was beautiful."

"*You're* beautiful," he said in a husky voice that made her blood flow like warm honey through her veins.

His fingers weren't quite steady as they touched the curve of her cheek, then trailed along the side of her jaw as he leaned toward her.

He's going to kiss me. He's going to kiss me. He's going to kiss me.

As if wanting to give her a chance to say no, Joel paused. Though his lips were so close that she need only to move a fraction of an inch for his mouth to be on hers, this was her opportunity to sit back and pretend nothing had almost happened.

But Kate's center for rational thought had gone silent and a smoldering heat had begun to build inside her. A sensation she didn't bother to fight. She wound her hands around his neck and squeezed out the last of the distance between them.

Twining strands of her hair loosely around his fingers, he brushed his lips against hers, the slight hint of friction sending a delicious shiver all the way to her toes.

When she opened her mouth, he changed the angle of the kiss, deepening it, kissing her with a slow thoroughness that left her weak and trembling.

She murmured a protest when his lips left hers to trail down her neck to the soft hollow above her collarbone. All the while Joel ran his palms up along her sides, skimming the curve of her breast.

"Touch me," she whispered.

The words had barely passed her lips when he caught her mouth in a hard, deep kiss and his thumbs brushed across the tight points of her nipples.

Her body responded with breathtaking speed. Her need became a stark carnal hunger, one she hadn't known she was capable of feeling.

Then she heard it.

A faint whistling…coming closer.

Chapter Eight

Joel lifted his head. Very abruptly. Then swore.

"Someone's coming."

Kate wasn't sure if she said the words or if Joel did. She was too busy pulling the remaining pins from her bun and letting the hair fall loose to her shoulders. By the time she smoothed her skirt with the palm of her hand, there was a rustle in the nearby trees and Ryan stepped into the clearing. He stopped whistling when he saw them.

Dressed in gray pants and a charcoal-colored shirt, the young attorney looked more like an up-and-coming executive than the former championship bull rider he'd once been. Still, Kate could see traces of that cocky cowboy in his confident stance and his lean muscular body.

Ryan tilted his head to one side, hooked his thumbs in his belt loops as if he were wearing Levi's and rocked back on his heels. "What have we here?"

"A private conversation," Kate said in a cool, dismissive tone.

"Which we have finished," Joel said. "Come join us."

If he'd been sitting closer, Kate would have elbowed Joel in the ribs. Didn't he realize that if you gave Ryan an inch he'd take a mile? But Joel had already scooted away from her—too far for a jab of any kind—and waved Ryan over.

If Kate didn't know better she'd think the contractor was relieved Ryan had come along when he did. Kate knew she should probably be happy for the interruption, but right now all she felt was angry. Okay, and maybe a little disappointed.

"Great night." Ryan plopped himself down between her and Joel. "What did you say you two were doing out here? Oh, that's right. You were having a private conversation."

The humor in his voice, the twinkle in his eyes were her undoing.

While Joel might have been too far away, Ryan was close enough for Kate to give *him* a well-deserved jab in the ribs. Not only was he getting on her nerves, but he was also having a bit too much fun at her expense.

Even though she jabbed him as hard as she could, his smile only widened. Apparently her elbow was a slight tap compared to being speared by a bull.

"I like your hair hanging loose like that, Kate." Ryan's innocent look didn't fool her one bit. "But wasn't it in some sort of bun earlier this evening?"

He shifted his gaze to Joel for confirmation.

Joel leaned forward and peered her way. The passion that had been in his eyes only minutes earlier had disappeared. He shrugged. "I guess I hadn't noticed."

Kate could understand his not wanting to fuel Ryan's curiosity, but the way he was looking at her now—as if he was struggling to remember her name as well as her hairstyle—was too much to bear.

She pushed to her feet, not sure who she was angrier with—Joel for inviting the nosy intruder to join them and acting as though she meant nothing to him, or Ryan for his game playing or herself for caring.

"I'm going inside to check on Mitzi," she announced. "You boys have fun."

"I can walk you—" Joel began.

"I'll be fine." Kate turned and headed back to the house, her shoulders stiff. While she didn't like leaving Joel with Ryan, her emotions were too close to the surface to stay.

As Kate reached the French doors leading inside, she paused and took a deep breath. The brisk walk in the cool mountain air had cleared her head. She reluctantly admitted that what had happened with Joel tonight had been a mistake. Thankfully they'd been stopped before it had gone any further.

As much as it pained her to admit, Ryan had done her a favor by interrupting. Her actions had been reckless, driven by emotion and desire, not by logic.

The way Joel shut down when the attorney appeared told her he'd been equally horrified by his loss of control. *His* impulsiveness she could excuse. But hers? She alone knew the insurmountable secrets that stood between them.

Guilt sluiced through her. Over deceiving him. Over deceiving Chloe. But most of all, over deceiving herself. For allowing herself to believe, even for the briefest of seconds, that there could be something more between her and Joel than friendship.

Joel watched Kate's slim figure disappear from view. The tight set to her shoulders coupled with her abrupt de-

parture left him with a nagging sense that somehow he'd
let her down.

Ryan rose to his feet. "You have to be careful not to
get too close to that one."

He saw Ryan's lips move but the words barely regis-
tered. *How could I have kissed her? Touched her?* Normally Joel prided himself on being firmly in control of
his emotions and his actions. Yet, when he was around
the pretty doctor, he found it difficult to think clearly.

"Consider it friendly advice. One guy to another."

Joel lifted his gaze. While he agreed it would be easy
to get in over his head with Kate, he didn't appreciate her
former boyfriend warning him off.

"Sounds like you're telling me to keep my distance."
Joel lifted a brow. "Is that because you want her for yourself?"

"I like Kate. That's hardly a secret." Ryan walked over
to a nearby pine, a bundle of restless energy. "Do I think
I have a chance with her? Not at all. You've gotten closer
to her in two weeks of dating than I did in six months."

"We're not dating. We—"

"Kate isn't easy to get to know." Ryan turned to face
Joel. "All I'm saying is, if you're looking for something
more than a beautiful dinner companion, I'd look elsewhere."

Joel could tell the man was sincere. But the attorney
was so far off the money it wasn't funny. "I'm not looking for a wife, if that's what you're thinking. A woman
who'd be satisfied with an occasional dinner and a movie
is *all* I'm looking for."

Looking for? Whoa. Where had that come from?
Before this evening Joel had been perfectly content with
his life. He wasn't looking for more of anything.

Ryan thought for a moment, then grinned. "Well, then, I'd say you've found yourself the right gal."

Out of the corner of her eye, Kate saw Joel return to the party with Ryan. She shifted slightly so that her back was to the two men, and continued her conversation with Mary Karen and her sister-in-law, July Wahl.

Kate was still shaking over what had gone on outside. Thankfully no one appeared to notice. Over the years she'd become adept at hiding her emotions.

She refocused on the conversation and soon Mary Karen's hilarious hair-raising tales about life with five small children had her laughing. She was grateful the young mother was in a talkative mood because it took her mind off her SITUATION.

It was best to think of Joel that way. He was merely a SITUATION she needed to handle. Not a man who could make her forgo logic with a single touch or one glance from sexy hazel eyes.

She'd definitely given Joel the wrong impression tonight. Now she had to find a way to show him the interlude in the swing meant nothing. This would achieve two purposes. It would avoid an uncomfortable, sticky conversation, and put them firmly back on their previous level of mere social acquaintances.

After a few minutes Mary Karen was called away. In the next instant July's husband, David, stopped by, asking Kate if he could steal his wife away for a few minutes. And just like that, Kate stood alone in a sea of people. Until she reminded herself that alone was good. Being by herself gave her a chance to come up with a plan to deal with the SITUATION.

She'd gotten a few thoughts together when she caught

sight of Joel headed her way, a glass of white wine in each hand. Her heart flip-flopped.

Relief flooded her when Travis stepped in front of Joel and pulled him aside to introduce him to Benedict Campbell, one of the doctors in Mitzi's clinic. The son of the group's founder, Ben was a brilliant surgeon in his own right and a good friend of their host.

"I didn't get a chance to tell you earlier how lovely you look tonight."

Kate's heart took a dip. She quickly rallied and pasted a smile on her lips as she turned. "Ryan, you seem to be everywhere this evening."

He grinned. "Everywhere you don't want me to be?"

What could she do but laugh?

"I met your friend," he said.

From across the room Kate felt Joel's curious glance on her. It suddenly struck her that Ryan might be a help in *showing* Joel that she considered the kiss they'd shared to be no big deal. It might not reflect well on her, but that couldn't be helped.

"Mitzi told me she's always had this secret fantasy about riding a bull."

She pulled her thoughts back to the conversation at hand. What had Ryan said? Something about Mitzi and a bull? "Are you kidding?"

His smile faded at the surprise in her voice. "You think she was making it up?"

Kate blinked and shook her head. The pieces of the conversation fell into place. "Absolutely not. Mitzi is very adventurous."

"They have a mechanical bull at Wally's Place." Ryan's gaze met hers. "Would you mind if I invited her to go with me sometime?"

"Why are you asking me?"

"She's your friend." He shrugged. "We were involved until recently. I don't want there to be any weirdness between us."

Kate smiled. This was one of the things she'd liked most about Ryan. He didn't talk in lawyerese. He used words like *stuff* and *weirdness* instead of the usual legal lingo.

Handing her empty appetizer plate to a passing waiter, Kate stepped closer and touched Ryan's arm. "Ask her. She'll have fun and so will you."

From across the room, Joel stilled his forward progress, disturbed by the sight of Ryan and Kate together. Ryan had made it clear they weren't a couple. But he'd also said he still liked her.

They certainly appeared to be cozy. She was smiling up at him. Ryan's entire attention was focused on her. When she placed a hand on the attorney's arm, an unfamiliar emotion twisted a knife in Joel's gut.

It took him a second but he finally put a name to what he was feeling. Jealousy. He was jealous.

Joel took a gulp of wine, shaken by the realization. How could he be feeling such an emotion? He meant what he'd said to Ryan. He wasn't looking for a wife, or even a girlfriend. And despite what had happened on the swing, he and Kate were merely friends. Acquaintances, really.

"I always thought they made a nice-looking couple."

Turning his head, Joel found Lexi standing beside him. "Yes, they do," he said easily. "Looks like they may be getting back together."

"Perhaps." Lexi's gold dress brought out the amber in her eyes, her assessing gaze reminding him of a watchful lioness. "Is that extra glass for someone?"

For a second Joel wasn't sure what she meant. Then he realized he still had Kate's glass of white wine in his hand.

"It's for you." He handed it to Lexi and turned so that Kate was no longer in his field of vision. "In exchange for information."

Lexi's lips tipped up in a self-satisfied smile. "What do you want to know?"

"Tell me what those two beautiful daughters of yours have been up to."

Out of the corner of her eye, Kate saw Joel give Lexi her glass of wine. Irritation bubbled up inside her. No matter that she didn't want any more wine, Kate knew he'd gotten it for her.

If Lexi wanted a glass of wine, she could darn well get her own.

"If looks could kill," Ryan murmured.

Kate refocused her attention on the man at her side. "What did you say?"

"Your claws are showing." Ryan grinned. "It must be true."

Kate met his gaze. "If you have something to say, just say it, cowboy."

"I thought you had a thing for Joel," Ryan said in a matter-of-fact tone. "When you dissed us both earlier, I wasn't sure. But now I see I was right."

"Joel and I are friends," Kate said stiffly. "Just like you and I were friends."

"Were?" Ryan lifted a brow. "When was I denigrated to a past tense?"

"Oh, you know what I mean." Kate slapped the side of his arm with the back of her hand, relieved to get the conversation off her and Joel.

"That's okay." Ryan heaved a melodramatic sigh worthy of a Shakespearean actor. "I wasn't that interested in you anyway."

"Liar."

He looked at her and began to laugh. She quickly joined in.

"Seriously, Kate, what's he got that I haven't?" Ryan's tone might be light, but the look in his eyes told her he was serious. "Other than a kid, that is."

"Chloe." The name rolled off her tongue and she couldn't help but smile.

"Oh, I get it." Ryan shook his head. "With Joel you could have a ready-made family. No pregnancy stretch marks to mar that gorgeous bod. No messy diapers or pulling an all-nighter with a crying infant."

"You're talking crazy."

"Am I? I've seen the way you look at both of them. I think you like the kid as much as you do her dad."

"One word," Kate said. "Lunatic talk."

"That's two, but who's counting?" Ryan reached over and gently took her hands in his. "Don't you want children of your own?"

She is mine, Kate wanted to say, but she kept quiet knowing she was already treading on thin ice.

Ryan wasn't the most observant guy. If he'd noticed her interest in Chloe, others probably had, too. Which meant she was spot-on with her decision to step back and not let herself get too close to either Joel or Chloe.

In a way she was grateful to Ryan. Before he'd opened her eyes, she'd convinced herself there was nothing wrong with being Joel and Chloe's friend. Now, even that degree of closeness seemed too much.

Her plan—the one she'd made before she'd ever set foot in Jackson—had been the wisest course. Keep her distance. Observe from afar. Because, as she'd discovered, the more she saw and spoke with Chloe, the harder it was not to want more.

It was the same with Joel. She genuinely liked the man.

But being Joel's friend would definitely be a slippery slope. Thanks to Ryan, she now recognized the danger.

Sensing his eyes on her, she smiled. "Now, what were we talking about?"

"Children," Ryan said. "I asked—"

"Seriously?" Kate rolled her eyes. "We're at a fabulous party and you want to talk about kids? Why don't you dazzle me instead with all the exciting things you've been doing since we broke up?"

"As if you care." Ryan grinned. "You don't fool me. Not one bit."

Kate laughed out loud. She couldn't help it. Ryan had a razor-sharp mind and wit. He'd be a perfect match for Mitzi.

Impulsively she took his arm. "Let's check out the buffet table."

"You know, if we walk through the serving line like this—" Ryan glanced at her hand now resting on his forearm "—it'll be all over Jackson that you and I are back together."

"Are you worried about Mitzi?"

"No," he said. "I'm worried about you."

It was a sweet sentiment. Truth was, Kate was worried about her reputation, too. But acting interested in Ryan was the only way she could figure out how to extricate herself from the SITUATION. "As long as you and I know we're not involved, what does it matter what a few gossips say? Besides, if anyone asks, we'll tell them the truth."

"Which no one will believe." Ryan's brows pulled together. "What will Mitzi think?"

"She'll believe me when I tell her we're just friends."

"Are you doing this because you're afraid to get too close to Joel?" Ryan grimaced as if he couldn't believe those words had come from his mouth. "God, I hate that psychobabble crap."

Kate just smiled, not wanting to lie.

"He's a good man, Kate." Ryan began walking and she strolled beside him, ignoring the curious looks cast their way. "You better be careful. Whatever game you're playing may end up backfiring on you."

"I'm not playing any game." Kate cast a surreptitious glance in Joel's direction, but his back was to her.

This time it was Ryan's turn to laugh. "This ain't my first rodeo, sugar. I sure hope you know what you're doing."

Chapter Nine

Ever since she'd moved in, Kate had worked hard to make her townhouse a haven. In the living room, the gray-and-burgundy color scheme promoted a feeling of calm while the soft plush sofa and chair practically begged her to sink into them every evening.

The flat-screen television disappeared into a cabinet in the wall and more often than not, Kate left it there. At the end of a busy day she preferred listening to music instead. Like right now, relaxing "spa" music filled the room.

Immediately after getting home from the party she and Mitzi had changed into their sleepwear. Kate loved the feel of silk, so she'd pulled on her favorite silky blue pajamas. Mitzi had donned plaid boxers and a graphic tee.

"Now that I've had a few minutes to mull over what you explained to me, I want to simply say that you're crazy." Mitzi leaned back on Kate's sofa and slipped one leg under herself.

Dressed in an oversize T-shirt emblazoned with the words Doesn't Play Well with Others, and her face free of makeup, Mitzi looked much younger than her thirty-two years.

"Well, I guess I deserved that." Kate placed a steaming cup of hot cocoa with a big dollop of whipped cream on the coffee table in front of her friend, then dropped down on the other end of the sofa. "I did ask you to be honest."

Mitzi took a sip of the cocoa and sighed in ecstasy.

"Aren't you having any?" Mitzi looked up, whipped cream forming a milk mustache above her lips.

"It's summer," Kate reminded her, satisfied with her plain glass of cold milk.

"Give me chocolate in any form, anytime of the year." Mitzi took another big sip, but when she put the cup down and fixed her gaze on Kate, a chill traveled up Kate's spine. "I'm worried about you."

"You needn't be." Kate forced a bright tone. "I have everything under control."

Mitzi lifted a skeptical brow. "Really?"

"I was starting to get careless, sloppy even," Kate admitted, wishing the tightness in her chest would ease up a little. "I let my desire to get close to my...to Chloe cloud my good sense."

"What's wrong with wanting to know your own daughter?"

"We've been down this road before, Mitzi. Chloe is Joel's daughter, not mine." Kate rose and walked to the window, gazing out into the darkness. "I was allowing myself to get too close."

Mitzi raised a brow. "To her or to her father?"

Kate flushed. "I shouldn't have let him kiss me."

"Why did you?"

Kate gazed down at her hands, embarrassed by the

admission she was about to make. Until last night she'd always prided herself on being in control of her emotions. "I like Joel."

She raised her hand when Mitzi opened her mouth.

"I know I can't have him, which is a shame because I'm starting to think there could have been something meaningful between us." Kate gave a humorless laugh. "Just my luck, huh?"

"Perhaps you could be friends."

Kate shook her head. "It would be too dangerous. Too much of a chance that he'd break my heart—or I'd break his."

For a second Mitzi looked as if she might argue the point, then she shrugged. "It's probably a moot point anyway."

"What do you mean?

"You hurt him tonight, Kate." Mitzi took another sip of cocoa, her eyes serious. "By hanging out with Ryan, you may have slammed the door shut on having any kind of relationship with Joel."

Virginia's Café in Wilson, Wyoming, was a workingman's eatery. The seats in the booths were covered in orange vinyl and the cracked linoleum floor had clearly seen better days. Even though it was close to the home he was building in the mountains for Cole and Meg Lassiter, Joel regretted choosing it as a meeting place.

It didn't seem like the type of restaurant Dr. Kate would frequent and he wanted her to be relaxed when they spoke. But she'd already texted him that she was on her way, so there was no changing the location now.

For a Wednesday at one, the café was surprisingly busy. Thankfully he'd grabbed a booth at the back where it wasn't so noisy. Although there were any number of things Joel could be doing while he waited, he kept his gaze focused on the door. He didn't want Kate to come in and not see him.

When ten more minutes passed with no sign of her, he began to worry. Had she changed her mind? Gotten called back to the office for an emergency? Or perhaps simply decided she didn't want to have lunch with him? He'd picked up his phone to call her when the door opened and she stepped inside. She glanced around the crowded room, oblivious to all the admiring looks.

Even though most of diners were dressed in jeans and work shirts, Kate wore a black stretchy top and a black-and-white skirt in some swirly pattern. And, of course, her trademark heels were on her feet. She looked beautiful…and very out of place.

Joel pulled to his feet, wishing he'd thought to bring a change of clothes with him to the job site. The only consolation was that his jeans and T-shirt were clean. He'd spent more time talking with subcontractors than he had working this morning.

Kate had her own second thoughts. When she saw how the other diners were dressed, she wished that just this once she'd opted for more casual attire. But looking good gave her confidence. And today she needed all the confidence she could get.

She wasn't fully convinced that having lunch with Joel was a smart move. Yet, on Monday when she'd found a vase on her desk with a single red rose and an invitation to lunch, her heart wouldn't let her say no. Not after such a sweet gesture.

Oh, who was she kidding? She'd missed him. She felt bad about flirting with Ryan at the party last weekend. By coming here she wasn't saying she wanted to have a relationship with Joel—absolutely not—only that it was important he think well of her.

As she glanced around the small dining area, the smell of cooking grease assaulted her senses. Rather than being off-putting, it brought back memories of a place her grandmother had taken her as a child, a café that Gram swore served the best fries in the state of Pennsylvania.

"Kate."

She turned toward the sound and her breath caught in her throat. Even dressed for work and with hair tousled as though he'd just hopped out of bed, Joel looked magnificent.

Danger. Danger. Danger. Red flags popped up one after the other in her head. But it was too late to back out now.

She lifted one hand and wiggled her fingers in welcome and he immediately started weaving between the tables toward her.

Kate met him halfway. "I'm sorry I'm late."

"I wondered if you were going to make it," he said, moving close. He smelled like soap, sawdust and an indefinable male scent that made her insides quiver.

"There was an accident on the highway, where Moose-Wilson Road intersects with 22." Even though her voice was calm, her heart pounded so hard that it was a wonder he didn't hear it. "Thankfully no injuries."

"That's good." His fingers warm against her skin, he directed her to a booth at the back of the room.

The waitress, a no-nonsense type in her mid-forties, appeared immediately after they sat down, apparently used to serving men with short lunch hours. Thankfully Kate had been here once before and was familiar with the menu.

Until the waitress returned with their glasses of iced tea, Joel kept the conversation centered around the accident on the highway and when that topic dried up, on the weather.

He took a deep breath. "I appreciate you taking time out to come today."

"I've never been invited out for lunch so nicely before." Kate took a sip of the fresh-brewed tea. "Thank you for the beautiful rose."

"You're welcome." Joel shifted in his seat. Talk of the rose clearly made him uncomfortable. Obviously he wasn't a man used to making such gestures, which made receiving the flower even sweeter. "I wanted to apologize in person for last Saturday."

"I'm not sure what you're apologizing for."

"In the swing? When I kissed you?" he added when she continued to stare blankly at him.

"I didn't think you kissed badly enough to necessitate an apology," she said, trying not to smile. "Granted you may have been a bit rusty. But what you lacked in technique, you more than made up for in enthusiasm."

"My technique is just fine—" Joel sputtered, then stopped. She saw the corner of his mouth twitch. "You're joking."

"Am I?" Kate gazed at him through lowered lashes.

He chuckled. "Is this your way of telling me no apology is necessary?"

"That's right." As far as Kate was concerned, the lighter they kept this, the better. She waved a recently manicured hand in the air. "It was, after all, just a kiss."

"We went from zero to sixty in a second," he murmured, his brow furrowed. He looked up and met her gaze. "If Ryan hadn't shown up, it's hard to say what would have happened."

He blushed then. Honest to goodness blushed.

Kate blinked. Surely he didn't think it would have gone

that far. Of course, she grudgingly admitted—but only to herself—that wishing they both wore less clothing *had* crossed her mind.

"I loved my wife, Kate," he said while she was still formulating a response. "I don't know how I let things get so out of hand."

He looked so miserable that Kate swallowed the flippant reply poised on the tip of her tongue. Impulsively she reached across the table and laced her fingers through his.

She immediately realized her mistake. A bolt of heat traveled up her arm and her entire body began to hum.

"You're still a man, Joel," she said softly.

"But I'm not in the market for another wife. Or even a steady girlfriend." His tortured gaze met hers. "Once you've had the best, it's hard to settle for less."

His response was so honest and befuddled that she had to believe him. Kate knew she should have been cheering. After all, this is what she'd wanted: an assurance that he didn't expect more out of her than she was willing to give. Instead, the comment stung. She'd spent her whole life coming in second to her sister, and "settling for less" had a truly unpleasant ring. "You're in luck, bucko. I'm not in the market for a husband *or* a steady boyfriend."

"Because you have Ryan."

"What?" Then she realized that Joel had obviously bought her act Saturday night hook, line and sinker. For a split second she thought about continuing the charade. But she'd come to realize that wouldn't be fair to Ryan. Or to Mitzi. "No. I mean, Ryan is a friend. Just like you're my friend. That's all. Nothing more."

Joel rubbed his chin, his gaze thoughtful. "He said you weren't looking for commitment."

Kate pulled her brows together. "Who said that?"

"Ryan. After you'd left and gone inside."

Even though it was true, Kate didn't appreciate the attorney talking about her. And next time she saw him, she'd tell him just that.

"What happened at the party was simply a mistake." Joel nodded as if the extra emphasis would make it true.

"I wouldn't go so far as to say that." Kate clamped her mouth shut as the waitress appeared and placed a BLT in front of Kate and a hot beef sandwich in front of Joel.

"I don't follow," Joel said the second the waitress left. "Are you saying it wasn't a mistake?"

Let it go, the tiny voice of reason inside her head urged. *You've made your point. Don't blow it now.*

"I'm a woman. I have needs. You're a man. You have needs." Kate managed to keep her tone matter-of-fact, despite hearing her mother's shriek of disapproval in the back of her head. "Saturday, our needs converged."

A slight frown slipped over Joel's face. "Do you endorse casual sex?"

"I'm not endorsing anything." Kate lifted one shoulder in a careless shrug. "I'm simply saying there's no need to apologize for a kiss or something more between two consenting adults."

Joel forked off a piece of his hot beef sandwich and chewed, appearing to mull over her words. "What happens if our needs converge again?"

Kate wasn't sure who was more surprised by the question—her or Joel.

"I'm sorry again. I was out of line." Joel groaned and leaned back against the booth. "We need to talk about something else."

"Fine with me." Kate took a bite of her sandwich, noticing Joel had already pushed his plate aside. "What would you like to talk about?"

"Chloe."

The look on his face told her that something had him concerned. She dropped her sandwich and leaned forward. "Are the kids at day camp still being mean to her?"

"She hasn't said." He raked a hand through his hair.

"Tell me what's going on."

"Savannah's parents asked if she could come to Montana and spend a couple weeks with them."

"Does Chloe want to go?"

"Oh, she wants to go." Joel's lips twisted. "In fact, if I say no, she'll be hell to live with."

Kate searched his eyes. "Why would you say no?"

"These are the kids she goes to school with. Summer day camp is an opportunity for her to learn to get along with them."

"It takes two to tango," Kate muttered under her breath.

"Pardon?"

"I understand what you're saying and I see your point," Kate said in a normal tone of voice. She had her opinion but she wasn't sure if this was her business.

"But?"

"I didn't say 'but.'"

"Maybe not aloud," Joel said. "Yet I heard it clear as day. Please, Kate, you're Chloe's doctor. I'd appreciate your input."

If Joel wanted *Dr. McNeal's* opinion, she was happy to give it.

"As I've mentioned before, I didn't have an easy time growing up. I was a little older than Chloe when a friend I'd met at band camp asked me to go with her family to their time-share in Florida over Christmas."

"Christmas?" Joel's brows furrowed. "Your parents let you go?"

"They said no at first. My grandmother got them to reconsider." Her parents hadn't been easy to convince, but her grandmother had held firm. "She alone understood what a miserable time I'd been having at school."

Kate's lips lifted in a little smile. "I can't tell you how nice it was to hang out with a friend my age who liked me. One who thought I was funny and smart, all those things the kids at school couldn't see. I had a fabulous Christmas. Somehow, having such a great time made returning to school after the holidays easier."

"You're saying to let her go."

"I think you should at least consider it."

"You've given me a lot to think about."

"Chloe is a good kid," Kate said. "You said yourself that losing her mom and this move has been hard on both of you. I think we all need to do a better job of embracing pleasure where we can find it."

Kate settled her gaze on Joel. On his broad shoulders. On his firm, sensual lips. She remembered how his mouth had burned against hers. The electricity that had coursed through her at his touch.

Yes, it was too bad being intimate with him wasn't a possibility. Because if the way Joel kissed was any indication, making love with the handsome contractor was practically guaranteed to bring a whole boatload of pleasure her way.

Chapter Ten

The following Wednesday Joel left work early to make Chloe's favorite dinner: macaroni and cheese, peas and carrots and watermelon. He might not be the greatest cook, but this was one meal he could manage.

They talked during dinner, or rather his daughter entertained him by recounting all the adventures she and Savannah had enjoyed in the past. Then she moved on to speculating about all the fun she'd be having when she joined her friend in Montana.

After they'd finished eating, instead of helping him clear the table, he sent Chloe upstairs to change her clothes. Once the dishwasher was loaded, they were headed to the rink for a couple of hours of ice skating. Joel wasn't particularly excited about it, but Chloe had squealed when he told her of the plan.

"I'm almost done," he said, when she appeared in the kitchen doorway in her skating dress.

Chloe ground the toe of one shoe into the floor tile. "I was wondering if maybe Dr. Kate could come with us tonight?"

"Honey, I don't think—"

"Please, Daddy, please," Chloe pleaded.

"This is our last night together before we head to Billings." Letting Chloe visit her friend Savannah for two weeks had been a difficult decision. But it was the right one. His daughter hadn't been this happy since before her mother died. "I thought we'd spend it together, just the two of us."

The closer the time had come for her to leave, the more Joel realized just how much he was going to miss his little girl.

"I thought you liked Dr. Kate. Why don't you want to see her again?"

The truth was Joel yearned for Kate with an intensity that concerned him. Although it had been almost a week, he hadn't been able to get their conversation at Virginia's out of his mind.

Between consenting adults. Embracing pleasure where you can find it. Those two phrases she'd uttered were stuck on a revolving platter in his head. Could Kate have been hinting that she'd be open to a no-strings-attached affair?

His mouth went dry.

"Dr. Kate loves to skate." Chloe tugged at his sleeve. "Her friend said so."

He glanced down to find his daughter staring up at him.

"Will you, Daddy?" Chloe's dark eyes never wavered from his face. "Will you ask her?"

Ask Kate if she'd be interesting in sleeping with him? He'd always believed making love belonged in the context

of a committed relationship. But that was long ago when
life still made sense. And he and Kate were two consenting adults…

"Daddy," Chloe said. "Please ask her."

"Uh, ask her what, princess?"

"To go skating." His little girl might be only nine but
she had eye rolling down to an art form. "What else?"

If Mitzi hadn't been called to the hospital, Kate probably would have turned down Joel's last-minute offer. She
veered off the highway toward the ice rink and chuckled.
Who was she kidding? The second she'd heard that Chloe
had specifically asked for her to go skating with them,
wild horses couldn't have kept her away.

Seeing Joel again, now that was another story. The kiss
in the swing had changed the dynamics of their acquaintance. Even though lunch had ended quite amiably, when
Joel had walked her out to the parking lot and reached
around her to open the car door, she'd been this close to
kissing him.

The look in his eyes had told her she wasn't the only
one tempted. Unfortunately, er, fortunately, they'd both
acted as mature individuals. He'd shaken her hand and
said he appreciated the advice on Chloe. She'd politely
thanked him for the lunch, and that was that…until she
saw his name on her phone's readout tonight.

Joel had offered to pick her up, but Kate told him she'd
meet them. She pulled her car into the near-empty parking lot and swept the lot with her gaze. Joel's truck was
nowhere to be seen.

Because the night was warm, Kate had worn her skating outfit to the rink so she wouldn't have to change. Once
inside the large metal structure, she hauled the bag con-

taining her skates to a bench, sat down and slipped off her flats.

She'd just finished lacing up her skates when Joel and Chloe arrived. A big smile split Chloe's face and Joel lifted one hand in greeting. Kate's heart fluttered like tiny hummingbird wings.

While Joel was handsome as ever in jeans and a salmon-colored shirt, Chloe looked absolutely darling in her royal-blue skating dress. Her black eye had faded to a dull yellow and the cut on her forehead was barely noticeable. "You look especially pretty tonight, Chloe."

"So do you," the child said, then blushed and ducked her head.

Kate couldn't remember a nicer compliment. By the look of heat in his eyes, Joel found her black georgette wrap skirt and form-fitting silvery top very much to his liking.

While the two put on their skates, Chloe told Kate all about her upcoming trip to Montana.

"You're going to have so much fun," Kate told the child, smiling at Joel. She couldn't believe he'd taken her advice.

"I'm so happy you came tonight," Chloe said with an excited little wiggle. "You can help me with my camel spin."

"Chloe." Joel's voice was stern. "If you'd like Dr. Kate to help you with your camel spins, you *ask,* not *tell* her."

"I'm sorry." The tips of Chloe's ears turned bright red and she shifted her gaze to her feet.

"I love doing spins," Kate said. "I'd be happy to help you."

Chloe lifted her head. "You would?"

Kate nodded. "And if your dad is interested, I can teach

him how to do Michael Jackson's moonwalk. It's super-easy on skates."

Chloe pulled her brows together and cocked her head. "Who's Michael Jackson?"

Joel met her gaze and smiled. Kate wondered if he was aware that when he smiled, even his eyes lit up. This guy was the real deal. What you saw was what you got. No phony posturing. No "I'm so important" swagger.

"He was a popular singer who also danced really well," Kate said when she found her voice. "He did this dance step called the moonwalk, only not on ice, of course. Shall I show you both how to do it?"

"Thank you, Kate. That's nice of you," Joel said, though the look of apprehension in his eyes told her he wasn't completely sold on the idea.

"Sounds like fun," Chloe said with enthusiasm, apparently not sharing Joel's reservations.

Kate led the father and daughter to a corner of the ice when Sarabeth Brown skated up. Her dress was the same style as Chloe's, except in hot-pink. "I didn't know you skated."

It was hard to tell who the child was speaking to, but when Chloe remained mute, Kate smiled at the girl. "Sarabeth, how nice to see you again. Is your mom here?"

"Mommy is having a purse party," Sarabeth informed her. "My sister is here, but she's too busy texting her friends to skate with me."

"Dr. Kate is going to show me and my dad how to do a moonwalk. It's this old-time dance thing," Chloe said, apparently finding her voice. "Do you want her to show you, too?"

Kate heard the hesitation in Chloe's voice but was proud of the child for having the courage to make the offer.

"Sure," Sarabeth said immediately. "That'd be cool."

The smile on Chloe's face could have lit up the entire building.

With a lighter heart, Kate skated farther out on the ice, then spun around to face the threesome. "Place one skate's toe pick slightly behind the heel of the other skate, then lift up the heel."

Kate continued to illustrate while teaching them the technique.

Chloe and Sarabeth caught on right away.

Joel tried. And tried. And tried.

Chloe hadn't been lying when she'd said her dad wasn't good on the ice. After he'd fallen for the third—or was it the fourth time?—Sarabeth had clearly had enough.

"Let's go practice our spins," she said to Chloe. "You can do spins, right?"

Chloe snorted. "I've been doing them for-ev-er. Since I was like…four years old."

Somehow Kate managed to keep from smiling.

Beside her, Joel hid his laughter behind a cough.

"Awesome," Sarabeth said, clearly impressed. "None of our other friends can do 'em."

Our friends? Joel nudged Kate, telling her he'd caught the nuance, too.

Chloe's lips lifted and her eyes gleamed with satisfaction. "Do you want to do a haircutter spin first?"

Sarabeth's eyes widened. "You can do a haircutter?"

"They're supereasy." Chloe held out her hand. "Come on, I'll show you."

The two girls set off hand in hand for the area in the middle of the ice reserved for practicing specific moves. Because it was a slow night, they had the entire area to themselves.

"Looks like Chloe's making progress in the friend

department." The sound of giggles from the two girls brought a smile to Kate's lips.

"Yep." Joel grinned. "Which means you're stuck with me."

He looked inordinately pleased at the prospect.

"How about we skate for a while?" Even though she was standing still, Kate suddenly felt out of breath. "Build your confidence up a bit."

"Sounds good." Joel took her hand and slipped it through the crook in his arm as if it was the most natural thing in the world.

For a second his gaze settled on his daughter as she spun around and around, her head back, her right leg pulled to her head.

Once she was done, Sarabeth applauded.

Joel smiled proudly.

"She's pretty good," Kate said.

"Yes, she is, but she's not what I want to talk about right now." Joel's gaze met hers. "I've been thinking a lot about what you said last week at Virginia's."

Kate lifted a shoulder in a careless shrug, even as her heart pounded like a bass drum in her chest. "I said a lot of things."

"About us being consenting adults and there being no shame in embracing pleasure where we can find it," he reminded her.

Shame? Kate couldn't remember using that word.

Joel leaned close, his breath warm against her ear. "I'm attracted to you, Kate. I have the feeling the attraction isn't all one-sided. Am I right?"

Her breath caught, then began again. Dear God, were they really going to have this conversation in a skating rink?

"Well, um," she stammered, "yes, I admit I do find you, uh, incredibly sexy."

Incredibly sexy? He'd simply asked if she was attracted to him. Yet, she'd skipped all the way to sexy? Kate stifled a groan.

Joel didn't seem to mind the jump. His smile broadened. "Sexy, huh?"

"A little sexy."

"Little isn't a word a man normally wants to hear." A light danced in his eyes. "Besides, I believe your exact words were '*incredibly* sexy.'"

He was having way too much fun at her expense.

Heat crawled up Kate's neck. "I'm prone to exaggeration."

"Well, I'm not," Joel said as they completed another circle of the rink. "And may I say that I find you incredibly sexy, too."

Kate's knees went weak. If he hadn't been holding on to her, she'd have stumbled.

He tightened his grip and it felt as if he'd never let her go. But, of course, Kate knew that wasn't true. He'd made that very clear at the diner.

"Any suggestions on how we, uh, deal with this attraction?" The second the words left Kate's mouth, her entire body began to hum as she considered the possibilities.

"That's a tough one," he said, his expression suddenly serious.

"We could sleep together," Kate said, as casually as if she was suggesting another turn around the rink. "See if that gets this out of our system. This heat between us may be simply the case of two young healthy people not having had sex in a long time."

Joel was silent for a long moment, then cocked his head in an inquiring tilt. "Didn't you just recently break up with Ryan?"

For a second Kate wasn't sure what that had to do with

this discussion. Then it hit her. Like almost everyone else in the world, Joel connected dating with sexual activity. While Ryan had made it clear he wanted to sleep with her, the desire had never been there for her.

"Ryan and I weren't intimate," she said simply.

"Apologies," he said with a sheepish expression. "I shouldn't have assumed that you and he were—"

"No worries," Kate said. "It was a logical assumption."

But Joel was no longer listening. His gaze had dropped and now lingered on the scooped neckline of her top. Her nipples stiffened, straining toward the remembered delight of his touch.

"I don't think once will be enough to get you out of my system," he murmured, stepping close and twining a strand of her hair loosely around his fingers. "But we can't be sleeping together with Chloe around."

It was strange, yet oddly reassuring, that they were discussing this with the same care they would give any other major decision. She had to appreciate his concern for the example he'd be setting for Chloe.

It was too bad she found it so difficult to concentrate. Her eyes, which seemed to suddenly develop a mind of their own, zeroed in on the area directly below his belt buckle. "She'll be out of town for two weeks."

He grinned. "You're a genius."

"I am?"

"You're right. We've got two whole weeks. More than enough time for you to get me out of your system and for me to get you out of mine."

Kate thought back to her previous less-than-satisfying lovemaking sessions. "It won't take anywhere near that long."

The look on Joel's face would have been funny at any other time. "You sound so…confident."

"While I haven't had many sexual relationships, all of them were very short-lived." Actually Kate could count on one hand the number of men she'd been with, most of them during that tumultuous year after the adoption. The counselor she'd finally seen at student health told her she was trying to fill the emptiness in her life with sex.

"I've had only one," Joel said.

Kate pulled her brows together. "You've never been with anyone but…with anyone else?"

For some reason Kate refused to bring his wife's name into whatever was happening between them.

"We were childhood sweethearts."

"Oh." Kate wasn't sure what to say to that. "Well, before you ask, I don't have any diseases or anything. I've been fully checked out."

He studied her for several seconds, his steady gaze shooting tingles down her spine.

She moistened her lips with the tip of her tongue. "I want to kiss you."

"I want to make love to you." His voice was a husky caress and his eyes seemed to glitter, suddenly looking more green than brown. He tucked a stray curl behind her ear, then trailed a finger down her jawline. "I want to fulfill all of your fantasies and desires—"

"Daddy, I did a perfect haircutter," Chloe called out, skating up to a stop beside them. Her cheeks were pink and her eyes sparkled.

"Congratulations," Joel said in a hearty voice, his hand dropping to his side.

"Good for you, Chloe." Kate pulled her gaze from Joel to focus on the child. "That's a hard spin to master."

Joel glanced around. "Where's Sarabeth?"

"She had to leave. Guess what?" A tiny smile tugged at the corners of Chloe's mouth.

Joel lifted a brow.

"Sarabeth asked me to a sleepover when I get back." Chloe did a little happy jig on her skates. "I said yes. This will be my very first sleepover."

Kate gave her a quick hug. This was definitely good news. While reuniting with her friend in Montana was wonderful, Chloe needed friends in Jackson Hole, too. "I'm happy you and Sarabeth had fun."

"How about you?" Chloe asked. "Did you and Daddy have fun?"

"We did," Joel said easily. "Kate agreed to keep me company while you're out of town."

Kate didn't remember formally agreeing, unless discussing kissing, fantasies and desires counted as coming to a consensus. Still, what did it matter? The bottom line was he wanted her. And she wanted him.

"Daddy is going to miss me so much," Chloe announced.

"I will miss you, princess." Joel shifted his gaze to Kate. "But I'm going to do my best to keep busy while you're gone."

Chapter Eleven

"You're really going to have a two-week affair with him?" Mitzi's eyes were as wide as Kate had ever seen them. And she was sitting up on the cushions of Kate's sofa as straight as any soldier. "That's a complete turn-around for you."

Kate shrugged.

"Why?" Mitzi pressed. "Why would you settle for second best?"

Kate fixed an icy stare on her friend. "I'll pretend I didn't hear that."

"You deserve so much more. You're *worth* so much more than a couple weeks of being some man's sex toy."

"It's not like that. Did it ever occur to you that he'll be my toy, not the other way around?"

Mitzi ignored her. "When does this two weeks start?"

"Tomorrow."

Joel would be back from dropping off Chloe later tonight. Of course, Kate didn't expect to hear from him until tomorrow. That's when the countdown clock would begin ticking.

"Not to be a Debbie Downer—" Mitzi's voice broke through her thoughts "—but this is a bad idea. A very bad idea."

Kate understood her friend's concerns. She shared those worries, but it didn't change her decision. "I'm not going to apologize to you or to anyone else. I've denied myself too much over the years. I dedicated myself to my career and there was no time to indulge myself. Yes, I am settling for less than I deserve, but ours is a unique situation."

"Because of Chloe."

"And because he's still not fully over Amy." Somehow Kate managed to keep her tone matter-of-fact. "The bottom line is, Joel is a growing addiction I can't deny. So for two weeks I'm going to grab the brass ring and say to hell with logic."

"Because you've obviously made your decision, I'll support you. I might not agree, but you know I'm here for you." Mitzi tilted her head and met Kate's gaze. "I have just one piece of advice."

"What's that?"

"Don't waste one second of your time together thinking too hard. For once live fully in the moment and make this an adventure you'll look back on with fondness. You'll have plenty of time for reflection once the fourteen days are up."

Joel sat on his porch, newspaper in hand, and waited. He resisted the urge to check the time on his phone... again. All the way back from Billings he'd been pre-occupied with thoughts of his upcoming affair. While he wouldn't be getting emotionally involved, Joel had decided he and Kate couldn't meet solely for sex. That would be tacky. They should be able to enjoy each other's company for the next fourteen days, too.

His initial concern had been her reputation. It had taken a hit when she'd dropped Ryan so abruptly. Joel certainly didn't want their friends to think she'd done it again with him when they parted ways. By the time he'd reached the Wyoming state line, he finally concluded that as long as he and Kate saved any displays of affection for the bedroom, it should be okay. Everyone would assume she was merely keeping him company while his daughter was out of town…especially if that's what he and Kate told them.

Today Jackson Hole was celebrating the Fourth of July in a big way. He and Kate had a whole day's worth of events to attend, beginning with the Pancake Breakfast on Center Street. The Jaycees served a hearty meal of eggs, sausage and pancakes every year prior to the big parade.

Initially Joel had thought Mitzi might impact their plans for the next fourteen days. After all, Kate couldn't abandon her friend. But the orthopedic surgeon had unexpectedly returned to Los Angeles this morning after receiving a frantic call from her sister. Apparently Mitzi's niece, the one who'd been involved in a car accident, had developed some complications.

It appeared he and Kate had clear sailing beginning today. The only thing Joel didn't like was Kate insisting on meeting him at his house. Granted, it'd have been out of his way to pick her up, but he'd have gladly done it. Making her drive to Jackson to meet him didn't seem, well, gentlemanly. But he hadn't been able to change Kate's mind. She was one stubborn lady.

While Amy had been satisfied—happy, really—to let

him make most of the decisions, Kate had a more inde-
pendent spirit. Joel wondered if that same spirit would
show up in bed. He grinned, realizing he was looking
forward to finding out.

At the sound of a car engine, he glanced up and set
aside the newspaper. Kate's Subaru rounded the corner
and came to a halt in front of his house. By the time she
stepped out of the car and removed a large wicker basket
from the back, he was at the curb, lifting it from her arms.

"What's in here?" He pretended to stagger from the
load. "It weighs a ton."

"Sandwiches, fruit and wine, among other things." The
sun glinted off her jet-black hair and her shiny red lips.
Her hazel eyes looked more green than brown in the light.
"Mind if I put the perishables in your fridge?"

"Not at all." Joel glanced down at the basket in his
hand. "Is this our picnic dinner for Music in the Hole?"

Presented by the Grand Teton Music Festival, Music
in the Hole was an Independence Day tradition. He and
Chloe had gone last year to listen to the patriotic music
and enjoy the kid-friendly activities. When they'd seen the
families with their blankets, eating out of wicker baskets
on the Alpine Field lawn, Joel had promised his daughter
that when they went this year they'd pack a picnic basket.

But Chloe was in Montana and Kate would be the one
on the blanket with him this year. He slanted a sideways
glance as he followed her up the sidewalk to the steps.
Today, instead of dressing up, she wore tiny white shorts
that hugged her backside and a blue shirt with several
bold red and white brush strokes across her breasts.

"We don't have to eat this stuff. We can get food
from one of the vendors, if you prefer." Kate climbed
the steps to the porch with grace. "Everyone in the clinic

was talking about taking a picnic basket. I'd never gone before, so—"

"I'm glad you thought of it." His response ended her nervous chatter. Opening the screen door, he stepped aside to let her enter.

She smiled her thanks and brushed past him.

His body tensed at the brief contact but he pretended he hadn't felt it. Or caught a whiff of her light, flowery fragrance.

Once inside, Kate paused. Her gaze swept the room. She nodded. "A kitchen–living room combination. An efficient use of space."

Even though there was only approval in her voice, if she'd expected his home to be as nice as the ones he'd built for several of her friends, she had to be disappointed. While his house had shiny hardwood floors and an open floor plan, it was more of a cottage with only two bedrooms and one bathroom.

"The plan was to live here just long enough to give me time to build a home in the mountains. Then everything changed."

Joel didn't explain more. The look in Kate's eyes told him she understood.

"It's in a great location." She took the basket from his hands and placed it on the floor next to the fridge. When she bent over to put the sandwiches and fruit salad away, Joel couldn't help but stare.

He wouldn't be a red-blooded male if he didn't take the opportunity to admire her long shapely legs. Or notice that the vee of her shirt gave a glimpse at underlying curves. Anticipation coursed through him. Soon those legs would be wrapped around him and those soft curves would be like putty in his hands.

It was still hard for him to believe she'd agreed to a

two-week affair. A woman like her could have any man, but she'd chosen him, insisting short-term was all she wanted, too. Was she aware that the clock had already begun counting down the hours and minutes of those days?

What would she do if he took her hand and led her to the bedroom? Would she be shocked? Outraged? Or... flattered that he found her so irresistible?

"All done." Kate straightened.

"If you'd like," he said, resisting the urge to adjust his jeans, "I can give you the grand tour."

"You have a nice place here, Joel." She leaned back against the countertop.

His eyes lingered on the breasts that appeared to be straining against the front of her shirt.

"Like I said, it's nothing fancy." He paused, cleared his throat, then began again. "But I've tried to make it feel like a home."

"Feeling is good." Kate slowly slid her hand across the shiny granite countertop. "Smooth. Hard."

His mouth went dry at the image that popped into his head. A vivid image of her stroking him...

Joel swallowed, his throat like sawdust. "I wanted this place to be a refuge that Chloe and I would enjoy coming home to at the end of a long day."

"Well, from what I've seen so far," she said, "you suc-ceeded."

But he'd stopped listening, except to the words running through his head. *Touch her. Touch her. Touch her.*

There was no reason he shouldn't. No reason at all. He took her hand. The long slender fingers were warmer than his and twice as soft.

A large red oval stone rested on her right ring finger.

He couldn't believe he hadn't noticed it before. He touched the stone. "What is this?"

Two bright spots of pink dotted her cheeks. "A fire opal."

Given to her by an old boyfriend, no doubt. Joel's gut clenched. Not your business, he told himself. "It's unique."

Although he hadn't asked a single question, Kate must have sensed his curiosity. "I bought it the summer after my first year of medical school. Fire opals are supposed to bestow courage, stamina, willpower and energy on the wearer and overall have a positive effect on the psyche." Kate took a breath. "Aren't you glad you asked?"

"Let me see if I got this correct." He ran a hand down her arm. "You bought it to celebrate that you'd survived that year and to give yourself the energy to get through the rest of your schooling?"

Kate hesitated for only a second before flashing a brilliant smile. "Something like that."

"It's a large stone." For a second old memories surged, threatening his resolve to keep today about the present. "Amy didn't like big rings. Thought they were too showy. I couldn't even get her a diamond. A simple gold band was all she'd accept."

The minute the words left his lips, the smile slipped from Kate's face and Joel knew it had been the wrong thing to say. Why should Kate care what Amy liked or didn't like? And bringing up your deceased wife the day you started an affair, well, there was probably some rule against that, too.

"I'll show you the rest of the house," he said, thankful she hadn't pulled her hand from his. Not yet anyway.

"Please," she said, her eyes searching his.

Please what? Please show me the rest of the house?

Please make love to me now? Or please quit talking about your wife?

Time to take a tour. Once they finished, hopefully all would be forgotten. He rested his hand against the small of her back. "The bedrooms are this way. I'll make it quick."

Kate made a snorting sound. When he turned, she tried to cover it with a cough. She looked as if she was trying very hard not to laugh.

Joel raised a questioning brow.

"Uh, not too quick, I hope."

Was she referring to... Nah. "It's not that big, so it won't take long—"

He stopped when he saw her lips twitch.

"The house," he said loudly. "The house isn't that big."

"I knew what you meant." She batted her eyelashes at him, her expression all wide-eyed and innocent. Too innocent.

She was obviously having fun at his expense, but he didn't care. The light he'd almost extinguished was back in her eyes. That's what mattered.

He shot her a wink. "You'll find out soon enough about the other."

"Promises. Promises." She waved a hand in the air and heaved an exaggerated sigh.

Surely she wasn't intimating that he was trying to delay their lovemaking. Hell, if he wasn't trying so hard to be civilized, she'd be slung over his shoulder and they'd be headed to the bedroom right now.

"I don't want you to miss breakfast," he said, cursing himself for stumbling over the words. "I'm sure you're as hungry as I am."

"*Hungry* is an understatement," Kate murmured as they stopped at his bedroom door.

She peered into the bedroom, conscious of Joel standing at her shoulder, of his warm breath against her neck. He was so big. So masculine. For one second she simply stood there, reveling in the intoxicating scent of his cologne.

So far he'd been so restrained, so gentlemanly. It felt almost as if she'd arrived with a game plan in place only to find the rules had changed. Instead of this being the beginning of an affair, it felt like a first date.

Heck, he hadn't even kissed her yet, which made her feel even more like a wanton. Because from the moment she'd seen him standing on his front porch in his worn jeans and red shirt, all she could think of was kissing him. Didn't he realize they had only fourteen days? Didn't he realize they were wasting precious time being so, well, so proper?

"What do you think?" he asked.

Kate realized she'd been staring unseeing into the room. She blinked and refocused. His sanctuary had a welcoming, comfortable feel with a multicolored quilt on the four-poster bed and the rag rugs on the shiny hardwood.

While warmth and comfort were all well and good, it wasn't what she wanted—no, needed—from him.

She and Joel could go and eat their pancakes and sausage, then watch the parade. Comment on the funny cars and ooh and aah over the floats. But even though she'd present a bright face to the world, she wouldn't really enjoy it because her thoughts would be on tonight. When they returned to his house. When they no longer had to pretend what it was they really wanted from each other. When they would finally make love…

Kate spun around and faced him, leaving little space

between them. She placed her hands on his shoulders and met his surprised gaze.

Electricity sizzled between them.

His fingers played with her hair. "Something on your mind?"

Although his expression was serious, there was a smile in his voice.

"I'm hungry, all right." Even to her own ears, Kate's voice sounded husky and more than a little sultry. "But not for pancakes and eggs."

Joel tilted his head slightly to the right.

She trailed a finger down his arm. "I want *you* for breakfast. And I'd like to indulge my craving right now, if you please."

"I do please." A hint of a smile touched his lips. "Great minds and all that."

"What do you mean?"

"Right before you spoke I was thinking that if I could have anything on a menu this morning, it would be you." He bent and kissed her softly on the mouth.

Now, this was more like it. Kate wound her arms around his neck, sliding her fingers into his hair.

She'd thought after her declaration that he'd sweep her into his arms, take her to the bed and make mad, passionate love. Instead he lifted her chin with his finger.

"Are you absolutely certain this is what you want?" His voice was a hoarse and throaty rasp.

Kate nodded, breathing in the clean fresh scent of his shampoo mixed with the spicy tang of his cologne. His eyes searched hers, and whatever he found must have reassured him because he took her hand and his thumb caressed her palm. "I'm a little rusty at all this."

Shivers of desire traveled up her arm at his touch.

He cleared his throat. "But I am prepared."

Kate cocked her head in an inquiring tilt.

"I picked up condoms on my way back from Billings," he said. "The way I see it, safe sex is everyone's responsibility."

A warmth that had nothing to do with room temperature enveloped her. "I hope you bought enough," she said in a breathless tone.

"Count on it." He returned her smile and tugged her to him.

Desire rose and swamped her. Simply being so close made her body ache with longing. She wanted this man in a way that defied logic.

He lowered his head and pressed his mouth against hers. His hand flattened against her lower back, drawing her up against the length of his body. He spread his hands over her buttocks and pressed her against his erection.

Oh, my.

Suddenly her arms were around his neck. Her fingers caressing the soft texture of his hair as his mouth closed over hers.

His lips lingered, drawing her into a whirling spiral of emotions and sensations that seemed profoundly different. There was chemistry here, an intimacy and spark that she'd never experienced before.

Kate splayed her hands across his back, feeling the muscles tighten beneath the fabric. She explored his body with a kind of wonder, as if it was the first time she'd ever touched a man. It was new, this desire to linger. When his hands touched her through the soft cotton of her shirt, her skin quivered.

The shadows in the hall deepened and the world seemed to be bathed in a golden glow, creating a sweet intimacy made for two.

"You're gorgeous." Had she said that? Or had he? Did it matter?

Joel explored the soft skin behind her ears and down her neck, his mouth open against her skin. Everywhere his lips touched, she sizzled. She pressed herself against him, lifting her face to his, cursing the fabric that still separated them.

His mouth once again closed over hers, and this time the kiss turned wild, a lush openmouthed mating of lips and tongues. When she came up for air, they were both naked on the bed.

Kate drew back and looked her fill. He had a working-man's body—corded with muscle, lean and tan. Dark hair converged on the flat planes of his stomach.

A curious humming filled her body.

"I wondered what you looked like," he said with something akin to awe in his voice.

She ran her hands over his biceps, then trailing them over his chest. "So strong, so—"

"Soft," he said, cupping her large breasts in his palms, his fingers brushing the tips. Her nipples puckered and tingled as he continued his exploration, skimming his hand over intimate dips and hollows.

His touch was gentle and caring. He asked, rather than demanded, and she responded without reservation. Her passion, her need for him grew with each touch, with each tender caress. By the time Joel rolled over and retrieved the condoms from the bedside table, every nerve ending was on high alert.

He entered her slowly, pushing in a little and then retreating, as if making sure she was ready for him. He was big and thick, stretching her. She wrapped her arms around him, pulling him against her, reveling in the wonder of being filled by a man intent on pleasing them both.

They moved in perfect rhythm in an age-old ritual that somehow seemed new. She loved the way his hard body felt over hers. She loved the way his body trembled with pent-up need as he waited…for her.

Her pleasure mounted with each thrust. She closed around him, arched to him. Kate couldn't remember the last time she'd been so happy. She celebrated her happiness noisily, determined to wring every last drop of pleasure from the moment.

Kate rode the building pressure until their bodies were damp and sweaty, and still she clung to him. When the combination of physical and emotional sent her crashing over the edge, it seemed right that she was in this man's arms.

Chapter Twelve

When Kate had fantasized about making love with Joel, she'd worried she might feel ill at ease or awkward afterward. But she didn't.

Lying next to him with the sunlight streaming through the half-open blinds felt somehow...right. He wrapped his arms around her shoulders and pulled her to him, kissing the top of her head.

"That," he said, exhaling a satisfied breath, "was amazing."

It *had* been amazing and fantastic and incredible and another dozen words with similar meanings. And now it was done. Over. Ended. For a second Kate was tempted to slip out from under his arm and hurriedly get dressed. It's what she'd done any other time she'd had sex. Besides, feeling so close, so comfortable with this man had to be a mistake.

Then Kate remembered what Mitzi had said about seizing these fourteen days. Not mucking them up with worry or second-guesses. Really, what was there to worry about? Joel was Chloe's father. That made him off-limits for anything more than a brief fling. What she should be focusing on was all the fun they could be having now.

"Penny for your thoughts." His gaze raked over her and a spray of goose bumps pebbled her skin.

The fire that had burned in her, hot and hungry, only moments before, began to build again. Instead of immediately answering, she placed her hand against the broad planes of his chest, her fingers toying with the dusting of dark hair. "Remember that old potato-chip commercial that said you couldn't eat just one?"

A smile slowly spread across his face. "Let me guess. You were the one who always had to have the second chip?"

"Actually—" Kate placed an openmouthed kiss on his belly, his skin salty beneath her tongue "—I've never had the desire to go past one. Until now."

His smile became a grin. "That good, eh?"

"And—" Kate gave a husky little laugh "—I'm warning you now, I can't promise I'll be satisfied at two."

She wasn't sure if she had more to say but it didn't matter. The last word barely made it past her lips when he reached out and captured her hand, drawing it toward his mouth. At the last second, he turned her fingers and pressed his lips into her palm.

The hot, damp contact provided the final fuel to the fire burning hot and deep inside her. Suddenly he was kissing her, touching her with a fierceness that both thrilled and excited her. She could tell from the urgency of his mouth, the roughness of his touch, the feverish light in his eyes that he was on fire, too.

She pulled his mouth down to hers as she began to move underneath him.

"I want to make love to you slowly," he whispered. "But if you keeping moving like that—"

"What? What is big bad Joel going to do?" She ran her tongue up the side of his neck and wrapped her legs around him, pulling him closer. She could feel his arousal against her. It wouldn't take much for him to be inside her again.

"This." Joel thrust into her hard and deep, filling her so perfectly, making her feel impossibly complete.

He looked down into her eyes, the muscles in his arms and shoulders tight as he held himself above her. For a second concern furrowed his brow. "I forgot the condom."

"I'm on the pill," she reassured him. "No worries."

And as he began to move inside her, Kate forgot all her worries. Forgot everything except the pleasure. And the passion. And the joy of being thoroughly loved.

Afterward, Joel followed Kate into an exhausted slumber. The loud boom of an illegal M-80 firework outside pulled him awake. He glanced over and found Kate curled up beside him.

Her lips still looked like plump, ripe strawberries even though he'd long ago kissed the red lipstick off them. The hair, which normally fell in sleek, stylish strands to her shoulders, now lay tousled around her face. Even so, she had to be the most beautiful woman he'd ever seen.

What about Amy? a tiny voice whispered in his ear.

But Joel couldn't, wouldn't, think of Amy now. Not with Kate lying naked in his bed. Later he'd reflect on what had happened today. Not now.

Kate stirred and her lids fluttered open. For the first time he noticed she had flecks of gold mixed with the brown and green, just like Chloe. She pushed herself up to her elbows, not seeming to care that the sheet fell to her waist, baring her breasts. With one hand she brushed the hair back from her face, with the other she covered a yawn. "I fell asleep?"

"We both did." He leaned forward and brushed a kiss across her lips. "But the noise woke me."

A look of alarm crossed her face. "Please don't tell me I snore."

Joel laughed. "It was the neighbor kid shooting off a firecracker."

"Whew," she said, her eyes dancing with good humor. "That's a relief."

His gaze dropped to her breasts. They were surprisingly large with rosy pink tips. Joel remembered how they'd felt in his hands. How they'd tasted in his mouth. In an instant he was hard. With great effort he forced his eyes upward to her beautiful face and those luscious lips. "We missed the pancake breakfast."

"Disappointed?" she asked, a watchfulness in her eyes that belied her casual tone.

"Me? Heck no." He let his gaze linger. "Actually I'm afraid I wouldn't have enjoyed it much. Because all the time I'd have been wishing I was here. In bed. With you."

"I had...fun." A tiny smile tugged at the corners of her lips. "You?"

At the last second, he pulled back the teasing reply from his lips. Something in the set of her shoulders told him Kate wasn't as confident as she appeared. "You exceeded my wildest expectations."

Her shoulders relaxed and a smile hovered on her lips. "Which time?"

"Both times."

She laughed then, a low throaty chuckle that stirred his senses. "We did go a bit overboard."

"I enjoyed it," he said. "If you're hungry I could rustle us up some breakfast."

"I don't need to stay."

He tilted his head, not sure what she meant.

"I mean, if the purpose of our hanging out today was so we'd be more comfortable tonight when we—"

Joel waited.

"—you know...did it," she stammered.

"When we made love?"

"When we had sex," she clarified.

Whatever you called what they had shared, he wasn't ready to let her go. Not yet. Not until the two weeks were up. Joel realized with a jolt of awareness how much he'd been looking forward to spending time with her.

Unable to keep his hands off her, he cupped her face with his hand and kissed her again, murmuring against the corner of her mouth, "Stay. Please."

She smiled and kissed him back. "Because you put it so nicely, yes."

Satisfaction flowed through his veins. "What do you want for breakfast?"

Her gaze flickered to the clock on the bedside table. "The pancake breakfast ended at ten."

"I am not without culinary skills," he informed her.

"You're a true jack-of-all-trades, Joel Dennes," she replied. "The things you can do with those hands are mind-boggling."

"Hey, babe—" Joel shot her a wink "—you ain't seen nothin' yet."

She arched a brow. "Are you saying you were holding back on me?"

"I guess you'll have to wait and see."

Kate's hand slid beneath the sheet that rode low on his hips. Her smile widened when she encountered the evidence showing that he wasn't completely worn out by their morning activities. "I prefer not to wait."

"But Kate, three times," he protested weakly, secretly pleased by her desire.

"Poor Joel." She pursed her lips and shook her head, but the twinkle in her eye gave her away. "Look at this. You've already risen to the occasion."

He thought about telling her that he'd wanted her again five seconds after he'd awakened. Instead, when she pushed the sheet aside and lowered her head, he moaned.

"You're going to be the death of me, Kate."

Her only reply was a wicked laugh.

By the time she showed him a few handy things she could do with her hands—and her mouth—they were both famished. They ate quickly, then dressed and headed to the field by Jackson Hole Middle School.

They had to park several blocks away but Kate didn't mind. The sky was a vivid blue with only a few wispy clouds. She lifted her face to the sun as they walked to the field and talked. Their easy familiarity was at odds with the pre-sex jitters of the morning.

The field was in sight when Joel's phone rang. He pulled it from his pocket and glanced down. A smile lifted his lips. "It's Chloe."

"Answer it," Kate urged. "I can't wait to hear how she's doing."

While the child was with her best friend, she was still far from home. A little homesickness was to be expected.

"Hello, princess." Joel switched over to speaker phone. "How's Montana? Are you having fun?"

"We're having oodles of fun. Aren't we, Savannah?"

Chloe's voice bubbled with excitement as she told her dad everything she and her best friend had done yesterday. "What have you been doing?"

"Well—" Joel slanted a sideways glance at Kate "—Dr. Kate is keeping me company today. We're headed to Music in the Hole now and then we're going to stop by a party that Mr. and Mrs. Delacourt are throwing."

Kate had reservations about their showing up at the party together. But Joel insisted that with their spending so much time together the next couple of weeks, it would result in more talk if they showed up separately.

She listened to the father-daughter conversation, marveling at their camaraderie, knowing she couldn't have picked a better parent for Chloe.

"Do you want to speak with Dr. Kate?" Joel asked his daughter.

"Yes, please."

He handed her the phone.

"Hi, Chloe."

"Thank you for keeping my dad company, Dr. Kate," Chloe said. "I know he misses me lots."

"It's my pleasure." Kate glanced at Joel, the devilish twinkle in his eyes making her smile. "Sounds like you've been having a blast with your friend."

Kate asked the child a few more questions. Although almost three hundred miles separated them, the happiness in Chloe's voice eased her worry. "I'm going to give the phone back to your dad."

"Try not to miss me too much, Daddy," Chloe said to Joel. "I'll be back before you know it."

As she and Joel continued their trek to the field, Kate decided they'd been wise to seize the morning. Because Chloe *would* be back before they knew it. Then she'd go back to being Dr. Kate, a family friend. And Joel would go back to being a social friend and a man with whom she'd secretly once had a fling.

It was a depressing thought.

"Is your sister's little girl doing better?" Joel asked.

"She is," Kate said simply. "Thank you for asking."

"You do that a lot."

"What do you mean?"

"Shut people out," he said. "You barely answered my question."

Kate stiffened. "I was being considerate. I'm sure you don't want a blow-by-blow of Elle's recovery."

"Maybe I do." He took off his sunglasses and his dark eyes met hers. "Did you ever think of that? Perhaps I'd like to get to know you better."

"Why?"

"Because you're my friend." Even though they'd agreed to no public displays of affection he took her hand. "What's important in your life is important to me."

A tightness gripped Kate's chest. Oh, how she wished that were true. But he was her temporary lover, not her friend. And she had to guard her heart. Pretend she didn't care. Because, despite her cavalier comments to Mitzi, Kate knew she was playing with fire.

"Elle simply had a very bad virus. She was released from the hospital yesterday." It was easier to give him a little information than argue about something that wouldn't matter in two weeks.

"I'm happy to hear it." Joel sounded as if he actually appreciated the information. "Did your sister have you speak with the doctor?"

Kate swallowed her irritation. His question opened a wound that had already begun to scab over. She'd left several messages for Andrea but had never heard back. Her aunt had been the one to finally call her with an update.

If she had any doubts she was outside her family's inner circle, this latest incident confirmed it.

"I didn't speak with Andrea." She tugged her hand from his. "But like I said, it worked out."

"You don't want to hold my hand?"

"No PDA. It's what we decided."

He scowled. "I don't like it."

"It makes sense." Kate gasped as a large intoxicated man bumped into her. Hard. When she tried to move aside, he stumbled and the heel of his cowboy boot came down on the top of her toes. Pain shot through her foot. She cried out.

"Watch where you're going," Joel called out to him, then turned to Kate. "Are you okay?"

She tried to be strong, but the tears filling her eyes gave her away. "I think I'm going to have a nasty bruise."

Joel swore. His eyes narrowed and his head jerked in the direction where the man had gone. But the drunkard had already disappeared into the crowd. When Joel turned back, worry filled his eyes. "There's a first-aid tent not far from here. I'll carry you."

His concern warmed her heart. But the last thing either of their reputations needed was for him to be seen carrying her in his arms.

"I've got a better idea." Kate gestured to a large wooden bench about twenty feet away in the shade of a large cottonwood. "Help me over there. I can put up my foot while you go to the first-aid station and get me some supplies."

He frowned.

Kate forced a smile, despite the stabbing pain in her foot. "Trust me. It's the best plan."

Before she knew what was happening she was in his arms. He strode to the bench, depositing her on the wooden slats as if she was the most precious of cargo, setting the picnic basket beside her.

He stood beside the bench for a long moment. "I don't like leaving you."

"I'll be fine." She rattled off the items she wanted him to pick up for her, wishing the throbbing in her toes would ease.

"I'll be right back." He gently brushed a strand of hair back from her face. "Stay here."

"Don't worry." Kate chuckled, then winced. "I'm not going anywhere."

He said something when he left. It sounded like "good sport" but she couldn't be sure.

Slipping her sandal off her foot, Kate leaned over and carefully inspected the rapidly swelling toes. It appeared to be the fourth and fifth distal phalanges that had taken the brunt of the man's weight. The sooner she got the foot elevated and ice on it, the better.

Kate swiveled her body and lifted her right foot onto the armrest at the far end of the dusty bench. All she could hope for now was that

1. No one she knew would stop by;
2. Joel would hurry and bring everything she'd requested and
3. the dirt would come out of her new white shorts.

"Dr. Kate."

She heaved a resigned sigh. Of course she should have known that in this sea of people someone would recognize her. She lifted herself up to her elbows and turned in the direction of the voice.

Holding the leash of a golden retriever, with her brow furrowed in concern, stood Emilie Hyland. "Are you okay?"

"Doing great," Kate quipped. "And you?"

The second the words left her mouth, Kate wished she could pull them back. The girl had really "blossomed" since Kate had seen her in the office several weeks ago. There was no hiding her pregnancy now.

Emilie ignored the question, focusing her bright blue eyes on Kate's foot. "What happened?"

"A drunk stepped on me. Big guy. Cowboy boots."

The teen's eyes widened. She glanced around as if ready to sound an alarm. "Can I get you something? Call someone?"

"Thank you, Emilie, but a friend is off getting me some items from the first-aid tent," Kate said quickly, offering a reassuring smile. "Give me a little tape and ice and I'll be good as new."

Relief skittered across Emilie's pretty face. "Cool."

Since Kate had last seen the teenager, Emilie had cut her blond hair to a sleek bob. She was as attractive as ever, but the sparkle that normally danced in her blue eyes was noticeably absent. With her pregnancy now apparent, Kate knew the past couple weeks couldn't have been easy. Unfortunately it would only get more stressful.

"How do you like Dr. Fisher?" Kate had referred the girl to Travis. Not only was he the best ob-gyn in Jackson, but he also had a warm and caring personality. She'd thought he and Emilie would be a good fit.

"He's nice." Emilie shifted from one foot to the other. "Last week we talked about my...options."

Because her pregnancy was so advanced, Kate knew that at this point, the girl had only two: keep the baby or give it up for adoption.

"My mom wants me to keep him." The words spilled from Emilie's mouth. "But I'm sixteen, Dr. Kate. What kind of mother would I be? I want to go to college. If I keep him, I'll be lucky to finish high school. My parents don't make enough money to support us all."

"You have some difficult choices to make in the next couple months." Kate gentled her tone. "It might be helpful if you talked to someone about your feelings. Dr. Peter Allman is someone I trust. He's very easy to talk with and I think he could help you to consider the pros and cons of your options."

Emilie's eyes searched Kate's face. "What do you think I should do?"

"What I think doesn't matter," Kate said softly. "It's a difficult decision and a very personal one. It's one you—and the baby's father—have to make."

"Dylan doesn't want anything to do with me or the baby." Bitterness colored Emilie's words.

"You'll make the right deci—"

Kate's words were drowned out by the retriever's staccato barks.

"I'd better go." Emilie jerked on the leash. "I hope you feel better."

Joel walked up just as Emilie turned to leave. He smiled, but the girl brushed past him.

"Isn't that Emilie Hyland?"

"You know her?"

"I know her dad, Dave. He's a bricklayer who does a lot of work for me." Joel frowned. "Is she pregnant?"

"Did they by any chance give you ibuprofen?" Kate sidestepped the question.

He jerked his gaze back to her. "They did. I picked up a bottle of water, too."

Joel squatted down beside her, Emilie and her bulging belly thankfully forgotten. He opened the small packet and pressed the pills in her hand. Once she'd popped them into her mouth he handed her the water. "How are you feeling?"

Kate took a big drink, touched by his caring. "My foot throbs like someone took a sledgehammer to it. Other than that, I feel wonderful."

His hazel eyes flashed. "I could punch the guy."

Kate lifted a shoulder in a slight shrug. "He was drunk. He didn't know what he was doing."

"No excuse." Joel pressed his lips together. "I'm not putting all the blame on him. I should have been watching out for you. I should have protected you."

Kate thought about pointing out that she'd managed to take pretty good care of herself for thirty-one years. But she kept her mouth shut. The thought of his watching out for her was...nice.

"What are you going to do with these?" In his outstretched hand the cotton balls looked amazingly small and fluffy.

"I'll show you." Kate clenched her teeth together and gently moved her smallest toe and the one next to it apart, then carefully placed the white fluff between the two toes. She repeated the procedure with the next two toes.

"What's the purpose?" Joel leaned close, his clean-shaven face right next to hers.

Her heart skipped a beat. Despite their "no PDA" vow—and her pain—she was tempted to kiss his cheek and tell him how much his concern meant. Instead, she forced a smile, then returned her attention to her foot, wrapping her toes together with the tape.

"The cotton keeps the toes from rubbing together." Kate held out her hand and he handed her the ice pack. She draped the red-and-white-checkered napkin she'd snagged from the picnic basket over her toes. "Now I'll put the ice bag in place and...it's all good."

A muscle in his jaw jumped. "All good except you have three broken toes."

"Two." She closed her eyes briefly against the pain. "And they're bruised, not broken."

"How can you be sure?"

"I broke a toe once," she said. "Trust me, I know the difference."

"Are you ready to head home?"

"Is that what you want?"

"I'm not the one in pain," he pointed out.

"I don't want to go home." Despite her aching foot, Kate wasn't ready for the day to end. "Let's go to Lexi's house. We promised her and Nick we'd stop by. If I need more ibuprofen or ice, they'll have it."

"Okay," he said. "But just so we're clear about later, you're staying at my house tonight."

"Overnight?"

"I want to take care of you. Make sure you don't overdo it."

"I don't have any pajamas with me," she sputtered.

A slow smile spread across his face. "Is that a problem?"

Kate wasn't convinced spending the night with Joel was a wise thing to do. Yet the excitement coursing through her veins told her she'd already made her decision.

"You're right. It's not." Her heart beat a sultry rhythm against her chest wall. "But I need my makeup and curling iron."

"No worries. We'll stop by your place and grab whatever you need."

"Anyone ever told you that you can be a bit bossy?"

"I'm taking care of you, Kate." He tipped her chin up with his finger and brushed a kiss across her lips. "Whether you want me to or not."

Chapter Thirteen

By the time she and Joel reached the mountains surrounding Jackson, the throb in Kate's foot had morphed into a dull ache. He pulled the truck into the circular driveway in front of the large stone-and-log home, stopping right in front. He wanted to carry her into the house but Kate refused. Still, she did lean on his arm as she hobbled from the truck to the front porch.

Joel rang the bell, his worried glance shifting between her and the closed door. Clearly unhappy about having her stand for so long, Kate swore if the door hadn't opened when it did, he'd have scooped her up into his arms and walked in unannounced.

"Happy Independence Day," Lexi greeted them as the door swung open. Her welcoming smile faded as she caught sight of Kate's one-legged stance. "Oh, my goodness, what happened to you?"

With the area around the toes turning black-and-blue,

Kate knew her foot wasn't a pretty sight. Still, she managed a smile as she shuffled onto the marble flooring in the foyer. "A drunken cowboy stepped on my foot when Joel and I were walking to Alpine Field."

Joel muttered something uncomplimentary about the man. Even though Kate didn't catch it all, she got the gist. Bottom line, the guy was lucky he'd gone on his drunken merry way by the time Joel realized what had happened.

"So you two—" Lexi paused and brought a finger to her lips "—were at Music in the Hole together?"

Joel looked at Lexi as if she'd spoken gibberish. "Of course we were together."

"Of course you were together." That familiar matchmaking spark flickered in Lexi's eyes. A spark that Kate knew must immediately be extinguished.

"Didn't you hear, Lexi? Chloe asked me to keep her dad company while she's out of town." Kate forced a laugh. "Whether he wants me around or not."

Joel opened his mouth to protest but Kate shot him a warning glance. This was the agreement. For both of their sakes it was important to stick to the plan.

"Nick, David and Travis are trying to get a baseball game going," Lexi said to Joel. "They told me to send you back when you arrived."

He began shaking his head. "Kate needs—"

"She'll be fine." Lexi put her hand on Joel's shoulder and gave him a little shove. "I'll take care of her."

To Kate's surprise, Joel planted his feet and fixed his gaze on her. "Will you be okay?"

A lump formed in Kate's throat. She blinked rapidly, keeping the tears at bay. How long had it been since someone wanted to care for *her?* Still, this was a game and she had a part to play.

"I'll be fine." She gave a dismissive wave, her voice casual and offhand, just as she'd intended.

"If you do need anything—"

"If I do—" Kate slanted a pointed glance to the brunette who'd been silently taking in every nuance "—I have Lexi."

"Absolutely," the social worker said. "I'm extremely dependable."

"Thank you," he said, finally satisfied.

As Kate watched him stride off, the ache in her heart became stronger than the ache in her foot. It was crazy. She'd slept with the guy once—okay maybe more than once—and spent a few hours with him. It didn't make sense that she felt so alone without him by her side now.

"Joel seems to be taking a personal interest in your welfare." Lexi's voice broke through Kate's thoughts. "What's that about?"

"I don't know." Kate shrugged. "It must be because I was injured while we were together. You know how men are...."

To her relief, Lexi laughed. Yet, Kate noticed a hint of suspicion remained in her amber eyes.

Lexi held out her arm for Kate to grasp. "There's a chair with an ottoman on the back deck. You'll be able to put up your foot and watch the ball game in comfort."

Kate leaned on Lexi, but it wasn't the same as having Joel beside her. He was like a rock. Strong and solid, a man a woman could depend on....

Lost in her thoughts, Kate didn't say much until they reached the porch. "I'm sorry, Lex. I really hate being a bother."

"Stop that talk." Lexi helped Kate ease into the chair. "That's what friends are for. You'd do the same for me."

"Yes." Kate choked out the word. "In a heartbeat."

Friends. Why had she fought so hard against accepting the fact that this woman—and the others in their group—were her friends? Was it because she feared having to confide in them? Of seeing the disappointment in their eyes when they learned she'd chosen her career over her daughter?

Yet, everyone had secrets, private regrets. Friends didn't need to be privy to everything that had ever gone on in one's life.

Lexi slipped a throw pillow under Kate's foot, then straightened. "What can I get you to drink?"

Before Kate had a chance to answer, footsteps sounded on the steps. Mary Karen rushed to Kate's side, looking like a college student in her peasant top and jean skirt, her blond hair pulled back into a ponytail. "Are you okay? I saw Joel out on the ball field. He told me you got into a fight with a drunk."

Something told Kate it was Mary Karen—not Joel—who'd embellished the story. Still, she had to admit, Mary Karen's account made it more interesting. "I'm afraid it was nothing that exciting. Some guy—who, yes, appeared to be intoxicated—stumbled. The heel of his cowboy boot came down on my toes."

"That's horrible." Mary Karen plopped down in the chair beside her, her blue eyes filled with sympathy. "I bet it hurts like the blazes."

"It does." Kate shifted slightly, trying to get comfortable. "I took ibuprofen right away—"

"You should have ice on it by now," a deep masculine growl came from the steps.

Kate's heart flip-flopped.

Joel crossed the deck in long, purposeful strides.

"I thought you were up to bat." Mary Karen's gaze

drifted to the far end of the lush lawn where the men were gathered.

"I hit a home run." The hard lines on Joel's face eased. He grinned. "Now Travis and David are arguing about changing the field boundaries. While they're occupied, I thought I'd check on Kate."

"My *friends*—" Kate's mouth lingered on the word "—have been taking excellent care of me."

Lexi rose to her feet with an ease Kate had always envied. What was even more unfair than her natural elegance was the fact that her wicker-colored linen shorts showed no trace of wrinkles.

"I was just headed inside to refill her ice pack." The social worker tossed the words over her shoulder as she headed inside.

"Sounds like everything is under control." Joel gave a satisfied nod, then turned to Kate. "Remember I have my cell on, so if you need anything…"

"She won't," Mary Karen asserted with a teasing smile. "We're going to ply her with chocolates, conversation and a whole lot of wine."

"Chocolate and wine." Kate laughed. "What more does a woman need?"

Joel's gaze met hers and held. Her mouth went dry. Ah, yes, there was something more a woman needed. At least she did. Forget the injured foot. *Soon,* Kate told him with her eyes, *soon.*

"Dennes, get down here," Travis bellowed from the makeshift field.

"Sounds like they've got the boundaries figured out." Joel's lips lifted in a slight smile. "Later."

To Kate's ears the word sounded more like a promise than a goodbye. She followed him with her eyes until he was on the lawn and headed toward his friends.

"What's up with you two?" Mary Karen leaned forward in her chair.

Kate played dumb. "What do you mean?"

"The way he looks at you." Mary Karen pretended to shiver. "Gives me goose bumps."

"Yeah, right." Kate laughed, but the intense possessive look in his eyes had given her goose bumps, too.

Lexi returned with a tray containing an ice bag, a bottle of merlot, wineglasses and a bowl filled with chocolates. A dish towel lay over one arm. After placing the tray on a nearby table, Lexi draped the checkered cloth over Kate's foot, then carefully positioned the ice bag on her injured toes.

"Mary Karen, you pour the wine and chat with Kate for a few minutes." Lexi turned back toward the house. "I need to check on how the babysitter is doing with the little ones."

Kate assumed *the little ones* referred to Lexi's youngest daughter, Grace, and Mary Karen's youngest set of twins, Ben and Sophie.

"Don't take too long. The wine might be gone by the time you get back," Mary Karen called after her.

In less than a minute, both Mary Karen and Kate had a glass of the burgundy liquid in one hand and a piece of chocolate in the other.

Kate took a small sip of wine, racking her brain for how she would change the subject if Mary Karen chose to take up the conversation where they'd left off. She liked Mary Karen but wasn't interested in playing twenty questions with her.

When the pretty nurse began talking about her older boys' latest escapades, Kate let out the breath she'd been holding and took another sip of merlot.

Mary Karen had just finished recounting an amusing

story involving her oldest set of twins—two very rambunctious boys—and a rope and bucket of water, when her gaze narrowed on Kate.

Oh, no, Kate thought, *here it comes.*

"Did you know Travis and I were friends with benefits for almost three years before we married?" Mary Karen spoke in the same tone she might use to announce what she was serving for dinner.

Kate choked on the peanut cluster. When she'd first moved to Jackson Hole, she and Travis had met at Wally's Place several times for drinks. That was before his marriage. She had no idea he and Mary Karen had an arrangement.

"I'm sorry." Kate took a fortifying gulp of wine. "When Travis and I were hanging out, I thought he was unattached."

Kate couldn't imagine how she'd feel if Joel was dating someone now, while she was sleeping with him.

"Per the terms of our arrangement, Travis was free to date. He just couldn't sleep with anyone."

"We didn't have sex," Kate hastened to reassure Mary Karen, just in case there was any question in her mind.

"I know that." Mary Karen leaned forward and squeezed her hand. "What kind of arrangement do you and Joel have?"

Zing. Kate hadn't seen that one coming. Heat rose up her neck even though she managed to keep her tone offhand. "I'm not sure what you mean."

"You told Lexi that you're just keeping Joel company while Chloe is out of town. Two friends simply hanging out." Mary Karen brought the glass of wine to her lips. "Isn't that what you said?"

"That's right." Kate spoke through suddenly dry lips.

"I don't buy it."

"Excuse me?"

"I see the way he looks at you," Mary Karen continued in a matter-of-fact tone.

"And, um, how is that?"

Mary Karen's lips curved up in a sly smile. "Like he could eat you up."

A flush of pleasure washed over Kate even as she shook her head. "I'm sure you're mistaken."

The look in Mary Karen's blue eyes told Kate she hadn't been convincing. At least not enough. Still, Mary Karen didn't press for a confession and Kate was grateful for that.

"When I first suggested to Travis that we give the friends-with-benefits thing a try, I was all for it."

Kate blinked. "You were?"

"I'd been in love with him since I was sixteen." Mary Karen's eyes took on a faraway glow. "We dated for a while when I was in college and he was in residency."

The two seemed so perfectly matched that Kate was having trouble figuring out why they hadn't married back then. "What happened? Why did you break up?"

"He didn't want children," she said simply. "I did. I couldn't see how a marriage between us could work."

Kate had heard bits and pieces of this story before but couldn't recall all the details. "So you married someone else, then had the twins—"

"Then got divorced when I was pregnant with Logan." Mary Karen paused. "Actually I got pregnant, *then* got married."

"Really." Kate didn't know what else to say.

"My sister-in-law, July, got knocked up, too," Mary Karen said with a rueful smile. "Only, my brother loved her as much as she loved him and was thrilled about the baby. I wasn't as lucky with Steven. But I did hit the jackpot with Travis."

Mary Karen laughed at her own joke, obviously recalling her whirlwind Vegas wedding.

It was mind-boggling to realize that three of her friends, all beautiful, educated women, had faced unplanned pregnancies. But unlike her, they'd kept their babies. Two had married.

"Lexi never married Addie's father," Kate murmured then stopped. Lexi hadn't said the information she'd shared was in confidence, but what if it was? Kate pressed her lips together, but it was pointless because the words had already slipped out.

"It's okay." Mary Karen patted her hand. "That's old news."

"I don't like to gossip—"

"Well, I do, but only in the nicest way." Mary Karen grinned. "The fact is, nothing stays a secret in Jackson Hole for long. So if you've got some deep dark secret, might as well spill now."

Kate let a laugh be her reply. But then, because Mary Karen was looking at her as if she expected something more, Kate lied through her teeth. "I'm afraid my life is an open book."

Except, of course, for that one chapter years ago.

"You know, Kate—" although they were the only ones on the deck, Mary Karen's voice lowered to a confidential whisper "—there's no reason for you and Joel to hide your relationship. Granted, he lost his wife, but that was a couple of years ago now. If you two are a couple, we'll all be happy for you."

Kate fought a surge of frustration. It hadn't even been one day and Mary Karen—and probably Lexi, too—had seen through their act.

Reaching over, Kate removed the ice from her foot and considered her options. She could continue to deny everything. Unfortunately she feared that would only encourage Mary Karen to keep on digging until she found out exactly what *was* going on. Or she could take Mary Karen into her confidence and ask her to convince the others there was nothing between her and Joel.

She pinned Mary Karen with her gaze. "If I tell you something, will you promise not to tell anyone?"

Mary Karen blinked and Kate saw that whatever her friend had expected to come out of her fishing expedition, it wasn't a confession.

"Could I tell Travis? I'd swear him to secrecy. You can absolutely trust his discretion."

Kate hesitated. One more person who might slip up.

"The only reason I ask is, Travis and I don't have any secrets. Really, you could trust him with your life."

A laugh bubbled up inside Kate. "Well, what I'm about to tell you isn't that serious."

Mary Karen remained silent, her eyes watchful. Kate sensed she wouldn't press. If Kate decided to walk away from this conversation, that would be okay. Still, because of Mary Karen's experience with Travis, she should understand.

"Joel and I are simply at the beginning of a two-week affair, which will terminate when Chloe returns." The words tumbled from Kate's lips. "At that time we'll go back to being social friends."

Mary Karen didn't look surprised at the admission. Of course, with five small children—four of them boys—it probably took a lot to shock her.

"Sounds like a fun interlude," Mary Karen said in an easy-breezy tone. "Travis and I never made love when the kids were in the house, so I understand that part. But why hide your relationship from your friends?"

"It's not really a—" The words died in Kate's throat. "Joel, is everything okay?"

He was back. Kate's heart gave an excited leap even as guilt sluiced through her veins. Here, she'd insisted he not tell a soul, yet what was she doing? Blabbing to Mary Karen.

Two lines of worry appeared between his brows. His gaze dropped to the ice bag next to her ankle and he cocked his head. "Why isn't the ice on your foot?"

"I had it on, but removed it a few minutes ago." Kate was surprised he was so worried. She wondered if his concern had anything to do with his wife's illness and subsequent death. She'd heard rumors that Amy Dennes had delayed going to the hospital when she'd become ill. "Ice isn't meant to be on an injury continuously. Just for fifteen minutes or so."

"How's the game going?" Mary Karen glanced at Joel. "We've been too busy gabbing to notice."

"The kids are now playing ball," Joel said with an indulgent smile. "Your Connor is quite a slugger."

Mary Karen sighed. "He's very active. And any of his siblings can attest to his 'slugging' abilities."

Joel smiled but his eyes remained on Kate.

"I'm feeling *much* better," Kate assured him. Okay, it was a bit of an exaggeration, but she wanted him to enjoy the day.

"That's all I need to know." He shot her a wink and headed back to the field.

"Now, where were we?" Mary Karen said once he was out of earshot. "Oh, yes. You were about to tell me why you and Joel decided to keep your relationship a secret."

Mary Karen, Kate decided, was the perfect woman to

be blessed with five children. She had a memory like a steel trap and could zero in without notice.

"Because we don't have a *relationship*." Kate emphasized the word. "We're only together for the sex."

"Only together for the sex? Ooh, this sounds interesting."

Kate looked up and stifled a groan.

Lexi pulled up a chair and took a seat. Her amber eyes snapped with curiosity. "Back up. Tell me everything. Well, the interesting parts anyway."

After swearing her to secrecy, which was beginning to seem rather pointless considering soon their entire group of friends would be under the Code of Silence, Kate caught her up to speed. "When you interru—er, walked up, I was telling Mary Karen that Joel and I have no relationship, it's just about the sex."

Mary Karen and Lexi exchanged a glance.

Lexi's brows pulled together in confusion. "I thought you liked Joel."

"I bet it's his first wife." Mary Karen shifted her gaze to Lexi. "You think he's still hung up on her."

"Well, yes," Kate said, "but that isn't—"

"Don't you want it to be about more than sex?" Mary Karen asked.

"M.K.," Lexi said, rather sharply, "isn't that a little personal?"

Mary Karen lifted her hands. "Just wondering. No obligation to answer."

"Of course we already know you think he's hot," Lexi mused.

Mary Karen tilted her head. "We do?"

"Yes." Lexi gave a decisive nod, then focused on Kate. "You must like him somewhat. If you were simply in the mood for a fling, you'd have shagged Ryan. I'm sure he'd have happily obliged."

Mary Karen shook her head. "C'mon, Lex, we all know Ryan would never have been satisfied with a fling."

Lexi thought for a second. "You're right."

"Of course I'm right." Mary Karen's self-satisfied smirk faded. "But I'm also confused."

Kate knew she'd regret it, but she opened her mouth anyway. "Confused about what?"

"Do you want to be Joel's girlfriend?" Mary Karen tilted her head.

Kate couldn't tell them about Chloe, so she tried the simple approach. "For reasons I prefer not to go into, we both knew the boyfriend-girlfriend thing wouldn't work for us. Because this will be only a two-week thing, why get everyone confused?"

"Makes sense," Lexi said slowly.

Mary Karen shook her head. "I'm worried."

"That our secret will get out?" Kate asked.

"No. That your heart will get broken." Mary Karen leaned forward, resting her hands on her thighs. "In theory your plan makes perfect sense. But trust me on this one, when you're sleeping with a guy you like and admire, keeping your emotions out of the equation is very, very difficult."

"It won't be a problem for me." Kate gave an emphatic nod. And it wouldn't. She had no choice. She couldn't fall in love with Joel Dennes.

Chapter Fourteen

Joel's eyes shone dark with concern. "Are you sure you're up to staying for the firework display?"

"Absolutely." At least, Kate would be once she got her hands on a glass of water and popped a few more ibuprofen. "Besides, the way I look at it, my foot will feel the same whether I'm here or at home."

They stood off to the side in a darkened corner of Mary Karen and Travis's large deck. Joel had appeared surprised when moments earlier she'd told him she was tired of sitting and wanted to take a stroll. It had felt good to stretch her legs and mingle.

But by the time they drew close to the doors leading inside, her toes had begun to make known their displeasure at the increased activity. She'd moved to the rail without comment, not wanting to complain, concerned if she did that Joel would insist on taking her home.

Kate inhaled the pungent scent of pine and let the cool

mountain air caress her face. A CD from the patriotic musical *George M!* played in the background. She found the music, mixed with the soft hum of conversation, as soothing as a bubbling brook. "It's so peaceful out here."

The words had barely left her lips when Mary Karen burst onto the deck, her husband mere steps behind her. She hadn't gone three feet when she stopped and whirled.

"You knew better than to give him that juice," Mary Karen hissed, her voice tight with anger.

Joel glanced at Kate. She shrugged.

Mary Karen's shoulders were rigid. The spunky blonde's eyes flashed blue fire. "There's an ugly purple stain all over the rug."

"Logan was thirsty, M.K." Travis's calm voice was in sharp contrast to his wife's. "He wanted grape juice."

By now the two had attracted the attention of everyone on the deck, including Ryan, who'd arrived only minutes earlier.

"Logan knows he has to sit at the table when he has grape juice." Her voice shook with emotion. "You know that, too, Trav."

"Cut him some slack, Mary Karen," Ryan called out. "You have four boys. Spills go with the territory."

"Shut up, Harcourt." Mary Karen pinned him with her gaze. "When you have kids, you may offer your opinion. Until then, mind your own beeswax."

Mary Karen turned back to her husband. "Lexi's grandmother made that rug." She angrily swiped back the tears filling her eyes. "Now it's ruined."

"Ah, honey, don't cry." Travis tugged his wife to him, holding on tight despite her efforts to pull away. "I'll take it to the cleaners on Monday. They'll work their magic and it will be good as new."

Kate told herself this was a private moment. But her gaze remained fixed on the couple.

"I'm sorry," Travis whispered, planting a kiss at the corner of his wife's lips. "So very sorry."

Only when Mary Karen's arms wrapped around his neck and their mouths melded together did Kate look away. It wasn't nearly soon enough. The raw emotion and sexual energy given off by the two was like an incendiary device. A smoldering heat ignited in her belly. It sputtered, then flared, fueled by the testosterone rolling off Joel in waves.

"Get a room," Mary Karen's brother, David, yelled.

Out of the corner of her eye, Kate saw his wife, July, swat him in the arm. Everyone laughed.

Travis turned toward his openly staring guests, a big smile on his face. One arm remained around his wife's waist. "Thanks for the suggestion, bro. If we disappear, you know where we'll be."

Two bright patches of pink dotted Mary Karen's cheeks, but Kate noticed she pinched her husband's backside before she stepped forward to mingle.

"My dad used to kiss my mom like that," Kate mused. "My sister and I thought it was gross. In retrospect it was rather sweet."

"I've never seen my parents kiss." Joel leaned against the rail. "I'm extremely thankful."

"Not even under the mistletoe?"

"Not even then." He sounded amused.

Although Kate had attended many Christmas parties, she'd never once been kissed under a sprig of berries and leaves. Perhaps that's why it still seemed like the ultimate romantic gesture. "If I asked, would you do it?"

He studied her for several seconds. "Because it's barely

July, I doubt we'll be encountering mistletoe anytime soon."

He was right and she wasn't about to push further. Besides, her relationship with Joel would be over long before Christmas, so it scarcely mattered.

Instead of saying more, Kate changed the subject. Movies, television shows, tastes in music and wine kept the conversational ball rolling.

As they talked, the fire inside Kate continued to build. Each time Joel touched her arm, her skin sizzled. From the way his gaze kept dropping to her mouth, she wasn't the only one feeling the heat.

The evening breeze kicked up, sending the light floral scent of her perfume wafting in Joel's direction. He inhaled deeply. Big mistake.

Keeping his passion for the pretty brunette under control tonight had been harder than Joel expected. It didn't help that their lovemaking this morning had been off the charts. He could still feel Kate's soft skin against his and hear the soft mew of pleasure when he touched her in key spots. The taste of her mouth was permanently seared on his lips.

When Travis had kissed Mary Karen, Joel wanted to say to hell with their agreement and kiss Kate until *they* were the ones needing a room. But he didn't. That wasn't him. He kept his emotions under control.

He glanced around the increasingly crowded deck. One thing for sure, there was no privacy here.

They could go back to his house, but he hated for Kate to miss the display over Snow King. What he needed was somewhere with a great view where they could be alone....

His lips curved up in a smile.

"I know the perfect place to watch the fireworks," he whispered in Kate's ear. "Interested?"

"A better spot than here?"

He dropped his gaze to the vee of her shirt. "More private."

"Well, if I can't have mistletoe—" Kate heaved an exaggerated sigh, but the twinkle in her eyes gave her away "—I'll settle for private."

When Joel turned the truck into the circular drive in front of the abstract-looking home in the mountains, Kate was certain he'd taken a wrong turn. Then he pulled to a stop and hopped out.

The fact that the home was completely dark inside didn't appear to concern him. He flung a blanket over his shoulder and tucked a pillow under each arm. In his left hand he carried a high-intensity flashlight.

Kate glanced around the professionally landscaped lawn. "Who lives here?"

"It recently sold." Joel took her arm and led her down on a rock path that curved around the side of the large home. "The new owners won't arrive until after the first of the year."

Kate stepped onto the back flagstone patio and motion sensors flooded the manicured lawn with light. Her breath caught in her throat. She looked up. And up. And up. At the far end of the yard, a steel observation tower soared forty feet into the air. Metal fencing encased a large deck area at the top.

Joel looped an arm around her shoulders and lifted his gaze. He smiled. "The perfect place to watch the fireworks."

"I'm sure it is, once you get up there." Kate stared at

the zillion steps that appeared to wind all the way to the heavens. "Please tell me there's an express elevator."

Joel's smile disappeared. "If you think climbing the steps will be too much—"

"I was just kidding. It's not a problem." Even though Kate knew the climb would put stress on her toes, if she was careful to lead with the ball of her foot she should be fine. She had no doubt the view would be worth the effort.

Joel cocked his head. There was a beat of silence. "Are you sure?"

She slipped her arm through his. "Absolutely positively sure."

He laughed and offered her his arm.

Once Kate reached the last step, she breathed a sigh of relief, then moved to the rail. Although the mountain property was surrounded by trees, up here she had an un-obstructed view of Snow King. "This is amazing."

Joel placed the light on the deck, then came up from behind her, slipping his arms around her waist, nuzzling her neck. "A-ma-zing."

Somehow she didn't think he was talking about the view. As Kate arched her neck, scenery was the last thing on her mind. All she could think was how good Joel smelled and how right it felt to have his body next to hers. She wondered if he'd ever made love under a star-filled sky. If not, perhaps they could both make tonight a first.

He must have read her mind because he gave her a deep, toe-curling kiss, then tugged her to the plaid blanket he'd spread in the center of the deck.

Kate settled herself on the soft flannel with a casual-ness at odds with the anticipation coursing through her. "How do you know about this place?"

Joel sat beside her, looping an arm over her shoulders, his fingers dangling just above her right breast. "The home needs a lot of updating on the inside and they wanted a bid."

She gazed into his eyes. Could he hear her heart pounding? "I didn't know your company did remodeling."

"New-home construction is our primary focus." His gaze remained on her lips. "But when it gets slow, having indoor work keeps the subcontractors I work with happy."

"Well, I'm happy you found this place." Kate liked it here. Liked being alone with Joel. Liked knowing that she could kiss him whenever she wanted.

"We have a good ten minutes before the fireworks start."

Was that a smile lurking in his hazel depths? Kate trailed a finger down his arm, her gaze never leaving his. "Any suggestions on how we pass the time?"

"We could talk."

Her heart plummeted in her chest. She dropped her hand to her side. "I guess we *could*."

He chuckled then, a low pleasant rumbling sound. "Or we could get naked."

Before she could respond, Joel placed an openmouthed kiss on her neck. The mere touch of his smooth, moist lips sent blood surging through Kate's body.

"You are so beautiful." His voice was soft and gentle as a caress. His hand slid beneath her shirt.

Kate's skin turned to gooseflesh and anticipation skittered up her spine.

"So soft," he said in a low soothing voice, rubbing his palm lightly over her skin. His fingers were strong, yet gentle, and her entire body tingled at his touch. Warm shivers of sheer pleasure coursed through her veins as several loud booms shattered the stillness. A spray of glittering gold stars rained down on them.

"Want to continue? Or would you prefer we stop for the fireworks?" His deep voice held a teasing lilt.

"Just steer clear of the toes," was all Kate could manage.

Thankfully Joel understood. While scattering kisses across her shoulders and up her neck, he continued to gently move his hand over her lower back. With each slow stoke, each unhurried touch, her desire grew. When he slid his hand upward, she moaned and arched her spine against him.

He played her like a fine violin, drawing her out, making her respond as she'd never responded before. The darkness and solitude lent a dreamlike air. By the time the sky over Snow King was painted in broad swaths of red, white and blue, their clothes were strewn across the deck. And the only fireworks Kate cared about were the ones she found in Joel Dennes's arms.

After ten nights together, Kate had to admit it felt strange locking up alone. She liked falling asleep in Joel's arms. Liked waking up to find his leg flung possessively over hers. Liked making love before she'd had her morning coffee.

Today, just after she'd added cream and sugar to her morning brew, Joel had called to tell her the morning hadn't been the same without her. Satisfaction flowed like warm honey through her veins. It appeared seeing her every day had become a habit for him, too.

Kate couldn't imagine going days or, gulp, weeks without talking to Joel. Soon that would be a reality, but she refused to worry about that now.

Because she and Mitzi had agreed to meet at the Jackson Chamber of Commerce's monthly event for young professionals, Kate happily accepted Joel's offer of a ride. With one stipulation. They had to stop at Carl's Jewelry on the way.

Her day quickly sped by and Kate had just finished with her last patient when Joel texted he was waiting in the parking lot. On the drive downtown, conversation flowed easily as she updated him on her day and he updated her on his.

Next to being in bed with him, this was what she liked the most. She couldn't believe how comfortable she felt around him. When he pulled into the parking lot and shut off the truck, Kate impulsively leaned over and kissed him.

He smiled, clearly pleased. "What was that for?"

"Just because." Kate shot him a wink and unbuckled her seat belt. "You can wait in the truck if you want. I'm only dropping something off, so it shouldn't take more than a couple of minutes."

"I'll go with you." Joel pushed open the truck door and rounded the front of the vehicle. "I've been wanting to check out their merchandise for weeks."

Kate's heart skipped a beat. "You have?"

"Chloe's birthday is coming up. July twenty-fifth."

Kate didn't need the reminder. The date was permanently seared into her memory.

"I've been thinking about getting her a ruby necklace." Joel cupped Kate's elbow as they started down the sidewalk. "Or maybe a ring."

"Ruby being her birthstone," Kate murmured.

He slanted a sideways glance. "How'd you know that?"

I know everything there is to know about Chloe would be a comment guaranteed to elicit all sorts of questions.

Kate smiled and sidestepped. "My sister's birthday is July twenty-seventh."

"Do you think Chloe is too young for jewelry?" he asked when the jewelry store awning came into view.

"For some children, ten might be too young." Kate spoke slowly, not because she was unsure of what to say, but because she wanted to savor the moment. To allow herself to pretend—for this brief moment in time—that they were parents considering what was best for *their* daughter. "But Chloe is more mature than most. She'd take good care of a necklace or ring."

He appeared pleased by her assessment. "I agree."

"And she's sensitive." Kate's heart overflowed with love for the child. "She'd cherish such a special gift."

"I believe you're right." Joel opened the door to the jewelry store and stepped aside, allowing Kate to enter first. "There isn't time to pick out something today, but at least I'll get an idea what their selection is like."

Kate thought about offering her assistance, but only two days of their affair remained. Two days and she'd go back to simply being his friend.

The past couple of weeks had been heaven with a little bit of hell thrown in. She'd enjoyed her time with Joel, both in and out of bed. Yet, the knowledge that this "affair" was only temporary made every lovemaking session, every pizza date, every phone call "just to say hello," bittersweet.

"Lexi." Joel's greeting pulled Kate from her reverie.

Kate shifted her gaze and saw the social worker standing next to a glass-topped counter filled with rings. Ignoring a twinge of pain in her toes, Kate crossed the room quickly and gave her friend a hug. "What brings you here this afternoon?"

The brunette looked stunning in a sleeveless linen

sheath of periwinkle blue. Her obviously curious gaze shifted from Joel to Kate. "I might ask you two the same question."

Kate pulled a tiny cloth drawstring bag from her purse, opened it and let the necklace slide into her palm. "Getting a new clasp put on this."

"Oh." Was that disappointment she saw in Lexi's eyes?

"How about you?" Joel asked. "What brings you downtown?"

"I'm picking up my wedding ring. One of the prongs had broken off." Lexi made a face.

A smartly dressed woman in a capped-sleeve black dress with silver spectacles hanging from a chain around her neck approached them. "May I help you?"

Joel slanted a sideways glance at Lexi.

"I've already been helped," Lexi told them. "Carl is in the back getting my ring."

Kate opened the bag and the necklace slid into her open palm. "The clasp on this is broken."

"That's a beautiful stone." Lexi leaned close. "What is it?"

"A fire opal." Kate extended her palm so her friend had a better view. "Just like my ring."

"Your ring is red." Lexi studied the stone encased in ornate filigreed silver. "This is more of a burnt orange."

"The color can vary from a hot-yellow to a brilliant red." The clerk's comment told Kate that the woman knew her stuff. "Yours is one of the largest fire opals I've seen."

"Gram knew I liked big, showy jewelry." A slight smile lifted Kate's lips. "Which makes no sense considering both my mother and sister prefer the simpler pieces. My sister didn't even want a diamond engagement ring. A simple gold band was good enough for her."

"That's how Amy was," Joel said, his tone heavy with approval.

Kate's smile faded.

"Forget simple and small," Lexi said. "I adore my big diamond."

"Mrs. Delacourt, I hope you don't mind, but after I repaired the prong, I took the liberty of cleaning the ring." A thin older man with a shiny bald head and wire-rimmed glasses leaned across the counter and slipped the ring on Lexi's finger.

Set in a platinum setting, the multifaceted diamond glittered and sparkled beneath the large chandelier. Even though Kate was no expert on rings, she realized the stone had to be at least two carats.

"That *is* big," Joel said.

Kate fought a pang of envy. "It's lovely."

"I think it's beautiful." Lexi held her finger up to the light. "But what makes it extraspecial is that Nick knew I'd never ask for such an expensive ring. He bought it simply because he knew I loved big stones and he wanted to make me happy. Is it any wonder I adore him?"

"You're a lucky woman, Mrs. Delacourt," the clerk said, a hint of envy in her tone.

Kate agreed wholeheartedly. She was happy for her friend, she really was. But she couldn't help but wonder when it would be her turn. Would she ever find a man who loved her that much?

Chapter Fifteen

The monthly Jackson After-Hours event was in full swing by the time Kate and Joel arrived. The popular brewery on the edge of the downtown business district teemed with young men in khakis and cotton shirts and women in colorful dresses and skirts.

Joel knew the purpose of coming to the monthly event sponsored by the local chamber of commerce was to mingle and network, but at the moment he didn't feel like doing either. He grabbed another handful of mixed nuts and washed them down with a sip from the bottle on the table before him.

Just before he and Kate walked through the brewery door, it struck him that in a little over twenty-four hours he'd be leaving for Montana to pick up Chloe. Once she was home, he'd go back to his old life and Kate would go back to hers. The trouble was he'd grown accustomed to having her around, to sharing the events of his day with her, to kissing her like she'd kissed him earlier, *just because.*

Kate was smart and fun with a strong sense of integrity. A woman he could trust. That didn't mean he'd fallen in love with her. Amy was still the only woman he would ever love. But he liked Kate, liked her a lot. And Chloe adored her.

Joel had spoken with his daughter at least twice a day since she'd left. He could tell by her happy chatter that she was having a blast with her friend in Montana. Still, as he'd told Kate on the way over here, he was relieved she'd finally started to sound excited about coming home. He liked hearing that she missed him and that she was looking forward to her sleepover with Sarabeth.

He wasn't sure if it was good or bad that she'd gotten into the habit of asking to speak to Kate once they finished talking. It was as if she just expected the doctor to be with him. Of course, he had to admit that three out of four times she'd asked, Kate *had* been there to take the phone call.

In less than fourteen days Kate had become a part of his life. He took another sip from the bottle and wondered what she'd say if he asked to see her after their time was up.

Of course, he'd make it clear that it would be as a friend and they wouldn't really be dating, much less dating exclusively. Unfortunately that would mean he'd have to accept that what happened tonight would continue to occur.

He'd had high hopes for the evening, especially when he learned Mitzi wasn't coming after all. He and Kate would get a drink, mingle for a half hour or so, then find a quiet table and catch up on each other's day.

But he and Kate had barely stepped up to the bar to get

a drink when Lexi had appeared and whisked Kate away to mingle. Or rather, to deposit her into the waiting arms of Benedict Campbell.

Joel took a sip of his Guinness and made a concerted effort not to glare at the respected surgeon.

"Not liking the view?"

Joel stifled a curse. Just when he thought the night couldn't get any worse, his not-so-favorite attorney had to make an appearance. To top it off, Ryan's hand snaked in front of him and grabbed the rest of the mixed nuts.

"The open bar is thataway." Joel gestured with his head to a spot across the room, then returned his attention to Kate and her new "friend."

The attorney plopped into the chair Joel had saved for Kate. "Don't worry about him."

Even though the Guinness now tasted like sawdust, Joel took another sip before responding. "I don't know what you're talking about."

"Yeah, right." Ryan chuckled and motioned to a college-aged blonde waitress, ordering a beer before turning his attention back to Joel. "Like I said, Kate's not interested in Ben."

Kate looked interested. In fact, if Joel didn't know better, he'd think she and the surgeon were already a couple by the way she was laughing with him, her hand resting on his arm.

Ben couldn't seem to take his eyes off her. That wasn't surprising considering how sexy she looked this evening. Her bright yellow dress hugged her curves and the sandals she wore made her legs look as though they went on forever. Last night those legs had been wrapped around him.

Why had they come tonight when in two days it would be all over? They should be at his house right now, feasting on each other rather than on cold hors d'oeuvres. It seemed ironic that Kate had wanted to attend because it would be Mitzi's first time. Yet her friend was stuck in surgery and they'd ended up at this event when they'd rather be elsewhere.

Joel watched Kate brush a strand of hair back from her face. A muscle in his jaw jumped. He'd seen that gesture many times in the past two weeks. Usually it occurred when the pretty doctor was tired of talking and ready for some action. Could she want...Benedict?

Joel's gut felt like someone had driven a spike into it. To make matters worse, Ryan had taken up permanent residency at his table. Instead of mingling, the attorney sat sipping the beer the pretty waitress had dropped off.

"Don't you have any other friends?"

"Kate." A smug smile lifted Ryan's lips. "But she's busy right now."

Busy with Benedict.

Joel kept his expression impassive. "Okay, tell me. What makes you think she's not interested in him?"

Ryan snagged another handful of nuts from a nearby table and ate every single one of them before answering. "Because she's in love with *you*."

According to everyone, this month's Jackson After-Hours event was a rousing success. Even though Kate had done her part by showing up, all she could think of was that she and Joel had only two evenings left and they were wasting one of them here.

To make matters worse, she'd hardly seen him all evening. For some unknown reason Lexi had appeared to make it her personal mission to encourage Kate to mingle. When she protested that she'd come with Joel, the popular social worker had just laughed and dragged her over to speak with Benedict Campbell.

Finally, after two long hours apart, she and Joel had been able to reunite and make their escape. She had so much to tell him. While Benedict seemed reserved and aloof, he'd regaled her with funny and interesting stories. Joel didn't seem to find them as amusing. When she quit talking, silence filled the truck cab. Definitely odd. Still, she told herself, last night had been a late one for both of them.

Her spirits perked up when, instead of taking her straight home, Joel turned in the direction of his place. Once inside, Kate slipped off her shoes and took a seat on the leather sofa. She patted the spot beside her.

He shook his head.

Kate pulled her brows together. Tired was one thing. This was something else. "What's wrong?"

He jammed his hands into his pockets and rocked back on his heels. "What makes you think something is wrong?"

"Well, for starters, you haven't said ten words since we left the brewery." A feeling of unease wrapped itself tight around her shoulders but she managed to keep her tone light. "Not to mention we've been inside five minutes and we still have our clothes on."

His lips curved upward at that observation, but the smile didn't quite reach his eyes.

Instead of filling the silence with nervous chatter, Kate pressed her lips together and waited for his response.

"We've gotten to know each other pretty well these past couple of weeks," he said after several long heartbeats. His brows pulled together in a frown and he began to pace. "I can't believe Ryan knows you better than I do."

"He doesn't." Even though Kate liked the attorney,

having Joel bring his name into a conversation raised any number of red flags. "Tell me what he said."

Joel's gaze met hers. "He said you're in love with me."

When Kate was twelve she'd fallen off her bike and had the air knocked out of her. She remembered that feeling. She felt the same way now.

Although she cursed Ryan for interfering, she realized he'd spoken the truth. A truth she hadn't even admitted to herself until this moment. If she didn't feel so much like crying, she'd laugh at the irony. She'd fallen in love with the one man who could never be hers.

But if she confessed that love, it would be over between them. Kate knew that as well as she knew her own name.

"Of course it isn't true." She kept her tone matter-of-fact. This wasn't, after all, a hearts-and-flowers moment. "But I do *like* you. I hope that's okay."

A tousle of hair had fallen across his forehead. She wanted nothing more than to brush it back. How foolish she'd been to think she could keep herself from falling in love with him.

Joel expelled a ragged breath and dropped down beside her on the sofa. "I like you, too."

He reached over and took her hand and Kate let out the breath she'd been holding. When she was with him like this, she could almost believe everything was okay. And it appeared to be, at least for now.

"I did a lot of thinking tonight. There's really no reason we can't continue to see each other when Chloe returns. As friends, of course," he quickly added.

"Friends *without* benefits," Kate clarified.

"If that's the way it'd have to be—"

"It would be too complicated for us and too confusing to Chloe any other way." Kate didn't want the stipulation any more than he did, but she had to figure out how to keep some distance between them…for her heart's sake.

"But that won't start until Chloe gets back." He brought her hand to his mouth and pressed a kiss in the palm.

A smoldering heat flared through her. She gazed at him through lowered lashes. "Correct, again."

Her gaze met his. Time seemed to stretch and extend.

Joel's grin was a little lopsided, his fingers not quite steady as they touched the curve of her cheek, trailed along the line of her jaw. "I'm going to make this a night we'll never forget."

Excitement coursed through her when she saw the gleam in his eyes. There was a promise there, one that said there was more, much more to come.

She looped her arms around his neck and pressed a kiss against those lips she'd come to know so well. "See that you do."

As his lips closed over hers and his hand flattened against her lower back, drawing her close, Kate gave in to the emotion, to the feelings sweeping through her body like a wildfire.

If one more night was all they had, she was going to make it a night they'd *both* remember.

"Dr. Kate and I are going to paint our nails and toes today," Chloe announced over breakfast. "Then later we're going to meet Mrs. Delacourt and Addie for an Italian soda."

Joel added some more cream to his coffee and smiled. Because Kate wasn't on call today, Chloe was spending the day with her instead of with the teenage girl who normally watched her when he had to work on the weekend.

During the past few months, he and Kate had settled into a routine. One night during the week she'd make dinner for them, then later in the week, he and Chloe would make dinner for her. On the weekends he and Kate would go out Saturday night. Sundays were their family days.

It would have been a satisfactory arrangement except for one factor. They no longer slept together. Even though it had been part of the rules laid out, Joel couldn't help wishing it wasn't so, well, set in stone. He could understand when Chloe was in the house. But even when his daughter was away on a sleepover—which had been happening with increasing regularity—all clothes stayed on.

He supposed he could push the issue. During their good-night kiss, which sometimes lasted a half hour or more, it was apparent that celibacy was as hard on her as it was on him. With a little encouragement Joel knew he could have her in his bed. But it was better this way.

Or so he kept telling himself.

Their two-week affair had been simply a physical release. Continuing to date Kate didn't seem like a betrayal of what he and Amy had shared because they were merely good friends. No love involved.

The only concern he had was Chloe. She'd grown attached to Kate over the past couple of months. But he consoled himself with the fact that Kate wasn't the type of woman who'd ever abandon a child. Even if their relationship came to an end, he had confidence she'd remain Chloe's friend.

And it wasn't as if Kate was sitting around pining for him. Kate was now going on an occasional date with other men. She'd told him because they were simply friends that it was best they not get too dependent on each other. He'd agreed. But if it was for the best, why did it feel so wrong? And why couldn't he bring himself to ask anyone out?

"Can we go out for pizza tonight, Daddy?" Chloe hopped up, taking her bowl to the sink without being asked. Another good habit she'd picked up from Kate.

Joel took a sip of coffee. "Kate and I go out on Saturday night. Remember?"

"Not tonight, Daddy. She has a date with Dr. Campbell."

Joel slowly lowered his mug to the table. "I'd forgotten."

It wasn't that he hadn't been warned. Kate had told him weeks ago that Benedict had invited her to attend some medical-society function with him and that she'd accepted. No, he hadn't forgotten, but neither was it something he dwelled on. If he did, he'd have to confront the fact that sooner or later Kate would find someone else. And that was something he preferred not to think about.

Chapter Sixteen

Kate finished dressing and putting on her makeup while Chloe played happily in the living room. Even from her bedroom, she could hear the little girl singing to herself.

As she applied her copper-colored lipstick, she smiled. These Saturdays that they spent alone had given her a chance to get to know Chloe...and to fall even deeper in love with her daughter.

She knew she shouldn't think of her in that way, but it came so easy now. It might not be right, but she wasn't saying it aloud, so what did it hurt? After casting one last glance in the mirror, Kate retrieved her shoes from the closet and carried them with her into the living room. She dropped them next to the sofa.

Although her toes had completely healed, she tried not to squish them any sooner than necessary.

"I like your new shoes." Chloe picked up one of the

taupe peep-toe pumps with the pleated accent. "Very stylish."

Kate hid a smile. Those were almost the exact words Mitzi had used before she'd left the house to go shopping. Often when Chloe came over, Mitzi would stay and the three of them would spend the day together. But tonight was a big medical-society event at the Spring Gulch Country Club.

Mitzi swore she hadn't a thing to wear. Even though she was *just* going with Ryan—her words, not Kate's— she'd headed out for an afternoon of shopping. That left Kate alone with Chloe for the afternoon, a fact that suited Kate just fine.

In the past two months, she and Chloe had developed a relationship. The child sometimes came to her for advice, but most of the time they simply enjoyed doing "girl" things together.

"I'm glad you like them."

"You're going to look so pretty tonight." Chloe's gaze settled on the black dress, with a swath of tan down each side, draped over the sofa. Her smile faded. "I just wish—"

Kate looked up from the toenail she was painting a deep burgundy. "You wish what, sweetie?"

Chloe chewed on her lip, then ducked her head. "I shouldn't say."

After finishing the last nail, Kate put the applicator into the bottle and screwed it shut, then gave Chloe her full attention. "What have I always told you?"

"That there isn't anything I can't tell you."

"Okay, then." Kate gentled her tone. "Tell me what's on your mind."

"I wish you were going with my dad," Chloe blurted out. "He's every bit as handsome at Dr. Campbell and you two have so much fun together. I don't know why you're not taking him. It just seems so…wrong."

It felt wrong to Kate, too. But dating other men was a survival thing. Joel didn't love her. Oh, she knew he cared about her, but it wasn't enough. She'd spent too many years coming in second to her sister to settle for any man's leftovers.

Dating other men made it feel like she wasn't pining for someone she couldn't have. She was still out there keeping her options open. It seemed ironic—and more than a little sad—that the only man she wanted was the one she couldn't have. But that wasn't something Chloe could understand. Heck, she barely understood it herself.

"Your father—" Kate paused, praying for the right words "—loved your mommy very much. He may not ever marry again. But I've never been married and one day I'd like to have a husband and some children. So, while I admire your dad and enjoy his company, we're just friends."

To Kate's surprise, Chloe's face took on a mulish expression. She crossed her arms. "You kiss him. Friends don't kiss like that."

Heat rose up Kate's neck. Two nights ago, when she and Joel had both thought Chloe was asleep, they'd decided to begin saying good-night while sitting on the sofa in his living room. That had been a big mistake. If Chloe hadn't come in when she had, Kate had no doubt that she and Joel would have gone "all the way" instead of having a forced stop at second base.

"Not casual friends," she finally managed to choke out. "But your father and I are *good* friends."

Thankfully Kate was spared having to say more by the ringing of the doorbell.

Chloe hopped up and raced to the front door. "I'll get it."

Kate rose to her feet and followed behind. In a matter of seconds, the UPS guy had deposited the large box on the floor of the foyer and was sprinting to his truck.

"What's in it?" Chloe's eyes sparkled with curiosity.

"I don't know." Kate looked at the return address and sighed. "It's from my mother."

"Is it your birthday?"

Kate shook her head and lifted the box, relieved that it wasn't as heavy as it looked. "Let's open it and find out."

Chloe clapped her hands. "This is going to be so much fun."

For the little girl's sake, Kate hoped it wasn't a box of old sweaters. Because it appeared her mother had used a whole roll of packing tape, the child's anticipation had built to a fever pitch by the time they finally got it open.

"Toys," Chloe squealed. "And pictures."

There was a letter inside, written in her mother's perfect penmanship, telling Kate that because she would likely remain in Jackson Hole, she was sending the rest of her childhood memorabilia.

Chloe pulled out a Cabbage Patch doll with brown pigtails and freckles and clasped her to her chest. "She's beautiful."

"Her name is Lottie Rose." Kate remembered how she and her mom and sister had stood in line for an hour before a local department store opened in hope of getting one of the popular dolls. "She was my firstborn. I eventually got two more, but Lottie has always held a special place in my heart."

"Where are you going to put her?" Chloe looked at a glass-topped side table and then in the direction of Kate's bedroom.

"Actually I'll probably pack her away."

Chloe's face fell. Her hold on the doll tightened.

"Unless—" Kate swallowed against the emotion well-ing up in her throat "—you'd like to have her?"

A shriek burst from Chloe's throat. "Yes. Yes. Yes. I want her. Are you sure? Can I really have her?"

It had been an impulsive offer but it felt right. Lottie had been a special gift. She should be handed down from mother to daughter. "I can't think of anyone who would give her a better home."

Kate had barely choked out the words when Chloe flung herself at her, wrapping her arms around her neck and hugging her tight. "I love you, Dr. Kate."

Kate wrapped her arms around the child—*her child*—and blinked back tears. "I love you, too, sweetheart."

She'd thought Chloe would jump back, eager to play with her new doll. But she settled her head against Kate's chest, as if content to be simply held.

Kate stroked the girl's dark satiny hair and forced her-self to breath past the tightness gripping her chest. This was the first time she'd held her daughter this close since that last day in the hospital.

Oh, Chloe, I'm so sorry. I should never have let you go.

Chloe lifted her head and for a second Kate worried that she'd spoken aloud. But the little girl just smiled and laid her head back against Kate's chest.

When they finally broke apart, it was with none of the awkwardness Kate expected.

"Are you ready for a snack?" Kate's voice sounded husky, even to her own ears. She cleared her throat and tried again. "I have apples with caramel dipping sauce."

Because Joel wasn't picking his daughter up until five-thirty, Kate knew it would be six-thirty or seven before the two ate.

"Can we finish looking through your stuff first?" Chloe dropped a kiss onto the top of Lottie's head.

"Sure." Kate glanced at the large cardboard box, wondering what other old memories it held.

As they dived into the contents, it appeared that the box held a little bit of everything. More dolls, though none as special as Lottie Rose, a boatload of stuffed animals and lots of games. And in the very bottom, a shoe box filled with pictures.

Chloe's eyes widened at the picture of Kate in her band uniform. "You were so pretty."

Because orange and black had never been her best colors, Kate knew that was an overstatement, but she appreciated the compliment.

"I want to look at all these," Chloe said with a pleading expression. "Can we, Dr. Kate? Please, can we?"

The clock on the fireplace mantel said they had less than thirty minutes until Joel arrived to pick up Chloe. Ben was supposed to arrive shortly after.

Still, she was dressed and ready to go, so there was time.

After maneuvering the box by the sofa, Kate took a seat and Chloe hopped up next to her. She reached into the box and pulled out a picture. "This was me as a baby."

Chloe oohed and aahed over the pictures of Kate as an infant and toddler. Even though there were many pictures of both her and Andrea, the little girl never once commented on Kate's sister's pretty face.

By the time they reached the grade school ones, Chloe was totally engaged. They moved on to the upper-elementary grades when Chloe looked at the picture in her hands and gasped.

"You look just like me, Dr. Kate." Chloe's eyes were wide. "We could be twins."

Kate glanced at the picture the child held in her hands. She wore her favorite pink skating outfit and was staring unsmiling at the camera. A chill traveled up her spine. The child was right. It could have been Chloe in the picture.

"Don't you think we look alike, Dr. Kate?"

The door had been opened slightly and Kate took full advantage. "Well, we both have dark hair. I could easily imagine you in that skating outfit. So, in that aspect we do look alike."

"No," Chloe said. "Your face looks like mine."

"I guess I can see the resemblance...." Kate glanced at the clock, her veins humming with nerves. "Your father will be here any minute. Let's look at some of the pictures when I was in junior high."

Kate shoved the ones where she was closest to Chloe's age under the sofa cushion and pulled out another handful. By the time the doorbell rang, Joel was fifteen minutes late and they were laughing at pictures from the camping trip her family had taken Kate's senior year.

Without missing a beat, Kate dumped the rest of the pictures back into the shoe box and placed it in the cardboard box, between a Ronald McDonald doll and her Wonder Woman Underoos.

"I want to look at more pictures," Chloe whined.

Kate brushed a strand of hair back from the child's face and plopped a kiss on her forehead. "Next time you're here, we'll finish going through the box."

"Pinky swear?"

Kate locked little fingers with the girl and squeezed as the doorbell rang again. "Pinky swear."

"Okay." Chloe wrapped her arm around her new doll and headed for the door. "I can't wait for Daddy to meet Lottie Rose."

Joel meeting Lottie Rose was one thing, but Kate didn't want him being there when Benedict Campbell arrived. It felt awkward enough to be going out with another man after what she and Joel had shared, but being in the same room with both of them was something she preferred to avoid. She prayed Joel would make a quick exit.

"Daddy, Daddy." Chloe flung open the door. "Look what Dr. Kate gave me."

The child held out the doll for his inspection. He touched the yarn pigtails and smiled.

"She's pretty," Joel said. "But not as pretty as you, princess."

Chloe clapped her hands over the doll's ears. "Don't say that. You'll hurt her feelings."

Joel's jeans, chambray shirt and boots were covered with a fine layer of dust. He looked rugged, manly and totally magnificent.

He whipped off his hat. "I apologize for being late. It's supposed to rain heavily for the next few days, so we pushed to get the house closed up. I lost track of the time."

"It's okay, Daddy," Chloe answered before Kate could respond. "Dr. Kate and I were busy. We didn't even miss you."

"Is that so?" His lips curved up in a smile as his gaze settled on Kate. "You look nice. Are you going somewhere special?"

"Tonight is the Jackson Hole Medical Society's Annual Event at Spring Gulch." Kate wished he'd remembered so she didn't have to mention it.

"That's right." His smile faded. "Too bad. I thought it'd be fun to go out for pizza."

Even though his expression was innocent, Kate wondered if he'd *really* forgotten about her date. "Perhaps another time."

"Dr. Kate and I looked at pictures, Daddy." Chloe tugged on his sleeve. "In one of them she looks *just like me*."

Joel lifted a brow.

"I had on a skating outfit similar to the one Chloe owns." Kate waved a dismissive hand, wishing she could think of a way to graciously push them both out the door.

"No, no, it wasn't the dress," Chloe insisted. "When I looked at the picture I thought it was *me*."

Joel rocked back on his heels. "This I have to see."

"It's in the shoe box." Chloe turned toward the sofa, but Kate caught her arm.

"Sweetie, how about we show your dad the picture next time? I have company coming and—" Kate paused "—here he is."

Dr. Benedict Campbell paused in the open doorway. Impeccably attired in a dark suit and gray tie, his appearance a sharp contrast to Joel's dusty work clothes.

Ben was a little older than Kate, with hair more black than brown and gray eyes that could turn hard as steel in an instant. His build reminded Kate of Joel's, tall with broad shoulders and lean hips. Unlike Mitzi, who detested the man, Kate enjoyed his company. But she wasn't attracted to him.

"Perfect timing," she said with a smile. "Let me grab my wrap from the closet and I'm ready to leave."

Even though it probably wasn't smart to leave Joel and Ben together, the evenings had started cooling down and she knew she'd regret not taking a coat.

"I don't know if you've ever met my daughter, Chloe." Joel rested his hand on the child's shoulder. "Chloe, this is Dr. Benedict Campbell."

"How do you do, Chloe?" Ben smiled. "Who is that you're holding?"

Chloe smiled shyly. "This is Lottie Rose. She was Dr. Kate's doll when she was little. She gave her to me."

"You and Dr. Kate must be good friends to have her give you such a special gift."

Kate heard Ben's comment from the other room and she groaned. Nothing good could come out of this line of questioning.

"I love Dr. Kate very, very much," Chloe said. "I wish she was my mommy."

Kate stopped in her tracks, a lump rising to her throat. She blinked rapidly, trying to clear the tears that sprang to her eyes.

By the time Kate reached the living room, Chloe was telling Benedict about the picture.

"Sounds interesting." Ben turned to Kate. "I'd like to see it."

"Dr. Kate can't show it to us now." Chloe shook her head. "'Cause she's going to the party with you."

The tone in the child's voice made it clear she didn't approve.

"I definitely want to see the picture," Joel said. "Bring it to church tomorrow."

"If I make it," Kate murmured.

"You have to come," Chloe wailed. "I'm singing in the choir."

Dear God, could this get any more awkward?

"Time to leave," Kate announced, shooing Chloe and Joel out the front door, then bringing up the rear with Benedict.

Only when she was in his black Mercedes and they were gliding down the highway to the Spring Gulch Country Club did the tightness leave Kate's chest. Later, when she got home tonight, she'd decide what she was going to do about the picture. But for now she wasn't going to give it a second thought.

Benedict turned off the highway and slanted a glance in her direction. "You and Joel Dennes seem very close."

Kate's smile froze on her face. "He thinks of me as a friend of the family."

"Not if the look he shot me was any indication." Ben laughed. "I felt as if I was going out with a married woman."

What could Kate do but laugh along with him? But the incident in her foyer set the tone for the entire evening. By the time Ben dropped her off at her house at a respectable 11:00 p.m., Kate knew something had to change.

Mitzi plopped down on the sofa next to Kate, an oversize coffee mug in her hand. "How was your date with Benedict Arnold, oh, I mean, Campbell?"

"I don't understand why you don't like the guy." Kate leaned back, cradling her cup between her palms. "He's very nice. Reserved but nice."

"Arrogant." Mitzi spat the word. "Egotistical jerk."

"Ben?" Kate frowned, trying to reconcile the man she'd spent the evening with and the one her friend described.

"Lots of people think he's an okay guy," Mitzi grudgingly admitted. "He and I just aren't a good combination."

Kate took a sip of coffee, finding Mitzi's response very interesting. She hadn't seen her friend show so much emotion over a man in, well, never.

"How come you skipped church?" Mitzi lifted a perfectly tweezed brow. "Wasn't Chloe singing?"

"Her dad will be there."

"That doesn't answer my question." Mitzi slanted a

sideways glance. "By the way, you look like hell this morning."

Kate raked a hand through her hair. This morning, she'd pulled on her oldest pair of yoga pants and a faded blue T-shirt that should have been relegated to the trash years ago. Although she'd brushed her teeth, she hadn't bothered with makeup. "I couldn't sleep."

"Well, that explains the raccoon eyes." Despite Mitzi's flippant tone, Kate sensed her friend was concerned. "Did something happen with Benedict? Because even though he's the head of the group, I won't put up with him—"

"It's not him, Mitz. It's Joel."

Mitzi's eyes widened in surprise. "I thought things were good between you two."

"I've come to the conclusion that continuing to see him was a mistake." Kate glanced down at the picture she'd pulled out this morning. The one Chloe had wanted her to show her dad.

"But you're only dating him. You're not sleeping with him. Or has that changed?"

"That hasn't changed." Kate slouched back against the cushion. "Sometimes I think it'd be easier if we were and I could tell myself it's just sex."

"I don't under—"

"Yesterday I overheard Chloe tell Joel she loved me and wished I was her mommy."

"Oh."

"Yeah. Oh." Kate expelled a ragged breath. "I know what I want, Mitzi. I want it all, but I can't have it all. And soon I won't have any of it."

Mitzi leaned over and peered into Kate's cup. "What are you drinking?"

Kate couldn't even manage a smile. And when Mitzi

set down her cup and took her hand, she couldn't hide her tears.

"Tell me what's going on," Mitzi said softly.

"I can't be Joel's friend anymore, Mitzi. It's too hard. I love him. I know he cares for me, but caring isn't enough. That's why I started dating again. But when I was out with Benedict, all I could think of was how I wished I was with Joel."

"Then maybe you should just... see only Joel."

"Don't you understand? Even if he were willing to fall in love again, it couldn't be with me. There can never be anything between us."

"Because he doesn't know that you're Chloe's birth mother."

Kate nodded. "How could two people build a life together with such a lie between them?"

Mitzi lifted the mug but didn't drink. "Then I guess there's only one solution to your problem."

"And that is?"

"You're going to have to tell him, Kate. Come clean and tell him you're Chloe's mother."

"Are you sure you don't want to go for a run with me?" Mitzi stood by the open door, making one last appeal.

Kate shook her head. "I'm going to take a shower. By the time you get back, I'll be perfectly presentable."

"Then I'm taking you to lunch," Mitzi said. "And I don't want any argument. We'll check out that new Mexican place on the highway."

"You won't get any argument from me."

Kate rose from the sofa as soon as Mitzi left to put her cup in the dishwasher, too restless to sit any longer. On her way back to the living room she heard the front door open. Trust Mitzi not to take no for an answer. "I don't care how nice it is out there. If you keep badgering me, I'm not going—"

Her breath caught in her throat. It wasn't her temporary roommate who stood in the foyer but Joel.

"Mitzi told me to let myself in." His eyes widened. Apparently she looked worse than she realized. "Are you okay?"

"I'm fine." She gestured to a chair. "Please, make yourself at home."

He had her at a definite disadvantage. He'd obviously come from church. Every hair on his head was in place and instead of attire more suitable for a second-rate yoga studio, he wore dark brown dress pants and a cream-colored dress shirt that put her faded tee to shame.

His gaze searched hers. "Chloe and I missed you at church."

"Yeah, well, I had a late night." Despite drinking a glass of warm milk at midnight, it had been close to three before she'd fallen asleep.

A muscle in Joel's jaw jumped. "Sounds like things went well with Benedict."

"Benedict?" Kate's sluggish brain didn't immediately make the connection. Then it hit her. He thought she'd been up late carousing with the doctor. She almost laughed. "He had me home by eleven. I just had trouble falling asleep. Too many things on my mind."

Joel looked pleased. "Eleven, eh?"

Kate picked at a thread on her fraying shirt. "I've been thinking we should have a talk."

His eyes turned watchful. The smile slipped from his lips. "Sounds ominous."

"Not really." She glanced at the clock. "Do you have to leave soon?"

"Oh, you mean to pick up Chloe?" He shook his head. "She's going home with Sarabeth after Sunday school."

"Okay, well…" This was it. The perfect opportunity. The confession stood poised on the tip of Kate's tongue but she couldn't get the words out. How do you say "I'm the woman who gave up Chloe. I've been lying to you both for over two years"? There certainly weren't any etiquette books that dealt with this situation. At least none that Kate had ever seen.

"Hey, is this the picture Chloe couldn't stop talking about?" Joel picked up the photo from the coffee table and held it up. The smile on his face vanished.

Perhaps a confession wasn't going to be necessary after all.

Chapter Seventeen

Joel stared down at the picture in his hand. It was an older-style photograph. A thin dark-haired girl dressed in a pink skating outfit stared back at him. Chloe was right. If he didn't know this was Kate, he'd think it was his daughter.

How was it possible that they looked so much alike? A cold chill washed over him as the memories began flooding back. *The baby's parents are both medical students,* the attorney had said. The father wanted no contact. The mother requested regular reports on the child.

Although Kate was from Pittsburgh, she'd been a medical student at UC Irvine around the time Chloe was born. Just down the road from the hospital in Laguna Hills.

He lifted his gaze from the photograph. "You're Chloe's mother."

For a second Joel thought Kate might deny it. Thought he was crazy for even suggesting it. Then she nodded.

His blood turned to ice. "You used me to get to Chloe."

"No, it wasn't like that."

He clenched his fists and counted to ten. *It wasn't like that.* Yeah, right. As if he'd believe anything she said now. Not after she'd looked him in the eye for almost two years and lied every time she pretended to be his friend. He narrowed his gaze. "You knew she was your daughter, yet you didn't say a word."

When Kate clasped her hands together, they were trembling. He couldn't summon up an ounce of sympathy for her distress.

"When I signed those adoption papers I promised to stay out of your life."

"That's right. And you went back on your word. You came here. You became a part of her life." Joel raked a hand through his hair. How had he not seen it? Chloe had Kate's eyes. Her hair. He'd been stupid. No, *gullible.* Sucked in by a pretty smile and sweet lies.

Joel fought to rein in his anger. At her. At him. At the whole situation. "How did you find us? Those records were supposed to have remained sealed until Chloe was eighteen."

Kate shifted uncomfortably on the sofa. "I hired a detective. Amy had let slip some clues to your whereabouts in the letters she'd sent over the years. That's how he located you."

"So much for your promise to stay out of her life."

"What did you expect me to do?" She straightened and her hazel eyes flashed. "The reports had stopped. Suddenly. Without warning. After eight years of regular letters and pictures, I got nothing. I was out of my mind with worry, imagining something had happened to her. I had to know she was okay."

Joel refused to get sidetracked or let her heap the blame for this mess on him.

"Moving to Jackson Hole wasn't a coincidence," he said in a flat tone. "You came here with a purpose. You came here to insinuate yourself into her life. You decided the best way to get to her was through me."

"No." Kate leaped to her feet. "You don't understand."

"You're darn right I don't understand."

Kate was willing to admit she'd made some mistakes. Still, she wasn't the only one who'd broken their word. "Did you ever consider that if you'd sent the reports you *promised,* I wouldn't have had to come looking for her?"

"I was a little busy." His eyes were cold as steel, his tone heavy with sarcasm. "My wife had died, I was in the middle of planning a major move and I had a little girl who needed me."

Kate wasn't about to let him dismiss the months of needless pain he'd caused her. She hadn't slept a full night until the detective had finally located Chloe and told her she was okay.

"I lived for those reports." She met his gaze head on. "I haven't received one in over two years."

Something flickered in Joel's eyes. "Time may have gotten away from me, but that doesn't excuse you lying to me. To Chloe. To everyone."

Kate exhaled a ragged breath. It hadn't taken her long to realize that moving to Jackson had been a mistake. "When I came here I planned to keep my distance. I didn't know I'd end up with Chloe as one of my patients. Nor did I know that the community was so small and tight-knit. Aside from being her doctor, I never imagined we'd end up with the same group of friends."

He crossed his arms. "And our affair?"

"We shared the same goal. To scratch an itch that

wouldn't go away," Kate retorted, even as her heart cried out against such a simplistic explanation. Even though they'd probably both vehemently deny it, their affair had been about much more than sexual hunger.

"You said you liked me. I got the feeling you might even love me. Was that a lie, too?"

Kate's head was spinning. It felt as if the second she answered one question he popped out another. She wished he'd slow down. Give her a chance to catch her breath and gather her thoughts. But the set to his jaw and the look in his eyes said he wanted answers. Now.

"Of course I liked you," she said in a matter-of-fact tone. "That doesn't mean I ever thought you'd be a good partner for me."

"Because of the lie."

"Because I never stood a chance of measuring up to Saint Amy." Kate lifted her chin. "I grew up in the shadow of my sister. I could never be with a man who thought I was second-best."

"Well, we don't have to worry about that. I like my women honest."

At that moment Kate hated him. Hated his arrogant judgment. Hated him for making her feel as though her mother had been right all along.

"Where do we go from here?" Kate said finally.

"With the truth. I'll tell Chloe that you're her birth mother. There's bound to be fallout, but I'll deal with it."

"I can be there—"

"No." His hand cut a sharp swath through the air. "You've already done quite enough."

Before she could say another word, he was on his feet and out the door.

Kate sank back into the sofa. "Well, that went well," she muttered, then promptly burst into tears.

* * *

Joel hadn't even made it to the curb when he realized he'd let his anger make an important decision. Telling Chloe that Kate was her mother needed to be handled with kid gloves. She was sure to have a lot of questions. Questions only Kate could answer.

He turned on his heel and headed back to the townhouse, opening the door without knocking. She still sat on the sofa, her head in her hands.

"Kate."

She looked up, her lashes wet with tears.

Hardening his heart, Joel crossed the room and dropped into the chair he'd vacated only minutes earlier. "I've decided we need to tell Chloe together."

She simply stared.

"She may have questions that I can't answer."

"Like, 'Why did my mom give me up?'"

"Yeah, like that," he said absently as he imagined the shock on Chloe's face, the tears and questions that were sure to follow. "I want to make sure she understands that she wasn't a throwaway, that she was very much wanted."

"A throwaway?" Kate's voice rose. Anger snapped in her eyes. "You have no idea how hard—"

"Seven o'clock. My house." Joel wasn't interested in any more explanations, any more excuses. She could give those to Chloe. And they better be good.

Kate gestured toward the door with her head. "Show yourself out."

Joel gave a curt nod. He covered the distance to the door in several long strides, then turned. "If you're not there, I'll tell her myself."

"I'll be there."

He saw the pain beneath her lifted chin and stoic features. For a second he longed to sit on the sofa and pull her close. Comfort her. Assure her that all would be okay.

The realization that he still harbored feelings for her made him slam the door behind him with extra force.

Chapter Eighteen

"Dr. Kate is going to be surprised when I tell her that Sarabeth has a Cabbage Patch Kid, too. Her kid's name is Melody Anna. Next time I go over there, I'm going to bring Lottie Rose with me so they can get acquainted."

Joel rubbed the bridge of his nose as Chloe continued to prattle on about nothing and everything. She hadn't stopped talking since he'd picked her up just before supper. When she'd heard Kate would be stopping by, she'd gotten even more excited.

Chloe's obvious fondness for her biological mother made him realize it would be hard to banish Kate from his daughter's life. Not without harming Chloe in the process.

The doorbell rang. Chloe jumped up. "I'll get it."

Joel glanced at the clock. Right on time. Reluctantly he pulled to his feet as Kate entered the room.

Although he still wore the jeans and the long-sleeved

black T-shirt he'd changed into after church, he expected Kate to show up in a dress and heels. He'd noticed she tended to dress up when she was nervous. Once again she surprised him.

While she wasn't as casually dressed as she'd been that morning, the fitted black pants and cashmere red sweater was definitely a notch below her normal style. Even her shoes were different. Not a trace of heel on the simple black shoes that reminded him of Chloe's dance ones.

Sheesh. Joel stifled a groan. He must be more on edge than he realized to be so focused on Kate's footwear. "Thanks for coming."

"Thanks for inviting me."

Polite strangers. Just like goddamn polite strangers. Still, that's what he wanted. Distance between him and Kate. Between Kate and his daughter.

Chloe smiled at them both and pointed to the sofa. "Dr. Kate, you sit there. Daddy, you sit next to her. That way if you want to kiss, you can."

Joel and Kate exchanged glances.

"Kiss?" Kate finally choked out.

"Like Sarabeth's parents do, 'cept when they're fighting. Then they yell." Even though they were the only three in the room, Chloe lowered her voice. "Sarabeth hopes they kiss a lot more. She'd like to have a baby brother or sister."

Beside him, Kate inhaled sharply.

Joel was still figuring out how to respond to the comment when Chloe tugged on his hand. He moved automatically, wondering how he could explain to a ten-year-old that kissing didn't result in a baby without getting into a full-fledged birds-and-bees discussion.

"Uh, Chloe," he began. "You know that—"

"That's a discussion for another time." Kate shook her

head slightly, her voice gentle and soft. "Chloe, honey, your dad and I have something important to discuss with you."

Joy flashed across the little girl's face. She shrieked.

"You're getting married." Chloe jumped up and down, her voice trembling with excitement. "That's it, isn't it? Sarabeth said you'd probably ask me if it was okay. It's okay. I'd like it a lot."

"I'm not marrying Dr. Kate." Joel spoke in a firm tone that left no room for misunderstanding.

When Chloe's face crumpled, he decided he should have been a little less forceful. He certainly didn't want to make his child cry before they'd even gotten started.

"Then what?" The little girl's eyes, now anxious, flitted from him to Kate.

"Remember when your mommy and I told you how we'd wanted a baby for so long and couldn't have one?" Just saying the words brought a knot to Joel's stomach. They'd been devastated when Amy's doctor had told her it wouldn't be safe for her to get pregnant.

"But you went to California and got me," Chloe said triumphantly, her face brightening. The adoption story was one of her favorites.

"That's right." Joel started to sweat. Where did he go from here? "I became your daddy, and Mommy, your mother. But you had another mother. The one who gave birth to you."

The child nodded, though puzzlement now filled her eyes. She obviously sensed something was up.

"Chloe." Kate leaned forward, her hand wrapping around the small slender fingers that were so like her own. "I'm the woman who gave birth to you."

Joel noticed she didn't call herself Chloe's mother, though, he grudgingly admitted, she had the right.

Chloe's eyes widened. She immediately turned to her father. "Is that true?"

He nodded.

"That's why we look alike," Kate said.

The child was silent for a long moment. "Why did you do it?" Chloe pulled her hand away and sat back. "Mommy said you gave me to her and Daddy because you loved me. But if you loved me, how could you give me away? Was it because I'm ugly?"

The child's bottom lip began to tremble.

"You're not ugly, princess," Joel said. "You look just like…your mother. She's the most beautiful woman in Jackson Hole."

While Joel was speaking, Kate moved to the oversize chair where Chloe sat and slipped in beside her.

"I was in school when I got pregnant with you. My boyfriend wasn't ready to be a daddy, so he wasn't going to be any help." Kate paused for a long moment. "I wanted you to have both a mother and a father. I wanted you to have more than I could give you."

"I don't need a lot of things," Chloe said.

"But you wouldn't have had your daddy and your mommy. While I never knew your mommy, I think she was a special lady."

Chloe nodded. Two fat tears slipped down her cheeks.

"And your daddy is an okay guy." Kate's tone turned light and teasing. "Even if he can't skate worth a darn."

Joel expelled the breath he'd been holding when Chloe smiled through her tears.

"I love you, Chloe. I loved you when you were a tiny baby growing inside me. I loved you when you were born. I never stopped loving you. I never will."

There was a fierceness to Kate's expression that told Joel she meant every word.

Chloe tilted her head, her forehead furrowed. "Why didn't you tell me that you were my mommy sooner?"

"When I gave you to your parents I made a promise that I would stay out of your life until you were eighteen." Kate smoothed a strand of hair back from Chloe's face. "But once I knew where you were I couldn't stay away."

"Why didn't you tell me, Daddy?" Chloe turned toward Joel, her gaze sharp and accusing.

"He didn't know," Kate said quickly. "I told him only this morning."

Chloe wiped away her remaining tears with the back of her hand, her expression pensive. Joel knew this was a lot for a child to take in all at once. He wondered if he should set up a few sessions for her with Dr. Allman so she could work through any issues....

Chloe turned to Kate, her expression giving nothing away. "Can I have that picture of you when you were my age to show Sarabeth?"

Joel cast a glance in Kate's direction. From the look of surprise on her face, she didn't know how to decipher Chloe's reaction. Well, that made two of them.

"Do you have more questions?" Joel prompted.

Chloe turned to Kate. "What should I call you?"

Kate'e gaze flickered in his direction. He shrugged.

"Whatever you want," she said.

Chloe frowned. Confusion filled her eyes. "So it's okay if I still call you Dr. Kate?"

Kate offered a reassuring smile. "That would be just fine."

The child flung her arms around her neck. "I like you, Dr. Kate."

Kate touched Chloe's cheeks with the tips of her fingers. "I like you, too."

Joel experienced a whole gamut of emotions at the tentative mother-daughter bonding. Relief that Chloe didn't appear traumatized, though he knew there would be more questions, more anger, more tears. Gratitude that Kate had been sensitive to Chloe's needs. And sadness that it wasn't Amy sitting there with Chloe in her arms.

The two were still talking in hushed tones when Joel's cell phone rang. He considered letting it go to voice mail until he saw the call was from one of his crew who'd been injured on the job today.

"Thought you'd want to know I'm in the hospital," Larry Farrels said in lieu of a greeting.

Joel pulled his brows together. "Did the pain get worse?"

Larry had fallen off a ladder and landed across a saw-horse. He'd gotten up, dusted himself off and continued working. By the time the day ended, his only complaint was a sore left shoulder.

"Yeah, the pain got real bad. I went to the E.R. and they admitted me. Doc thinks I screwed up my spleen when I fell."

"Those sawhorses can be mean devils." Joel kept his tone light. "Especially when you jump 'em."

Larry laughed.

"Make sure the hospitals and doctors understand this is under workers' comp," Joel said, suddenly serious. "Will you need surgery?"

"Don't know yet. They want to keep me for a couple days. Maybe give me some blood. See if they can get it to heal without taking me under the knife."

Joel paused. Larry had recently moved to Jackson Hole. As far as he knew the guy didn't have any family in the area. "I was going to be in area of the hospital a little later. Feel good enough for company?"

"Yeah, absolutely." The man's eagerness for visitors told Joel he'd been right to offer. He got the room number and had just hung up when Chloe returned from the kitchen with two tall glasses of iced tea in her hands.

"Who were you talking to?" Chloe asked, handing one of the glasses to him and the other to Kate.

"One of the guys I work with," Joel said. "Took a hard fall but we thought he was fine. Seems he injured his spleen."

"Poor man," Kate murmured.

Joel shifted his gaze to his daughter. "Looks like we'll be making a quick trip to the hospital, princess."

"Aw, Daddy, do I have to go?"

"We can stop and look at the babies in the window," he said, sweetening the offer.

Chloe loved babies. Loved holding them. Loved seeing the newborns in the nursery window.

"Okay." Chloe turned to Kate. "Will you come over tomorrow?"

"Let me get back to you on that," Kate said, giving the child a hug. "After your dad and I talk."

But there ended up being no time for conversation. Kate received an urgent call from the hospital and was out the door before Joel had the chance to say goodbye. Or to decide where they went from here.

Chapter Nineteen

Kate arrived at the hospital just in time to witness Emilie Hyland deliver a seven-pound five-ounce baby boy. She examined him and pronounced him absolutely perfect.

When she started to hand him to Emilie, the girl turned her head. "I don't want to see him."

Kate knew Emilie had decided to give the baby up for adoption. She'd seen the adoptive parents waiting in the hall. Even though it was the teenager's choice whether or not to see her child, Kate wanted to make sure that she'd thought through her decision.

"Why don't you want to hold him?" Kate asked in a soft tone, devoid of any judgment.

Tears slipped down the girl's cheeks. "It will hurt too much."

Kate swallowed past the sudden lump in her throat. "It's going to hurt whether you hold him or not."

"You don't know." The girl's blue eyes flashed. "You

have no idea what this is like, how hard it is to give away your own flesh and blood."

"As a matter of fact, I do." Kate took a deep breath. "I gave up a baby for adoption ten years ago."

"You did?" Emilie's eyes widened. "Why?"

"The same reasons you're making this choice. I wanted to give my daughter a better life."

"Have you, I mean, did you ever regret not keeping her?"

"I questioned my decision many times." Kate refused to lie or sugarcoat the gravity of the decision. "But I wanted her to have two parents and a stable home. It wasn't a life I could have given her at that time."

"Paul and Robyn are wonderful people," Emilie said. "They'll be terrific parents. Because we're doing an open adoption, I'll be able to watch him grow up."

"Sounds like you've thought it all out."

The baby stirred in Kate's arms, emitting a soft cry.

Emilie stared at the blue bundle. "C-can I hold him?"

Kate answered by placing the baby in the girl's arms. Several minutes passed before Emilie reluctantly handed him back. "I'm sure Robyn and Paul are eager to see him."

"Let's get you up to your room and get you settled." The delivery room nurse placed her hand on Emilie's shoulder and smiled.

"I'll take the baby to the nursery," Kate told the nurse, then stepped out into the hall where a man and a woman in their mid-thirties stood. The tall broad-shouldered man and his petite blond-haired wife moved forward when they saw the blue bundle in her arms.

"Is that him?" The man's voice broke. He swiped at his eyes and cleared his throat. "Is that Nate?"

"How is Emilie?" the woman asked, though her eyes remained fixed on the baby.

"Doing well," Kate said. "And Nathan is a very healthy boy."

Paul slipped an arm around his wife's shoulder and gave it a squeeze. "We tried to have a baby for almost eight years."

"We'd given up hope." Robyn's voice trembled. "Nathan is truly a gift from God."

Kate held out the baby. "Would you like to hold your son?"

The two exchanged glances as if trying to figure out who got him first.

"You take him, Robyn," Paul said. "I've waited a long time to see you holding our baby."

Not long after Kate handed her the child, Paul's arms encircled his wife. He pulled her close until the three of them formed their own little circle of love.

As Kate stood back and watched them ooh and aah over their new son, she finally understood that giving Chloe to Joel and Amy *had* been a great gift and an unselfish decision.

The guilt that had been her daily companion for more than ten years slipped from her shoulders to pool at her feet.

After visiting with Larry, Joel and Chloe took the elevator to the maternity floor. They were almost to the nursery windows when they ran into Dave Hyland. "What are you doing here?"

"Emilie had her baby." A shadow fell over Dave's face. "Healthy little boy."

"Daddy, can I go and look at the babies?" Chloe interrupted, her gaze focused on the nursery window down the hall.

"Stay where I can see you." The words had barely left his lips when she took off running. "Walk," he called after her.

He turned back to Dave and clapped him on the shoulder. "Congratulations on your new grandson."

"Yeah, well, Emilie isn't keeping him." A muscle jumped in the bricklayer's jaw.

That's right, Joel thought. Emilie was in high school. Not married. Still a child herself.

"I'm sure it wasn't an easy decision for her to make," Joel said. "Chloe is adopted, so I have a special place in my heart for women with the courage to do what's best for the child."

"At least she's doing an open adoption," Dave acknowledged. "The couple who's adopting him live in Laramie, so we'll be able to get there for birthdays and special occasions. But I know my wife and Emilie are going to live for the monthly pictures and reports they've been promised."

Joel had no doubt Dave would be as eager for the pictures as his wife and daughter. He thought of Kate. Pictured her waiting for the reports and pictures that never came. Because he hadn't made keeping his promise a priority. He hadn't taken the time. Shame flooded him.

A door opened down the hall and Dave's wife motioned to him. "Emilie is on her way to the room."

"Daddy, Daddy," Chloe called to him when Dave walked away. "Come and look at this big baby."

There were only three babies in the nursery. Joel figured the "big one" had to be the little girl with the chubby cheeks in the front row. "She still looks small to me."

"If you and Dr. Ka—Mommy had a baby, I could be a big sister."

Joel's chuckle held no humor. He'd be lucky if Kate let him in her front door again, much less in her bed. "Dr. Kate and I aren't married, sweetheart."

"Then marry her," Chloe said as if the answer was obvious. "You love her, don't you?"

He did love Kate, Joel realized suddenly. Had loved her for quite a while. He just hadn't admitted it to himself. Until now. It was time to finally let Amy go and start his life again.

"It's not that simple." Joel remembered every word Kate had said. And every word he'd failed to say.

"Just because you loved Mommy doesn't mean you can't love Dr. Kate," Chloe said earnestly, sounding older than her years. "All you have to do is tell her."

Could it really be that simple? "When did you get to be so smart?"

Chloe tilted her head and carefully considered his words. Then she smiled. "When I turned ten."

Kate rose the next morning with a sense of peace in her heart. Chloe knew she was her mother and didn't hate her. Joel appeared agreeable to her seeing Chloe. Things were definitely looking up.

Yet sadness wrapped around her shoulders like a heavy cloak. Despite what she'd said to Joel, she still loved him. She tried to tell herself that it was good their relationship had ended. That in time she'd forget all about him. But she couldn't make herself believe the lie.

Since she didn't have to be in the office until noon, Kate stayed in her robe and slippers. She was enjoying a second cup of coffee when the doorbell rang.

Cinching the blue satin tie more firmly around her

waist, Kate strolled to the door with coffee in hand. She expected to see the FedEx guy with her new modem. Instead, Joel stood on the front stoop with a bakery bag in hand.

"May I come in?"

When Kate simply stood there, he brushed past her and stepped inside. "I'll take that as a yes."

Finally Kate's mouth caught up to her brain. "What are you doing here?"

"Almond bear claws." He pressed the bag into her hand and gestured toward her cup. "Got any more of that?"

"In the kitchen." Kate followed him. "Is Chloe okay?"

"She had a hard time sleeping, she was so excited." He poured some of the steaming brew into a cup, then reached into the refrigerator for the cream.

"I'm thankful she took the news so well." Kate dropped the sack of pastries on the table and automatically pulled two small plates from the cupboard.

Joel wrapped his hand around the large mug and took a sip. "Thank you."

"No problem. I made way more than I need—"

"I'm not talking about the coffee." His gaze never left her face. "I should have said this last night but I didn't. Thank you for Chloe. She meant the world to Amy and she means the world to me. Your sacrifice made it possible for us to be parents."

Kate opened her mouth and shut it.

"I'm sorry I didn't send the reports and pictures. It was inexcusable." True regret filled his eyes. He rocked back on his heels. "If I were you, I'd have hired a detective, too."

"You would have?"

"Absolutely."

Unsettled, Kate took a sip of her coffee. "This seems to be a complete turnaround."

"I've been doing a lot of hard thinking." He took a deep breath, but she spoke before he could continue.

"So have I. For all these years I've sold myself short. I felt I didn't deserve real happiness. That's why I was willing to settle for two weeks of no-obligation sex with you." As much as Kate had enjoyed their time together, the affair had been a mistake. Her heart was incapable of separating sex from love. "I deserve more. I want a man who loves and adores me and puts me first in his life. I want marriage. Perhaps children. I won't settle for less."

"I want those same things, Kate. And I want them with you."

To his chagrin, she began shaking her head even before he'd finished speaking. "I won't compete with a dead woman. Love isn't a competition. Or it shouldn't be."

"Amy is my past, Kate. I loved her as much as a man could love a woman. I don't deny that. But I love you now. And just as much. The comparisons were a way to keep you at arm's length," Joel said. "I fell in love with you so quickly that it made me feel disloyal to Amy."

"Really."

He heard the doubt in her voice, saw it in her eyes.

"Trying to compare you two is like comparing apples to oranges. I see you for who you are and I love—"

"Who am I, Joel?"

"You're a fighter. A woman who didn't let your family's expectations hold you back from following your dream of becoming a doctor."

Even though she didn't respond, Joel could tell she was listening, so he kept talking.

"You're a woman who loves deeply and wants the best

for those you love. That's why you chose to give your daughter a home where she could grow and thrive."

Kate shifted her gaze out the window. Her expression gave nothing away. He began to talk faster, not sure how much time he had left.

"You like big, flashy jewelry, making love under the stars and mistletoe. You're kind and smart and generous. You're the woman I love and you'll always be the most important woman in my heart."

He dropped to one knee and took her hand.

"What are you doing?" She tried to pull her hand back, but he wouldn't let go.

"I love you, Kate McNeal. I can't imagine my life without you in it. I want to spend the rest of my life making you happy. Will you do me the honor of being my wife and Chloe's mother?"

Kate blinked. Was she dreaming?

He slipped his hand into his jacket pocket and pulled out a tiny black velvet box. When he flipped it open, the overhead light scattered the rays, nearly blinding her.

"What is that?"

"It's an engagement ring, darlin'. The biggest, flashiest, most beautiful ring I could find. Do you like it?"

The uncertainty in his voice told her he wasn't nearly as confident as he appeared.

The stone was huge, an emerald-cut diamond surrounded by smaller diamonds. The thin platinum band allowed the stone to take center stage.

"It's beautiful. And big."

"Not nearly as big as my love, sweetheart."

Kate blinked. He was still there. She blinked again.

This time she saw clearly the love and promise in his hazel depths. Her heart rose to her throat.

"Will you marry me, Kate? Will you be a wife to me

and a mother to Chloe and to any other children we might have?"

"You want other children?"

"I'd love a whole houseful."

"Oh, Joel." She smiled through her tears.

He fought a surge of hope. "A simple *yes* will do."

"Yes," she said. "Yes, yes, yes."

He rose to his feet and pulled her to him, kissing her until she heard fireworks and cymbals and bells. Until her knees were so weak that he had to pick her up and carry her to the bedroom.

Epilogue

Kate pulled on her ice skates and expelled a happy sigh. Six months had passed since Joel had proposed. It had been three months since they'd married in a small ceremony surrounded by friends and family.

Her parents had arrived for the wedding, along with Andrea and her husband and children. Chloe had enjoyed playing with her new cousins. Kate had high hopes that her relationship with her sister would continue to improve.

Joel had just broken ground on their future home in the mountains, close to where several of their friends already lived. Life was good. And it was about to get even better.

Chloe was already out on the ice with her friends, so Kate had Joel all to herself. She wore the same black skirt and silver top she'd worn last summer at the rink.

"Where's Mitzi?" Joel asked. "I thought she was coming tonight?"

To Kate's surprise and delight Mitzi had chosen to remain in Jackson Hole. She'd become a permanent member of Spring Gulch Orthopedic. Kate didn't fully understand what had made her friend turn her back on her dream job in Beverly Hills. Especially considering that she and Benedict Campbell, the president of Spring Gulch Ortho, were always at each other's throats.

"Something came up." No need to tell him she'd asked Mitzi to stay home.

"Let's skate over there." Kate gestured with her head toward the other side of the rink. There were some seats not far from the ice where she and Joel often sat. Unlike where they were now, it was private. Even though his skating had improved, she had the feeling her news was better given sitting down.

Halfway across the rink, he changed course, pulling her along with him.

"Hey, where are we going?"

"To the center. I've always wanted to skate under a mirror ball."

The ice rink was a multipurpose facility. When it wasn't used for skating, the floor was covered and the place was rented out for dances and receptions.

"The ball looks funny tonight," Kate said as they approached the center of the ice. "There's something hanging from it. Why, it's a big sprig of mistletoe."

"Today is our three-month anniversary. I know how much you love mistletoe and I know how much I love you…." Joel pulled her close. He gave her a toe-curling kiss and somehow managed to remain standing in the process. "Happy anniversary, darling."

"I have a surprise for you, too," she said.

"It'll be hard to beat the mistletoe," Joel said, trying hard to be modest but not succeeding.

"You wanna bet?" She leaned up on her tiptoes and whispered in his ear.

His eyes widened. A grin split his face. "A baby?"

"Not for another seven months, but—"

"Hot damn." Joel grabbed and held her tight.

"What's going on?" Chloe skated up.

"We're going to have a baby," Joel said before Kate could get the words out. "You're going to be a big sister."

Chloe shrieked and flung herself at her parents. Joel cushioned his girls' fall when the three of them tumbled to the ice, the mirror ball shining brightly overhead, the mistletoe dancing in the air duct breeze.

Kate laughed. Because she was happy. Because she was in love. And…just because.

* * * * *

THE ANNIVERSARY PARTY

Dear Reader,

I am a big believer in celebrating milestones, and for Special Edition, this is a big one! Thirty years… it hardly seems possible, and yet April 1982 was indeed, yep, thirty years ago! When I walked into the Harlequin offices (only *twenty* years ago, but still), the first books I worked on were Special Edition. I loved the line instantly—for its breadth and its depth, and for its fabulous array of authors, some of whom I've been privileged to work with for twenty years, and some of whom are newer, but no less treasured, friends.

When it came time to plan our thirtieth anniversary celebration, we wanted to give our readers something from the heart—not to mention something from our very beloved April 2012 lineup. So many thanks to RaeAnne Thayne, Christine Rimmer, Susan Crosby, Christyne Butler, Gina Wilkins and Cindy Kirk for their contributions to *The Anniversary Party*. The Morgans, Diana and Frank, are celebrating their thirtieth anniversary along with us. Like us, they've had a great thirty years, and they're looking forward to many more. Like us, though there may be some obstacles along the way, they're getting their happily ever after.

Which is what we wish you, Dear Reader. Thanks for coming along for the first thirty years of Special Edition—we hope you'll be with us for many more!

We hope you enjoy *The Anniversary Party*.

Here's to the next thirty!

All the best,

Gail Chasan
Senior Editor, Special Edition

Chapter One
by RaeAnne Thayne

With the basket of crusty bread sticks she had baked that afternoon in one arm and a mixed salad—*insalata mista,* as the Italians would say—in the other, Melissa Morgan walked into her sister's house and her jaw dropped.

"Oh, my word, Ab! This looks incredible! When did you start decorating? A month ago?"

Predictably, Abby looked a little wild-eyed. Her sister was one of those type A personalities who always sought perfection, whether that was excelling in her college studies, where she'd emerged with a summa cum laude, or decorating for their parents' surprise thirtieth anniversary celebration.

Abby didn't answer for a moment. She was busy arranging a plant in the basket of a rusty bicycle resting against one wall so the greenery spilled over the top, almost to the front tire. Melissa had no idea how she'd

managed it but somehow Abby had hung wooden lattice
from her ceiling to form a faux pergola over her dining
table. Grapevines, fairy lights and more greenery had
been woven through the lattice and, at various inter-
vals, candles hung in colored jars like something out of a
Tuscan vineyard.

Adorning the walls were framed posters of Venice and
the beautiful and calming Lake Como.

"It feels like a month," Abby finally answered, "but
actually, I only started last week. Greg helped me hang
the lattice. I couldn't have done it without him."

The affection in her sister's voice caused a funny little
twinge inside Melissa. Abby and her husband had one
of those perfect relationships. They clearly adored each
other, no matter what.

She wished she could say the same thing about Josh.
After a year of dating, shouldn't she have a little more
confidence in their relationship? If someone had asked
her a month ago if she thought her boyfriend loved her,
she would have been able to answer with complete assurance in the affirmative, but for the past few weeks something had changed. He'd been acting so oddly—dodging
phone calls, canceling plans, avoiding her questions.

He seemed to be slipping away more every day. As
melodramatic as it sounded, she didn't know how she
would survive if he decided to break things off.

Breathe, she reminded herself. She didn't want to ruin
the anniversary dinner by worrying about Josh. For now,
she really needed to focus on her wonderful parents and
how very much they deserved this celebration she and
Abby had been planning for a long time.

"You and Greg have really outdone yourself. I love all
the little details. The old wine bottles, the flowers. Just
beautiful. I know Mom and Dad will be thrilled with your

hard work." She paused. "I can only see one little problem."

Abby looked vaguely panicked. "What? What's missing?"

Melissa shook her head ruefully. "Nothing. That's the problem. I was supposed to be helping you. That's why I'm here early, right? Have you left anything for me to do?"

"Are you kidding? I've still got a million things to do. The chicken cacciatore is just about ready to go into the oven. Why don't you help me set the table?"

"Sure," she said, following her sister into the kitchen.

"You talked to Louise, right?" Abby asked.

"Yes. She had everything ready when I stopped at her office on my way over here. I've got a huge gift basket in the car. You should see it. She really went all out. Biscotti, gourmet cappuccino mix, even a bottle of prosecco."

"What about the tickets and the itinerary?" Abby had that panicked look again.

"Relax, Abs. It's all there. She's been amazing. I think she just might be as scarily organized as you are."

Abby made a face. "Did you have a chance to go over the details?"

"She printed everything out and included a copy for us, as well as Mom and Dad. In addition to the plane tickets and the hotel information and the other goodies, she sent over pamphlets, maps, even an Italian-English dictionary and a couple of guidebooks."

"Perfect! They're going to be so surprised."

"Surprised and happy, I hope," Melissa answered, loading her arms with the deep red chargers and honey-gold plates her sister indicated, which perfectly matched the theme for the evening.

"How could they be anything else? They finally have

the chance to enjoy the perfect honeymoon they missed out on the first time." Abby smiled, looking more than a little starry-eyed. Despite being married for several years, her sister was a true romantic.

"This has to be better than the original," she said. "The bar was set pretty low thirty years ago, judging by all the stories they've told us over the years. Missed trains, lousy hotels, disappearing luggage."

"Don't forget the pickpocket that stole their cash and passports."

Melissa had to smile. Though their parents' stories always made their honeymoon thirty years ago sound dismal, Frank and Diane always laughed when they shared them, as if they had viewed the whole thing as a huge adventure.

She wanted that. She wanted to share that kind of joy and laughter and tears with Josh. The adventure that was life.

Her smile faded, replaced by that ache of sadness that always seemed so close these days. *Oh, Josh.* She reached into the silverware drawer, avoiding her sister's gaze.

"Okay. What's wrong?" Abby asked anyway.

She forced a smile. "Nothing. I'm just a little tired, that's all."

"Late night with Josh?" her sister teased.

Before she could stop them, tears welled up and spilled over. She blinked them back but not before her sharp-eyed sister caught them.

"What did I say?" Abby asked with a stunned look.

"Nothing. I just…I didn't have a late night with Josh. Not last night, not last week, not for the last two weeks. He's avoiding my calls and canceled our last two dates. Even when we're together, it's like he's not there. I know he's busy at work but…I think he's planning to break up with me."

Abby's jaw sagged and Melissa saw shock and something else, something furtive, shift across Abby's expression.

"That can't be true. It just…can't be."

She wanted to believe that, too. "I'm sorry. I shouldn't have said anything. Forget it. You've worked so hard to make this night perfect and I don't want to ruin it."

Abby shook her head. "You need to put that wacky idea out of your head right now. Josh is crazy about you. It's clear to anybody who has ever seen the two of you together for five seconds. He couldn't possibly be thinking of breaking things off."

"I'm sure you're right," she lied. Too much evidence pointed otherwise. Worst of all was the casual kiss goodnight the past few times she'd seen him, instead of one of their deep, emotional, soul-sharing kisses that made her toes curl.

"I'm serious, Missy. Trust me on this. I'm absolutely positive he's not planning to break up with you. Not Josh. He loves you. In fact…"

She stopped, biting her lip, and furiously turned back to the chicken.

"In fact what?"

Abby's features were evasive. "In fact, would he be out right now with Greg buying the wine and champagne for tonight if he didn't want to have anything to do with the Morgan family?"

Out of the corner of her gaze, Melissa saw that amazingly decorated dining room again, the magical setting her sister had worked so hard to create for their parents who loved each other dearly. She refused to ruin this night for Abby and the rest of her family. For now, she would focus on the celebration and forget the tiny cracks in her heart.

She pasted on a smile and grabbed the napkins, with their rings formed out of entwined grapevine hearts. "You're right. I'm being silly. I'm sure everything will be just fine. Anyway, tonight is for Mom and Dad. That's the important thing."

Abby gave her a searching look and Melissa couldn't help thinking that even with the worry lines on her forehead, Abby seemed to glow tonight.

"It is about them, isn't it?" Abby murmured. Though Melissa's arms were full, her sister reached around the plates and cutlery to give her a hug. "Trust me, baby sister. Everything will be just fine."

Melissa dearly wanted to believe her and as she returned to the dining room, she did her very best to ignore the ache of fear that something infinitely dear was slipping away.

"Hello? Are you still in there?"

His friend Greg's words jerked Josh out of his daze and he glanced up. "Yeah. Sorry. Did you say something?"

"Only about three times. I've been asking your opinion about the champagne and all I'm getting in return is a blank stare. You're a million miles away, man, which is not really helping out much here."

This just might be the most important day of his life. Who could blame a guy if he couldn't seem to string two thoughts together?

"Sorry. I've got a lot of things on my mind."

"And champagne is obviously not one of those things."

He made a face. "It rarely is. I'm afraid I'm more of a Sam Adams kind of guy."

"I hear you. Why do you think I asked you to come

along and help me pick out the wine and champagne for tonight?"

He had wondered that himself. "Because my car has a bigger trunk?"

Greg laughed, which eased Josh's nerves a little. He had to admit, he had liked the guy since he met him a year ago when he first started dating Melissa. Josh was married to Melissa's sister, Abby, and if things worked out the way he hoped, they would be brothers-in-law in the not-so-distant future.

"It's only the six of us for dinner," Greg reminded him. "I'm not exactly buying cases here. So what do you think?"

He turned back to the racks of bottles. "No idea. Which one is more expensive?"

Greg picked one up with a fancy label that certainly looked pricey.

"Excellent choice." The snooty clerk who had mostly been ignoring them since they walked in finally deigned to approach them.

"You think so?" Greg asked. "We're celebrating a big occasion."

"You won't be disappointed, I assure you. What else can I help you find?"

Sometime later—and with considerably lightened wallets—the two of them carried two magnums of champagne and two bottles of wine out to Josh's car.

"I, uh, need to make one last quick stop," he said after pulling into traffic. "Do you mind waiting?"

"No problem. The party doesn't start for another two hours. We've got plenty of time."

When Josh pulled up in front of an assuming storefront a few moments later, Greg looked at the sign above the door then back at him with eyebrows raised. "Wow.

Seriously? Tonight? I thought Abby was jumping the gun when she said she suspected you were close to proposing. She's always right, that beautiful wife of mine. Don't tell her I said that."

Josh shifted, uncomfortably aware his fingers were shaking a little as he undid his seatbelt. "I bought the ring two weeks ago. When the jeweler told me it would be ready today, I figured that was a sign."

"You're a brave man to pick a ring out without her."

Panic clutched at his gut again, but he took a deep breath and pushed it away. He wanted to make his proposal perfect. Part of that, to his mind, was the element of surprise.

"I found a bridal magazine at Melissa's apartment kind of hidden under a stack of books and she had the page folded down on this ring. I snapped a quick picture with my phone and took that in to the jeweler."

"Nice." Greg's admiring look settled his stomach a little.

"I figure, if she doesn't like it, we can always reset the stone, right?"

"So when are you going to pop the question?"

"I haven't figured that out yet. I thought maybe when I take her home after the party tonight, we might drive up to that overlook above town."

"That could work."

"What about you? How did you propose to Abby?"

"Nothing very original, I'm afraid. I took her to dinner at La Maison Marie. She loves that place. Personally, I think you're only paying for overpriced sauce, but what can you do? Anyway, after dinner, she kept acting like she was expecting something. I *did* take her along to shop for rings a few weeks earlier but hadn't said anything to her since. She seemed kind of disappointed when the dessert came and no big proposal. So we were walking around on the grounds after dinner and we walked past this water-fall and pond she liked. I pretended I tripped over some-thing and did a stupid little magician sleight of hand and pulled out the ring box."

"Did you do the whole drop-to-your-knee thing?"

"Yeah. It seemed important to Abby. Women remem-ber that kind of thing."

"I hope I don't forget that part."

"Don't sweat it. When the moment comes, whatever you do will be right for the two of you, I promise."

"I hope so."

The depth of his love for Melissa still took him by surprise. He loved her with everything inside him and wanted to give her all the hearts and flowers and romance she could ever want.

"It will be," Greg said. "Anyway, look at how lousy Frank and Diane's marriage started out. Their honeymoon sounded like a nightmare but thirty years later they can still laugh about it."

That was what he wanted with Melissa. Thirty years—and more—of laughter and joy and love.

He just had to get through the proposal first.

Chapter Two
by Christine Rimmer

"Frank. The light is yellow. Frank!" Diana Morgan stomped the passenger-side floor of the Buick. Hard. If only she had the brakes on her side.

Frank Morgan pulled to a smooth stop as the light went red. "There," he said, in that calm, deep, untroubled voice she'd always loved. "We're stopped. No need to wear a hole in the floor."

Diana glanced over at her husband of thirty years. She loved him so much. There were a whole lot of things to worry about in life, but Frank's love was the one thing Diana never doubted. He belonged to her, absolutely, as she belonged to him, and he'd given her two beautiful, perfect daughters. Abby and Melissa were all grown up now.

The years went by way too fast.

Diana sent her husband another glance. Thirty years

together. Amazing. She still loved just looking at him. He was the handsomest man she'd ever met, even at fifty-seven. Nature had been kind to him. He had all his hair and it was only lightly speckled with gray. She smoothed her own shoulder-length bob. No gray there, either. Her hair was still the same auburn shade it had been when she married him. Only in her case, nature didn't have a thing to do with it.

A man only grew more distinguished over the years. A woman had to work at it.

The light turned green. Frank hit the gas.

Too hard, Diana thought. But she didn't say a word. She only straightened her teal-blue silk blouse, re-crossed her legs and tried not to make impatient, worried noises. Frank was a wonderful man. But he drove too fast.

Abby and her husband, Greg, were having them over for dinner tonight. They were on their way there now— to Abby's house. Diana was looking forward to the evening. But she was also dreading it. Something was going on with Abby. A mother knows these things.

And something was bothering Melissa, too. Diana's younger daughter was still single. She'd been going out with Josh Wright for a year now. It was a serious relationship.

But was there something wrong between Josh and Melissa? Diana had a sense about these things, a sort of radar for emotional disturbances, especially when it came to her daughters. Right now, tonight, Diana had a suspicion that something wasn't right—both between Melissa and Josh *and* between Abby and Greg.

"Remember Venice?" Frank gave her a fond glance.

She smiled at him—and then stiffened. "Frank. Eyes on the road."

"All right, all right." He patiently faced front again.

"Remember that wonderful old hotel on the Grand Canal?"

She made a humphing sound. "It was like the rest of our honeymoon. Nothing went right."

"I loved every moment of it," he said softly.

She reminded him, "You know what happened at that hotel in Venice, how they managed to lose our luggage somewhere between the front desk and our room. How hard can it be, to get the suitcases to the right room? And it smelled a bit moldy in the bathroom, didn't you think?"

"All I remember is you, Diana. Naked in the morning light." He said it softly. Intimately.

She shivered a little, drew in a shaky breath and confessed, "Oh, yes. That. I remember that, too." It was one of the best things about a good marriage. The shared memories. Frank had seen her naked in Venice when they were both young. Together, they had heard Abby's first laugh, watched Melissa as she learned to walk, staggering and falling, but then gamely picking herself right back up and trying again. Together, they had made it through all those years that drew them closer, through the rough times as well as the happy ones....

A good marriage.

Until very recently, she'd been so sure that Abby and Greg were happy. But were they? Really? And what about Melissa and Josh?

Oh, Lord. Being a mother was the hardest job in the world. They grew up. But they stayed in your heart. And when they were suffering, you ached right along with them.

"All right," Frank said suddenly in an exasperated tone. "You'd better just tell me, Diana. You'd better just say it, whatever it is."

Diana sighed. Deeply. "Oh, Frank..."

"Come on," he coaxed, pulling to another stop at yet another stoplight—at the very last possible second. She didn't even stomp the floor that time, she was that upset. "Tell me," he insisted.

Tears pooled in her eyes and clogged her throat. She sniffed them back. "I wasn't going to do it. I wasn't going to interfere. I wasn't even going to say a word…"

He flipped open the armrest and whipped out a tissue. "Dry your eyes."

"Oh, Frank…" She took the tissue and dabbed at her lower lid. If she wasn't careful, her makeup would be a total mess.

"Now," Frank said, reaching across to pat her knee. "Tell me about it. Whatever it is, you know you'll feel better once we've talked it over."

The light changed. "Go," she said on a sob.

He drove on. "I'm waiting."

She sniffed again. "I think something's wrong between Abby and Greg. And not only that, there's something going on with Melissa, too. I think Melissa's got…a secret, you know? A secret that is worrying her terribly."

"Why do you think something's going on between Abby and Greg?"

"I sensed it. You know how sensitive I am— Oh, God. Do you think Abby and Greg are breaking up? Do you think he might be seeing someone else?"

"Whoa. Diana. Slow down."

"Well, I am *worried.* I am *so* worried. And Melissa. She is suffering. I can hear it in her voice when I talk to her."

"But you haven't told me *why* you think there might be something wrong—with Melissa, or between Abby and Greg. Did Abby say something to you?"

"Of course not. She wants to protect me."

"What about Melissa?"

"What do you *mean,* what about Melissa?"

"Well, did you *ask* her if something is bothering her?"

Another sob caught in Diana's throat. She swallowed it. "I couldn't. I didn't want to butt in."

Frank eased the car to the shoulder and stopped. "Diana," he said. That was all. Just her name.

It was more than enough. "Don't you look at me like that, Frank Morgan."

"Diana, I hate to say this—"

"Then don't. Just don't. And why are we stopped? We'll be late. Even with family, you know I always like to be on time."

"Diana…"

She waved her soggy tissue at him. "Drive, Frank. Just drive."

He leaned closer across the console. "Sweetheart…"

She sagged in her seat. "Oh, fine. What?"

"You know what you're doing, don't you?" He said it gently. But still. She knew exactly what he was getting at and she didn't like it one bit.

She sighed and dropped the wadded tissue in the little wastepaper bag she always carried in the car. "Well, I know you're bound to tell me, now don't I?"

He took her hand, kissed the back of it.

"Don't try to butter me up," she muttered.

"You're jumping to conclusions again," he said tenderly.

"Am not."

"Yes, you are. You've got nothin'. Zip. Admit it. No solid reason why you think Melissa has a secret or why you think Abby and Greg are suddenly on the rocks."

"I don't need a solid reason. I can *feel* it." She laid her hand over her heart. "Here."

"You know it's very possible that what's really going on is a surprise anniversary party for us, don't you?"

Diana smoothed her hair. "What? You mean tonight?"

"That's right. Tonight."

"Oh, I suppose. It could be." She pictured their dear faces. She loved them so much. "They are the sweetest girls, aren't they?"

"The best. I'm the luckiest dad in the world—not to mention the happiest husband."

Diana leaned toward him and kissed him. "You *are* a very special man." She sank back against her seat—and remembered how worried she was. "But Frank, if this *is* a party, it's still not *it*."

"It?" He looked bewildered. Men could be so thick-headed sometimes.

Patiently, she reminded him, "The awful, secret things that are going on with our daughters."

He bent in close, kissed her cheek and then brushed his lips across her own. "We are going to dinner at our daughter's house," he whispered. "We are going to have a wonderful time. You are not going to snoop around trying to find out if something's wrong with Abby. You're not going to worry about Melissa."

"I hate you, Frank."

"No, you don't. You love me *almost* as much as I love you."

She wrinkled her nose at him. "More. I love you more."

He kissed her again. "Promise you won't snoop and you'll stop jumping to conclusions?"

"And if I don't, what? We'll sit here on the side of the road all night?"

"Promise."

"Fine. All right. I promise."

He touched her cheek, a lovely, cherishing touch. "Can we go to Abby's now?"

"I'm not the one who stopped the car."

He only looked at her reproachfully.

She couldn't hold out against him. She never could. "Oh, all right. I've promised, already, okay? Now, let's go."

With a wry smile, he retreated back behind the wheel and eased the car forward into the flow of traffic again.

Abby opened the door. "Surprise!" Abby, Greg, Melissa and Josh all shouted at once. They all started clapping.

Greg announced, "Happy Anniversary!" The rest of them chimed in with "Congratulations!" and "Thirty years!" and "Wahoo!"

Frank was laughing. "Well, what do you know?"

Diana said nothing. One look in her older daughter's big brown eyes and she knew for certain that she wasn't just imagining things. Something was going on in Abby's life. Something important.

They all filed into the dining room, where the walls were decorated with posters of the Grand Canal and the Tuscan countryside, of the Coliseum and the small, beautiful town of Bellagio on Lake Como. The table was set with Abby's best china and tall candles gave a golden glow.

Greg said, "We thought, you know, an Italian theme—in honor of your honeymoon."

"It's lovely," said Diana, going through the motions, hugging first Greg and then Josh.

"Thank you," said Frank as he clapped his son-in-law on the back and shook hands with Josh.

Melissa came close. "Mom." She put on a smile. But

her eyes were as shadowed as Abby's. "Happy thirtieth anniversary."

Diana grabbed her and hugged her. No doubt about it. Melissa looked miserable, too.

Yes, Diana had promised Frank that she would mind her own business.

But, well, sometimes a woman just couldn't keep that kind of promise. Sometimes a woman had to find a way to get to the bottom of a bad situation for the sake of the ones she loved most of all.

By the end of the evening, no matter what, Diana would find out the secrets her daughters were keeping from her.

Frank leaned close. "Don't even think about it."

She gave him her sweetest smile. "Happy anniversary, darling."

Chapter Three
by Susan Crosby

Abby Morgan DeSena and her husband, Greg, had hosted quite a few dinner parties during their three years of marriage, but none as special as this one—a celebration of Abby's parents' thirtieth wedding anniversary. Abby and her younger sister, Melissa, had spent weeks planning the Italian-themed party as a sweet reminder for their parents of their honeymoon, and now that the main meal was over, Abby could say, well, so far, so good.

For someone who planned everything down to the last detail, that was high praise. They were on schedule. First, antipasti and wine in the living room, then chicken cacciatore, crusty bread sticks and green salad in the dining room.

But for all that the timetable had been met and the food praised and devoured, an air of tension hovered over the six people at the table, especially between Melissa and her boyfriend, Josh, who were both acting out of character.

"We had chicken cacciatore our first night in Bellagio, remember, Diana?" Abby's father said to her mother as everyone sat back, sated. "And lemon sorbet in prosecco."

"The waiter knocked my glass into my lap," Diana reminded him.

"Your napkin caught most of it, and he fixed you another one. He even took it off the tab. On our newlywed budget, it made a difference." He brought his wife's hand to his lips, his eyes twinkling. "And it was delicious, wasn't it? Tart and sweet and bubbly."

Diana blushed, making Abby wonder if the memory involved more than food. It was inspiring seeing her parents so openly in love after thirty years.

Under the table, Abby felt her hand being squeezed and looked at her own beloved husband. Greg winked, as if reading her mind.

"Well, we don't have sorbet and prosecco," Abby said, standing and stacking dinner plates. "But we certainly have dessert. Please sit down, Mom. You're our guest. Melissa and I will take care of everything."

It didn't take long to clear the table.

"Mom and Dad loved the dinner, didn't they?" Melissa asked as they entered Abby's contemporary kitchen.

"They seemed to," Abby answered, although unsure whether she believed her own words. Had her parents noticed the same tension Abby had? Her mother's gaze had flitted from Melissa to Josh to Abby to Greg all evening, as if searching for clues. It'd made Abby more nervous with every passing minute, and on a night she'd been looking forward to, a night of sweet surprises.

"How about you? Did you enjoy the meal?" Abby asked

Melissa, setting dishes in the sink, then started the cof-feemaker brewing. "You hardly touched your food."

She shrugged. "I guess I snacked on too many bread sticks before dinner."

Abby took out a raspberry tiramisu from the refrigera-tor while studying her sister, noting how stiffly Melissa held herself, how shaky her hands were as she rinsed the dinner plates. She seemed fragile. It wasn't a word Abby usually applied to her sister. The conversation they'd had earlier in the evening obviously hadn't set Melissa's mind at ease, but Abby didn't know what else to say to her tightly wrung sister. Only time—and Josh—could relieve Melissa's anxiety.

Abby set the fancy dessert on the counter next to six etched-crystal parfait glasses.

Melissa approached, drying her hands, then picked up one of the glasses. "Grandma gave these to you, didn't she?"

"Mmm-hmm. Three years ago as a wedding present. I know it's a cliché, but it seems like yesterday." Abby smiled at her sister, remembering the wedding, revisit-ing her wonderful marriage. She couldn't ask for a better husband, friend and partner than Greg. "Grandma plans to give you the other six glasses at your wedding. When we both have big family dinners, we can share them. It'll be our tradition."

Melissa's face paled. Her eyes welled. Horrified, Abby dropped the spoon and reached for her.

"I—I'll grab the gift basket from your office," Melissa said, taking a couple steps back then rushing out.

Frustrated, Abby pressed her face into her hands. If she were the screaming type, she would've screamed. If she were a throw-the-pots-around type, she would've done that, too, as noisily as possible. It would've felt *good*.

"I thought Melissa was in here with you," said a male voice from behind her.

Abby spun around and glared at Josh Wright, the source of Melissa's problems—and subsequently Abby's—as he peeked into the kitchen. He could be the solution, too, if only he'd act instead of sitting on his hands.

"She's getting the anniversary gift from my office," Abby said through gritted teeth, digging deep for the composure she'd inherited from her father.

Josh came all the way into the room. He looked as strained as Melissa. "Need some help?" he asked, shoving his hands into his pockets instead of going in search of Melissa.

"Coward." Abby began dishing up six portions of tiramisu.

"Guilty," Josh said, coming up beside her. "Give me a job. I can't sit still."

"You can pour the decaf into that carafe next to the coffeemaker."

Full of nervous energy, his hands shaking as much as Melissa's had earlier, he got right to the task, fumbling at every step, slopping coffee onto the counter.

"Relax, would you, Josh?" Abby said, exasperated. "You're making everyone jumpy, but especially Melissa. My sister is her mother's daughter, you know. They both have a flair for the dramatic, but this time Melissa is honestly thrown by your behavior. She's on the edge, and it's not of her own making."

"But it'll all come out okay in the end?"

The way he turned the sentence into a question had Abby staring at him. He and her kid sister were a study in contrasts, Melissa with her black hair and green eyes, Josh all blond and blue-eyed. They'd been dating for a

year, were head over heels in love with each other, seeming to validate the theory that opposites attract. It was
rare that they weren't touching or staring into each other's
eyes, communicating silently.

Tonight was different, however, and Abby knew why.
She just didn't know if they would all survive the suspense.

"Whether or not it all turns out okay in the end de-
pends on how long you take to pop the question," Abby
said, dropping her voice to a whisper.

"You know I'm planning the perfect proposal," he
whispered back. "Your husband gave me advice, but if
you'd like to add yours, I'm listening."

She couldn't tell him that Melissa thought he was about
to break up with her—that was hers to say. But Abby
could offer some perspective.

"Here's my advice, Josh, and it has nothing to do with
how to set a romantic scene that she'll remember the rest
of her life. My advice is simple—do it sooner rather than
later." She spoke in a normal tone again, figuring even if
someone came into the room, they wouldn't suspect what
she and Josh were talking about. "When Greg and I were
in college, I misunderstood something he said. Instead of
asking him to clarify it, I stewed. And stewed some more.
I blew it all out of proportion."

She dug deep into memories she'd long ago put aside.
"Here's what happens to a couple at times like that.
He asks what's wrong, and she says it's nothing. He
asks again. She *insists* it's nothing. A gulf widens that
can't be crossed because there's no longer a bridge between them, one you used to travel easily. It doesn't even
matter how much love you share. Once trust is gone,
once the ability to talk to each other openly and freely
goes away, the relationship begins to unravel. Some-

times it takes weeks, sometimes months, even years, but it happens and there's no fixing it."

"But you fixed it."

They almost hadn't, Abby remembered. They came so close to breaking up. "At times like that, it can go either way. Even strong partners struggle sometimes in a marriage."

"How do you get through those times?"

"You put on a smile for everyone, then you try to work it out alone together so that no one else gets involved."

"Don't you talk to your mom? She's had a long, successful marriage. She'd give good advice, wouldn't she?"

Abby smiled as she pictured her sweet, sometimes overwrought mother. "Mom's the last one I'd ask for advice," she said.

"I'm going to see what's taking so long," Diana said to her husband, laying her napkin on the table.

"Diana." Implied in his tone of voice were the words he didn't speak aloud—*Don't borrow trouble.*

"I'm sure they'll be right out," Greg said, standing, suddenly looking frantic. Her cool, calm son-in-law never panicked.

It upped her determination to see what was wrong. Because something definitely was.

"I'm going." Diana headed toward the kitchen. She could hear Abby speaking quietly.

"I adore my mother, but she makes mountains out of molehills. Greg and I are a team. We keep our problems to ourselves. And you know she would take my side, as any parent would, and that isn't fair to Greg. She might hold on to her partiality long after I've forgotten the argument. So you see, Josh, sometimes the best way to handle personal problems is to keep other people in the dark. Got it?"

"Clear as a bell."

Diana slapped a hand over her mouth and slid a few feet along the wall outside the kitchen before she let out an audible gasp. Her first born *was* keeping her in the dark about something, just as Diana had suspected. And Frank had pooh-poohed the whole thing.

Men just didn't get it. It wasn't called women's intuition for nothing—and she wasn't just a woman but a mother. Mothers saw every emotion on their children's faces, knew every body movement.

She'd *known* something was wrong with Abby. Now it'd been verified, not by rumor but by the person in question, no less. Abby and Greg were on the verge of separating. Her daughter had hidden their problems, not seeking advice from the one who loved her most in the world. Diana could've helped, too, she was sure of it.

Keep other people in the dark. The words stung. She wasn't "other people." She was Abby's mother.

And what about Melissa? What was her problem— because she definitely had one, something big, too. Had she confided in Abby?

Diana moved out of range, not wanting to hear more distressing words, not on the anniversary of the most wonderful day of her life. But she had to tell Frank what she'd learned, had to share the awful news with her own partner so that she could make it through the rest of the evening.

At least she could count on Frank to understand.

She hoped.

Chapter Four
by Christyne Butler

Don't think, don't feel.

Just keep breathing and you'll get through this night unscathed.

Unscathed, but with a broken heart.

Melissa squared her shoulders, brushed the wetness from her cheeks and heaved a shuddering breath that shook her all the way to her toes.

There. Don't you feel calmer?

No, she didn't, but that wasn't anyone's fault but her own.

She'd fallen in love with Josh on their very first date and after tonight, she'd probably never see him again.

The past two weeks had been crazy at her job. Trying to make it through what had been ten hours without her usual caffeine fix, having decided that two cups of coffee and three diet sodas a day weren't the best thing for her, had taken its toll. She'd been moody and pissy and okay, she was big to admit it, a bit dramatic.

Hey, she was her mother's daughter.

But none of that explained why the man of her dreams was going to break her heart.

Another deep breath did little to help, but it would have to do. Between helping her sister plan tonight's party and Josh's strange behavior, Melissa knew she was holding herself together with the thinnest of threads.

The scent of fresh coffee drifted through the house and Melissa groaned. Oh, how she ached for a hot cup, swimming in cream and lots of sugar.

Pushing the thought from her head, she picked up the gift basket that held everything her parents would need for a perfect second honeymoon in Italy. There was a small alcove right next to the dining room, a perfect place to stash it until just the right moment.

Turning, she headed for the door of her sister's office when the matching antique photo frames on a nearby bookshelf caught her eye.

The one on the right, taken just a few short years ago, was of Abby and Greg standing at the altar just after being presented to their friends and family as Mr. and Mrs. Gregory DeSena. Despite the elaborate setting, and the huge bridal party standing other either side of them, Melissa right there next to her sister, Abby and Greg only had eyes for each other. In fact, the photographer had captured the picture just as Greg had gently wiped a tear from her sister's cheek.

The other photograph, a bit more formal in monochrome colors of black and white, showed her mother and father on their wedding day. Her mother looked so young, so beautiful, so thin. Daddy was as handsome as ever in his tuxedo, his arm around his bride, his hand easily spanning her waist. The bridal bouquet was larger and over-the-top, typical for the early 80's, but her mother's dress…

Melissa squeezed tighter to the basket, the cellophane crinkling loudly in the silent room.

Abby had planned her wedding with the precision of an army general, right down to her chiffon, A-line silhouette gown with just enough crystal bling along the shoulder straps to give a special sparkle. Their mother looked the opposite, but just as beautiful wearing her own mother's gown, a vintage 1960 beauty of satin, lace and tulle with a circular skirt that cried out for layers of crinoline, a square-neck bodice and sleeves that hugged her arms.

A dress that Melissa had always seen herself wearing one day.

The day she married Josh.

Of course, she'd change into something short and sexy and perfect for dancing the night away after the ceremony, but—

"Oh, what does it matter!" Melissa said aloud. "It's not going to happen! It's never going to happen! Josh doesn't want to date you anymore, much less even think about getting down on one knee."

She exited the room and hurried down the long hall, tucking the basket just out of sight. They would have dessert, present the gift and then she would find a way to get Josh to take her home as soon as possible.

For the last time.

This was all Greg's fault.

As heartbreaking as it was, because she and Frank had always loved Greg, Diana knew deep in her heart that the man they'd welcomed in their home, into their hearts, was on the verge of walking out on their daughter.

How could Greg do this to Abby?

They were perfect together, complemented each other so well because they were so alike. Levelheaded, organized to a fault, methodical even.

Diana paused and grabbed hold of the stairway landing.

Could that be it?

Could Abby and Greg be too much alike? Had her son-in-law found someone else? Someone cute and bubbly who hung on his every word like it was gold?

Abby had mentioned a coworker of Greg's they'd run into one night while out to dinner. She'd said he'd been reluctant to introduce them, which seemed strange as the woman had literally gushed at how much she enjoyed working with Abby's husband when she'd stopped by their table.

The need to get to Frank, to squeeze his hand and have him comfort her, rolled over Diana. She needed him to tell her that everything would be all right, that she'd been right all along, and promise her they'd fight tooth and nail for their daughter so she didn't lose this beautiful home.

"Mom?"

Diana looked up and found Melissa standing there.

"Are you okay?" Melissa asked. "You look a little pale."

"I'm fine."

"You've got a death grip on the railing."

Diana immediately released her hold. "I just got a bit light-headed for a moment."

Concern filled her daughter's beautiful eyes. She motioned to the steps that led to the second floor. "Here, let's sit."

"But your sister is—"

"Perfectly capable of pulling dessert together all on

her own," Melissa took her arm and the two of them sat. "Disgustingly capable, as we both know."

Diana sat, basically because she had no choice, taking the time to really look at her daughter. She'd been crying. Her baby suffered the same fate as she did when tears came—puffy eyes. And while Melissa had been acting strange during dinner, this was the first true evidence Diana had that something was terribly wrong.

"Darling, you seem a bit…off this evening." Diana kept her tone light after a few minutes of silence passed. "How is everything with you? You didn't eat very much tonight."

Melissa stared at her clenched hands. "Everything is just fine, mother. It's been a long week and I'm very tired."

"Yes, you said you've been working long hours. That's probably cut into your free time with Josh."

"Y-yes, it has, but I don't think that's going to be a problem much longer."

"What does that mean?"

Melissa rose, one hand pressed against her stomach. "It's nothing. You were right. We should get back into the dining room. You know how Abby gets when things go off schedule."

Yes, she did know. Oh, the divorce was going to upset Abby's tidy world, but that didn't mean that Diana wouldn't be there for her other daughter, as well. She still had no idea what was bothering her youngest, but she would find out before this evening was through.

And she would make things right.

For both her girls.

She'd easily found the time to attend Abby's debates, girl scout meetings and band concerts and never missed a dance recital, theatre production or football game while

Melissa was on the cheerleading squad. Her daughters might be grown, but they still needed their mother.

Now more than ever.

Diana stood, as well. "Yes, let's go back and join everyone."

They walked into the room and Diana's gaze locked with Frank's. Her husband watched her every step as she moved around the table to retake her seat next to him. Thirty years of marriage honed his deduction skills to a razor-sharp point, and she knew that he knew she'd found out something.

"Okay, let's get this celebration going." Greg spoke from where he stood at the buffet filling tall fluted glasses with sparkling liquid, having already popped open the bottle. "Josh, why don't you hand out the champagne to everyone?"

Frank leaned in close. "What's wrong?"

Diana batted her eyes, determined not to cry as his gentle and caring tone was sure to bring on the waterworks. "Not now, darling."

"So you were worried for nothing?"

"Of course not. I was right all along—" She cut off her words when Abby came in with a tray of desserts in her hands. "Dear, can I help with those?"

"No, you stay seated, Mom. It'll only take me a moment to hand these out."

True to her words, the etched-crystal parfait dishes were soon at everyone's place setting and, immediately after, Josh placed a glass in front of Frank and Diana.

Diana watched as he then went back to get two more for Greg and Abby and one last trip for the final two glasses.

"Here you go, sweetheart." He moved in behind Melissa and reached past her shoulder to place a glass in front of her.

"No, thank you." Her baby girl's voice was strained.

"You don't want any champagne?" Josh was clearly confused. "You love the stuff. We practically finished off a magnum ourselves last New Year's Eve."

Melissa shook her head, her dark locks flying over her shoulder. "I'm sure. I'll just h-have—" She paused, pressing her fingertips to her mouth for a quick moment. "I'd prefer a cup of coffee. Decaf, please."

Oh, everything made sense now!

The tears, the exhaustion, the hand held protectively over her still flat belly, the refusal of alcohol. Her motherly intrusion might have been late in picking up on Melissa's distress, but the realization over what her baby was facing hit Diana like a thunderbolt coming from the sky.

Her heart didn't know whether to break for the certain pain Abby was facing over the end of her marriage or rejoice with the news that she was finally going to be a grandmother!

Her baby was having a baby!

Chapter Five
by Gina Wilkins

During the year he and Melissa Morgan had been together, Josh Wright thought he'd come to know her family fairly well, but there were still times when he felt like an outsider who couldn't quite catch on to the family rhythms. Tonight was one of those occasions.

The undercurrents of tension at the elegantly set dinner table were obvious enough, even to him.

Melissa had been acting oddly all evening. Abby and Greg kept exchanging significant looks, as though messages passed between them that no one else could hear. Even Melissa and Abby's mom, Diana, typically the life of any dinner party, was unnaturally subdued and introspective tonight. Only the family patriarch, Frank, seemed as steady and unruffled as ever, characteristically enjoying the time with his family without getting drawn in to their occasional, usually Diana-generated melodramas.

Josh didn't have a clue what was going on with any of them. Shouldn't he understand them better by now, considering he wanted so badly to be truly one of them soon?

He dipped his spoon into the dessert dish in front of him, scooping up a bite of fresh raspberries, an orange-liqueur flavored mascarpone cheese mixture and ladyfingers spread with what tasted like raspberry jam. "Abby, this dessert is amazing."

She smiled across the table at him. "Thank you. Mom and Dad had tiramisu the first night of their honeymoon, so I tried to recreate that nice memory."

"Ours wasn't flavored with orange and raspberry," Diana seemed compelled to point out. "We had a more traditional espresso-based tiramisu."

Abby's smile turned just a bit wry. "I found this recipe online and thought it sounded good. I wasn't trying to exactly reproduce what you had before, Mom."

"I think this one is even better," Frank interjected hastily, after swallowing a big bite of his dessert. "Who'd have thought thirty years later we'd be eating tiramisu made by our own little girl, eh, Diana?"

Everyone smiled—except Melissa, who was playing with her dessert without her usual enthusiasm for sweets. It bothered Josh that Melissa seemed to become more withdrawn and somber as the evening progressed. Though she had made a noticeable effort to participate in the dining table conversation, her eyes were darkened to almost jade and the few smiles she'd managed looked forced. As well as he knew her, as much as he loved her, he sensed when she was stressed or unhappy. For some reason, she seemed both tonight, and that was twisting him into knots.

Maybe Abby had been right when she'd warned him that his nervous anticipation was affecting Melissa, though he thought he'd done a better job of hiding it from her. Apparently, she knew him a bit too well, also.

Encouraged by the response to his compliment of the dessert, he thought he would try again to keep the conversation light and cheerful. Maybe Melissa would relax if everyone else did.

Mindful of the reason for this gathering—and because he was rather obsessed with love and marriage, anyway—he said, "Thirty years. That's a remarkable accomplishment these days. Not many couples are able to keep the fire alive for that long."

He couldn't imagine his passion for Melissa ever burning out, not in thirty years—or fifty, for that matter.

He felt her shift in her seat next to him and her spoon clicked against her dessert dish. He glanced sideways at her, but she was looking down at her dish, her glossy black hair falling forward to hide her face from him.

Frank, at least, seemed pleased with Josh's observation.

"That's it, exactly." Frank pointed his spoon in Josh's direction, almost dripping raspberry jam on the tablecloth. "Keeping the fire alive. Takes work, but it's worth it, right, hon?"

"Absolutely." Diana looked hard at Abby and Greg as she spoke. "All marriages go through challenging times, but with love and patience and mutual effort, the rewards will come."

Abby and Greg shared a startled look, but Frank spoke again before either of them could respond to what seemed like a sermon aimed directly at them. "I still remember the day I met her, just like it was yesterday."

That sounded like a story worth pursuing. Though everyone else had probably heard it many times, Josh encouraged Frank to continue. "I'd like to hear about it. How did you meet?"

Frank's smile was nostalgic, his eyes distant with the memories. "I was the best man in a college friend's wedding. Diana was the maid of honor. I had a flat tire on the way to the wedding rehearsal, so I was late arriving."

Diana shook her head. Though she still looked worried about something, she was paying attention to her husband's tale. "The bride was fit to be tied that it looked as though the best man wasn't going to show up for the rehearsal. She was a nervous wreck, even though her groom kept assuring her Frank could be counted on to be there."

Frank chuckled. "Anyway, the minute I arrived, all rumpled and dusty from changing the tire, I was rushed straight to a little room off the church sanctuary where the groom's party was gathered getting ready to enter on cue. I didn't have a chance to socialize or meet the other wedding party members before the rehearsal began. Five minutes after I dashed in, I was standing at the front of the church next to my friend Jim. And then the music began and the bridesmaids started their march in. Diana was the third bridesmaid to enter."

"Gretchen was first, Bridget next."

Ignoring the details Diana inserted, Frank continued, "She was wearing a green dress, the same color as her eyes. The minute she walked into the church, I felt my heart flop like a landed fish."

Diana laughed ruefully. "Well, that doesn't sound very romantic."

Frank patted her hand, still lost in his memories. "She stopped halfway down the aisle and informed the organist that she was playing much too slowly and that everyone in the audience would fall asleep before the whole wedding party reached the front of the church."

"Well, she was."

Frank chuckled and winked at Josh. "That was when I knew this was someone I had to meet."

Charmed by the story, Josh remembered the first moment he'd laid eyes on Melissa. He understood that "floppy fish" analogy all too well, though he'd compared his own heart to a runaway train. He could still recall how hard it had raced when Melissa had tossed back her dark hair and laughed up at him for the first time, her green eyes sparkling with humor and warmth. He'd actually wondered for a moment if she could hear it pounding against his chest.

"So it was love at first sight?"

Frank nodded decisively. "That it was."

"And when did you know she was 'the one' for you? That you wanted to marry her?"

"Probably right then. But certainly the next evening during the ceremony, after I'd spent a few hours getting to know Diana. When I found myself mentally saying 'I do' when the preacher asked 'Do you take this woman?' I knew I was hooked."

Josh sighed. This, he thought, was why he wanted to wait for the absolute perfect moment to propose to Melissa. Someday he hoped to tell a story that would make everyone who heard it say "Awww," the way he felt like doing now. "You're a lucky man, Frank. Not every guy is fortunate enough to find a woman he wants to spend the rest of his life with."

Three lucky men sat at this table tonight, he thought happily. Like Frank and Greg, he had found his perfect match.

Melissa dropped her spoon with a clatter and sprang to her feet. "I, uh— Excuse me," she muttered, her voice choked. "I'm not feeling well."

Before Josh or anyone else could ask her what was wrong, she dashed from the room. Concerned, he half rose from his seat, intending to follow her.

"What on earth is wrong with Melissa?" Frank asked in bewilderment.

Words burst from Diana as if she'd held them in as long as she was physically able. "Melissa is pregnant."

His knees turning to gelatin, Josh fell back into his chair with a thump.

After patting her face with a towel, Melissa looked in the bathroom mirror to make sure she'd removed all signs of her bout of tears. She was quite sure Abby would say she was overreacting and being overly dramatic—just like their Mom, Abby would say with a shake of her auburn head—but Melissa couldn't help it. Every time she thought about her life without Josh in it tears welled up behind her eyes and it was all she could do to keep them from gushing out.

Abby had tried to convince her she was only imagining that Josh was trying to find a way to break up with her. As much as she wanted to believe her sister, Melissa was convinced her qualms were well-founded. She knew every expression that crossed Josh's handsome face. Every flicker of emotion that passed through his clear blue eyes. He had grown increasingly nervous and awkward around her during the past few days, when they had always been so close, so connected, so easy together before. Passion was only a part of their relationship—though certainly a major part. But the mental connection between them was even more special—or at least it had been.

She didn't know what had gone wrong. Everything had seemed so perfect until Josh's behavior had suddenly changed. But maybe the questions he had asked her dad tonight had been a clue. Maybe he had concluded that he didn't really want to spend the rest of his life with her. That only a few men were lucky enough to find "the one."

She had so hoped she was Josh's "one."

Feeling tears threaten again, she drew a deep breath and lifted her chin, ordering herself to reclaim her pride. She would survive losing Josh, she assured herself. Maybe.

Forcing herself to leave Abby's guest bathroom, she headed for the dining room, expecting to hear conversation and the clinking of silverware and china. Instead what appeared to be stunned silence gripped the five people sitting at the table. Her gaze went instinctively to Josh, finding him staring back at her. His dark blond hair tumbled almost into his eyes, making him look oddly disheveled and perturbed. She realized suddenly that everyone else was gawking at her, too. Did she see sympathy on her father's face?

Before she could stop herself, she leaped to a stomach-wrenching conclusion. Had Josh told her family that he was breaking up with her? Is that why they were all looking at her like...well, like that?

"What?" she asked apprehensively.

"Why didn't you tell me?" Josh demanded.

It occurred to her that he sounded incongruously hurt, considering he was the one on the verge of breaking her heart. "Tell you what?"

"That you're pregnant."

"I'm—?" Her voice shot up into a squeak of surprise, unable to complete the sentence.

"Don't worry, darling, we'll all be here for you," Diana assured her, wiping her eyes with the corner of a napkin. "Just as we'll be here for you, Abby, after you and Greg split up. Although I sincerely hope you'll try to work everything out before you go your separate ways."

"Wait. What?" Greg's chair scraped against the floor as he spun to stare at his wife. "What is she talking about, Abby?"

Melissa felt as if she'd left a calm, orderly dinner party and returned only minutes later to sheer pandemonium.

"What on earth makes you think I'm pregnant?" she asked Josh, unable to concentrate on her sister's sputtering at the moment.

He looked from her to her mom and back again, growing visibly more confused by the minute. "Your mother told us."

Her mother sighed and nodded. "I've overheard a few snippets of conversation today. Enough to put two and two together about what's going on with both my poor girls. You're giving up caffeine and you're feeling queasy and we've all noticed that you've been upset all evening."

"Mom, I don't know what you heard—" Abby began, but Melissa talked over her sister.

"You're completely off base, Mom," she said firmly, avoiding Josh's eyes until she was sure she could look at him without succumbing to those looming tears again. "I'm giving up caffeine because I think I've been drinking too much of it for my health. I'm not pregnant."

Regret swept through her with the words. Maybe she was being overly dramatic again, but the thought of never having a child with Josh almost sent her bolting for the bathroom with another bout of hot tears.

She risked a quick glance at him, but she couldn't quite read his expression. He sat silently in his chair, his expression completely inscrutable now. She assumed he was deeply relieved to find out she wasn't pregnant, but the relief wasn't evident on his face. Maybe he was thinking about what a close call he'd just escaped.

Her mom searched her face. "You're not?"

Melissa shook her head. "No. I'm not."

"Then why have you been so upset this evening?"

Rattled by this entire confrontation, she blurted, "I'm upset because Josh is breaking up with me."

Josh made a choked sound before pushing a hand through his hair in exasperation. "Why do you think I'm breaking up with you?"

"I just, um, put two and two together," she muttered, all too aware that she sounded as much like her mother as Abby always accused her.

"Well, then you need to work on your math skills," Josh shot back with a frustrated shake of his head. "I don't want to break up with you, Melissa. I want to ask you to marry me!"

Chapter Six
by Cindy Kirk

Bedlam followed Josh Wright's announcement that he planned to propose to Melissa Morgan. Everyone at the table started talking in loud excited voices, their hands gesturing wildly.

Family patriarch Frank Morgan had experience with chaotic situations. After all, he and his wife Diana had raised two girls. When things got out of hand, control had to be established. Because his silver referee whistle was in a drawer back home, Frank improvised.

Seconds later, a shrill noise split the air.

His family immediately stopped talking and all turned in his direction.

"Frank?" Shock blanketed Greg DeSena's face. Though he'd been married to Frank's oldest daughter, Abby, for three years, this was a side to his father-in-law he'd obviously never seen.

Frank's youngest daughter, Melissa, slipped into her chair without being asked. She cast furtive glances at her boyfriend, Josh. It had been Josh's unexpected proclamation that he intended to propose to her that had thrown everyone into such a tizzy.

Even though Frank hadn't whistled a family meeting to order in years, his wife and daughters remembered what the blast of air meant.

"Darling." Diana spoke in a low tone, but loud enough for everyone at the table to hear clearly. "This is our anniversary dinner. Can't a family meeting wait until another time?"

Her green eyes looked liked liquid jade in the candlelight. Even after thirty years, one look from her, one touch, was all it took to make Frank fall in love all over again.

If they were at their home—instead of at Greg and Abby's house—he'd grab her hand and they'd trip up the stairs, kissing and shedding clothes with every step. But he was the head of this warm, wonderful, sometimes crazy family and with the position came responsibility.

"I'm sorry, sweetheart. This can't wait." Frank shifted his gaze from his beautiful wife and settled it on the man who'd blurted out his intentions only moments before. "Josh."

His future son-in-law snapped to attention. "Sir."

Though Frank hadn't been a marine in a very long time, Josh's response showed he'd retained his commanding presence. "Sounds like there's something you want to ask my daughter."

"Frank, no. Not now," Diana protested. "Not like this."

"Mr. Morgan is right." Josh pushed back his chair and stood. "There *is* something I want to ask Melissa. From the misunderstanding tonight, it appears I've already waited too long."

Frank nodded approvingly and sat back in his chair. He liked a decisive man. Josh would be a good addition to the family.

"If you want to wait—" Diana began.

Before she could finish, Frank leaned over and did what he'd wanted to do all night. He kissed her.

"Let the man say his piece," he murmured against her lips.

Diana shuddered. Her breathing hitched but predictably she opened her mouth. So he kissed her again. This time deeper, longer, until her eyes lost their focus, until she relaxed against his shoulder with a happy sigh.

Josh held out his hand to Melissa. His heart pounded so hard against his ribs, he felt almost faint. But he was going to do it. Now. Finally.

With a tremulous smile, Melissa placed her slender fingers in his. The lines that had furrowed her pretty brow the past couple of weeks disappeared. His heart clenched as he realized he'd been to blame for her distress. Well, he wouldn't delay a second longer. He promptly dropped to one knee.

"Melissa," Josh began then stopped when his voice broke. He glanced around the table. All eyes were on him, but no one dared to speak. Abby and Greg offered encouraging smiles. His future in-laws nodded approvingly.

His girlfriend's eyes never left his face. The love he saw shining in the emerald depths gave him courage to continue.

"When I first saw you at the office Christmas party, I was struck by your beauty. It wasn't until we began dating that I realized you are as beautiful inside out."

Melissa blinked back tears. Josh hoped they were tears of happiness.

"This past year I've fallen deeper and deeper in love with you. I can't imagine my life without you in it. I want your face to be the last I see at night and the first I see every morning. I want to have children with you. I want to grow old with you. I promise I'll do everything in my power to make you happy."

He was rambling. Speaking from the heart to be sure, but rambling. For a second Josh wished he had the speech he'd tinkered with over the past couple of months with him now, the one with the pretty words and poetic phrases. But it was across the room in his jacket pocket and too late to be of help now.

Josh slipped a small box from his pocket and snapped open the lid. The diamond he'd seen circled in her bride's magazine was nestled inside. The large stone caught the light and sparkled with an impressive brilliance. "I love you more than I thought it was possible to love someone."

He'd told himself he wasn't going to say another word but surely a declaration of such magnitude couldn't be considered rambling.

Her lips curved upward and she expelled a happy sigh. "I love you, too."

Josh resisted the urge to jump to his feet and do a little home-plate dance. He reminded himself there would be plenty of time for celebration once the ring was on her finger.

With great care, Josh lifted the diamond from the black velvet. He was primed to slip it on when she pulled her hand back ever-so-slightly.

"Isn't there something you want to ask me?" Melissa whispered.

At first Josh couldn't figure out what she was referring

to until he realized with sudden horror that he hadn't actually popped the question. Heat rose up his neck. Thankfully he was still on one knee. "Melissa, will you make me the happiest man in the world and marry me?"

The words came out in one breath and were a bit garbled, but she didn't appear to notice.

"Yes. Oh, yes."

Relief flooded him. He slid the ring in place with trembling fingers. "If you don't like it we can—"

"It's perfect. Absolutely perfect." Tears slipped down her cheeks.

He stood and pulled her close, kissing her soundly. "I wanted this to be special—"

"It is special." Melissa turned toward her family and smiled through happy tears. "I can't imagine anything better than having my family here to celebrate with us."

"This calls for a toast." Flashing a smile that was almost as bright as his daughter's, Frank picked up the nearest bottle of champagne. He filled Diana's glass and then his own before passing the bottle around the table.

Greg filled his glass and those of Josh and Melissa's but Abby, his wife, covered her glass with her hand and shook her head.

Frank stood and raised his glass high. "To Josh and Melissa. May you be as happy together as Diana and I have been for the past thirty years."

Words of congratulations and the sound of clinking glasses filled the air.

Nestled in the crook of her future husband's arm, Melissa giggled. Normally her mom knew everything before everyone else. Not this time.

"You thought I was pregnant because I wanted decaf coffee," she said to her mother, "but yet you don't find it odd that Abby hasn't had a sip of alcohol tonight?"

For a woman like Diana who prided herself on being in the "know," the comment was tantamount to waving a red flag in front of a bull. She whirled and fixed her gaze on her firstborn, who stood with her head resting against her husband's shoulder. "Honey, is there something you and Greg want to tell us?"

Abby's cheeks pinked. She straightened and exchanged a look with her husband. He gave a slight nod. She took one breath. And then another. "Greg and I, well, we're... we're pregnant."

"A baby!" Diana shrieked and moved so suddenly she'd have upset her glass of champagne, if Frank hadn't grabbed it. "I can't believe it. Our two girls, all grown up. One getting married. One having a baby. This is truly a happy day."

Everyone seemed to agree as tears of joy flowed as freely as the champagne, accompanied by much back-slapping.

"Have you thought of any names?" Diana asked Abby and Greg then turned to Melissa and Josh. "Any idea on a wedding date?"

Suggestions on both came fast and furious until Abby realized the party had gotten off track. She pulled her sister aside. "The anniversary gift," she said in a low tone to Melissa. "We need to give them their gift."

"I'll get it." In a matter of seconds, Melissa returned, cradling the large basket in her arms.

Josh moved to her side, as if he couldn't bear to be far from his new fiancée. Greg stood behind his wife, his arms around her still slender waist.

"Mom and Dad," Melissa began. "You've shown us what love looks like."

"What it feels like," Abby added.

With a flourish, Melissa presented her parents with

a basket overflowing with biscotti, gourmet cappuccino mix, and other items reminiscent of their honeymoon in Italy…along with assorted travel documents. "Congratulations on thirty years of marriage."

"And best wishes for thirty more," Abby and Melissa said in unison, with Josh and Greg chiming in.

"Oh, Frank, isn't this the best evening ever?" Diana's voice bubbled with excitement. "All this good news and gifts, too."

She exclaimed over every item in the basket but grew silent when she got to the tickets, guidebooks and brochures. Diana glanced at her husband. He shrugged, looking equally puzzled.

"It's a trip," Abby explained.

Melissa smiled. "We've booked you on a four-star vacation to Italy, so you can recreate your honeymoon, only this time in comfort and style."

"Oh, my stars." Diana put a hand to her head. When she began to sway, her husband slipped a steadying arm around her shoulders.

"I think your mom has had a bit too much excitement for one day." Frank chuckled. "Or maybe a little too much of the vino."

"I've only had two glasses. Or was it three?" Instead of elbowing him in the side as he expected, she laughed and refocused on her children. "Regardless, thank you all for such wonderful, thoughtful presents."

Abby exchanged a relieved glance with Melissa. "We wanted to give you and Dad the perfect gift to celebrate your years of happiness together."

"You already have," Frank said, his voice thick with emotion.

He shifted his gaze from Abby and Greg to Melissa and Josh before letting it linger on his beautiful wife, Diana. A wedding in the spring. A grandbaby next summer. A wonderful woman to share his days and nights. Who could ask for more?

* * * * *

HEART & HOME

Heartwarming romances where love can
happen right when you least expect it.

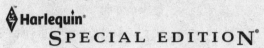

COMING NEXT MONTH
AVAILABLE APRIL 24, 2012

#2185 FORTUNE'S UNEXPECTED GROOM
The Fortunes of Texas: Whirlwind Romance
Nancy Robards Thompson

#2186 A DOCTOR IN HIS HOUSE
McKinley Medics
Lilian Darcy

#2187 HOLDING OUT FOR DOCTOR PERFECT
Men of Mercy Medical
Teresa Southwick

#2188 COURTED BY THE TEXAS MILLIONAIRE
St. Valentine, Texas
Crystal Green

#2189 MATCHMAKING BY MOONLIGHT
Teresa Hill

#2190 THE SURPRISE OF HER LIFE
Helen R. Myers

REQUEST YOUR FREE BOOKS!

2 FREE NOVELS PLUS 2 FREE GIFTS!

♦ Harlequin®

SPECIAL EDITION

Life, Love & Family

YES! Please send me 2 FREE Harlequin® Special Edition novels and my 2 FREE gifts (gifts are worth about $10). After receiving them, if I don't wish to receive any more books, I can return the shipping statement marked "cancel." If I don't cancel, I will receive 6 brand-new novels every month and be billed just $4.49 per book in the U.S. or $5.24 per book in Canada. That's a saving of at least 14% off the cover price! It's quite a bargain! Shipping and handling is just 50¢ per book in the U.S. and 75¢ per book in Canada.* I understand that accepting the 2 free books and gifts places me under no obligation to buy anything. I can always return a shipment and cancel at any time. Even if I never buy another book, the two free books and gifts are mine to keep forever.

235/335 HDN FEGF

Name	(PLEASE PRINT)

Address	Apt. #

City	State/Prov.	Zip/Postal Code

Signature (if under 18, a parent or guardian must sign)

Mail to the **Reader Service:**
IN U.S.A.: P.O. Box 1867, Buffalo, NY 14240-1867
IN CANADA: P.O. Box 609, Fort Erie, Ontario L2A 5X3

Not valid for current subscribers to Harlequin Special Edition books.

Want to try two free books from another line?
Call 1-800-873-8635 or visit www.ReaderService.com.

* Terms and prices subject to change without notice. Prices do not include applicable taxes. Sales tax applicable in N.Y. Canadian residents will be charged applicable taxes. Offer not valid in Quebec. This offer is limited to one order per household. All orders subject to credit approval. Credit or debit balances in a customer's account(s) may be offset by any other outstanding balance owed by or to the customer. Please allow 4 to 6 weeks for delivery. Offer available while quantities last.

Your Privacy—The Reader Service is committed to protecting your privacy. Our Privacy Policy is available online at www.ReaderService.com or upon request from the Reader Service.

We make a portion of our mailing list available to reputable third parties that offer products we believe may interest you. If you prefer that we not exchange your name with third parties, or if you wish to clarify or modify your communication preferences, please visit us at www.ReaderService.com/consumerschoice or write to us at Reader Service Preference Service, P.O. Box 9062, Buffalo, NY 14269. Include your complete name and address.

HSE11B

The heartwarming conclusion of

from fan-favorite author
TINA LEONARD

With five brothers married, Jonas Callahan is under no
pressure to tie the knot. But when Sabrina McKinley
admits her bouncing baby boy is his, Jonas does
everything he can to win over the woman he's loved
for years. First the last Callahan bachelor must uncover
an important family secret…before he can take
the lovely Sabrina down the aisle!

A Callahan Wedding

**Available this May
wherever books are sold.**

*After a bad decision—or two—Annie Mendes
is determined to succeed as a P.I. But her first assignment
could be her last, because one thing is clear: she's not cut
out to be a nanny. And Louisiana detective Nate Dufrene
seems to know there's more to her than meets the eye!*

*Read on for an exciting excerpt of the upcoming book
WATERS RUN DEEP by Liz Talley…*

THE SOUND OF A CAR behind her had Annie scooting off the
road and checking over her shoulder.

Nate Dufrene.

Her heart took on a galloping rhythm that had nothing to
do with exercise.

He slowed beside her. "Wanna ride?"

"I'm almost there. Besides, I wouldn't want to get your
seat sweaty."

His gaze traveled down her body before meeting her
eyes. Awareness ignited in her blood. "I don't mind."

Her mind screamed, *get your butt back to the house and
leave Nate alone.* Her libido, however, told her to take the
candy he offered and climb into his car like a naughty little
girl. Damn, it was hard to ignore candy like him.

"If you don't mind." She pulled open the door and
climbed inside.

The slight scent of citrus cologne, which suited him,
filled the car. She inhaled, sucking in cool air and Nate.
Both were good.

"You run often?" he asked.

"Three or four times a week."

"Oh, yeah? Maybe we can go for a run together."

Her body tightened unwillingly as thoughts of other
things they could do together flitted through her mind. She

shrugged as though his presence wasn't affecting her. Which it *so* was. Lord, what was wrong with her? *He* wasn't her assignment.

"Sure." No way—not if she wanted to keep her job. As he parked, she reached for the door handle, but his hand on her arm stopped her. His touch was warm, even on her heated flesh.

"What did you say you were before becoming a nanny?"

Alarm choked out the weird sexual energy that had been humming in her for the past few minutes. Maybe meeting him on the road wasn't as coincidental as it first seemed. "A real-estate agent."

Will Nate discover Annie's secret?
Find out in WATERS RUN DEEP by Liz Talley,
available May 2012 from Harlequin® Superromance®.

And be sure to look for the other two books
in Liz's THE BOYS OF BAYOU BRIDGE series,
available in July and September 2012.

INTRIGUE

DANGER LURKS AROUND EVERY CORNER WITH AUTHOR

PAULA GRAVES

CATCH A NEW INSTALLMENT OF

Four years ago, Megan Cooper Randall buried her husband, thinking he died a hero while battling rebels. The last thing she expects is former Pentagon lawyer Evan Pike to show up and state her deceased husband was a carefully targeted victim. With mercenaries hot on their heels, Evan and Megan have to work fast to uncover past conspiracies and fight for the chance to build a future together.

SECRET AGENDA

The truth will be revealed
May 2012

May is Mystery Month!

With six titles to choose from every month, uncover your love for breathtaking romantic suspense with Harlequin® Intrigue today!

Harlequin *Presents*®

Royalty has never been so scandalous!

THE SANTINA CROWN

When Crown Prince Alessandro of Santina proposes
to paparazzi favorite Allegra Jackson it promises
to be *the* social event of the decade!

Harlequin Presents® invites you to step into the decadent
playground of the world's rich and famous and rub shoulders
with royalty, sheikhs and glamorous socialites.

Collect all 8 passionate tales written by *USA TODAY* bestselling authors, beginning May 2012!